I0563578

Supernatural Medicine

Westlanders, Volume 1

Gabrielle Monego

Published by Gabrielle Monego, 2023.

This is a work of fiction. Similarities to real people, places, or events are entirely coincidental.

SUPERNATURAL MEDICINE

First edition. July 6, 2023.

Copyright © 2023 Gabrielle Monego.

ISBN: 978-0994295224

Written by Gabrielle Monego.

To my family, both of blood and of choice... Thank you

I love you

Chapter 1

Let me give you some advice, don't go drinking before your first day in a new school. Especially not if that first day isn't the first day of first term. I can hereby vouch for the fact that it isn't beneficial. I had arrived in Brisbane with my oldest brother and the twins, late last night. Then the rest of our subpack showed up in three cars, packed full of people, swags and food. They were supposed to let me leave. I was supposed to start a new chapter here. Alone. Richard and the twins had only come for a few days to help me settle in. Richard had some business to do in the city.

Dad is the top dog of our pack but our pack is huge and our territory takes up most of the north west of what used to be Queensland. Richard will most likely win the challenges and take over from dad when the time comes but for now he runs our subpack. We have three brothers, one set of feral twins and I'm their half-sister. I'll tell you about that some other time. There are also three others that we consider brothers and sister, they were adopted by the pack when their family died. They all showed up at my new, small apartment about half an hour after I got the keys.

They asked me to go out with them. I refused. Then they dared me. I refused. They had even begged me but I held my ground because I didn't want to show up on sleep deprived my first day. They finally resorted to blackmail but I could hold my own against that, we all held something over the others so they stopped.

When they resorted to bribery Maddie had ordered

them to leave me alone. I remember thinking that it was so nice of her to stand up to all the boys like that because she is in no way dominant compared to my real brothers. She hugged me, with tears in her eyes, she then said "I wish we didn't have to go yet, Juuls. It'll be a sad affair having to go out with this bunch of dogs without you. We'll find a place to let of some steam on the way home."

The tears had broken my resolve and I'd conceded defeat. The boys had whooped madly and congratulated Madd's on her performance. She smirked when I realised, too late, that they had played me. She collected her winnings because they'd made bets on who would break me first. We had started the evening in a human run bar then proceeded to a mixed species nightclub, The Pitt, and we hit it hard!! Zoë had bet on Maddie, so they shouted the first few rounds with their winnings. The boys never left for long before returning to the rest of the pack. We drank and danced and laughed until the early hours. When we got to my apartment we crashed on the pre-made swags that took up my whole living room floor. We woke up in a puppy pile when nine alarms went off. It seemed that nobody wanted me to be late. Madds packed my lunch while I tried to get presentable after a long scalding shower.

After a subdued breakfast I managed to convince them to let me go to school alone. It wasn't far from the apartment and I certainly didn't want to arrive on my first day with a pack of Westlanders on my tail. People might not recognise me alone but my family's reputation is well known everywhere. I had convinced dad to let me do this education as a human. There were ordinary humans studying supernatural medicine and I was going to be one of them. Fly under the radar and all that. That was the plan anyway.

The building was imposing, more so than it had been when I had been let through the empty building almost six months before. The tour didn't give any idea of how different the building would feel with so many different species lining the halls. As I swerved through the bodies lining the halls, I realised that people were staring. Curious about the unmarked, new girl in their territory, it was to be expected because I had missed the first two terms. The school head had made a rare exemption for me because I was actually ahead on the material that they were teaching first year students.

Then I walked past a group of people that all tried to intimidate me. I had been so close to my class, without any trouble, and then I was surrounded. Weres, I knew that look anywhere, I'd grown up with the man that owned that look. Arrogant with a hint of animal curiosity! They blocked me when I tried to get past them and surrounded me. They sniffed and growled as I stood there, deep in the large building that would take up the next four to six years of my life. I groaned in exasperation, this wasn't how I wanted to start my first day. On top of the differences with my last school and a major hangover, I was quickly becoming annoyed.

The guy that had stepped in my way had made sure not to touch me, lucky boy. I held my head high and ignored the need to be looking right at any of them. I wasn't here as the daughter of the pack leader and I had no right to make them submit, yet. It took an effort, reminding myself that wasn't in their pack.

One of the other boys lifted his hand, I saw what was coming, he grabbed for my breast. I grabbed the offending hand before it connected and broke his fingers, followed by his wrist, in one smooth motion. I never hesitated and despite the pain, he only whimpered softly as his body immediately tried to heal everything. The boy that had blocked me didn't speak but looked pleased by my response. As I expected, all were species respect strength, even humans. Looking at each of them for a second, right in the eyes, I said. "Listen you dumb mutts, I might be human but I'm not a chew-toy. You behave and I won't break anything else. I know my rights. You stay out of my way and I'll stay outta yours." I started walking and they backed out of my way. I heard them whisper. "She knows the term chew-toy."

"She knew what we are too." Said another.

"She is definitely human, I smelled nothing else on her scent and I didn't see her dog. If she was pack, I should have been able to see it."

Well, that had to be a top dog because only they could see the inner Dingo in other packs as well as his own. Good to know, hope I didn't piss them off too bad.

"Well, I smelled at least seven different dogs on her, she slept with them to smell that strong, under the smell of fresh soap."

"Guess she's someone else's chew-toy. I 'spose that might be why she knew the term."

"What a waste! I could have done with a piece of that!" A young voice piped up.

"Used trash." I heard another spiteful female voice

mumble as I walked away.

"Whatabout... that's none of our business. She's claimed rights, she knows the system. Show some respect." The voice was strong and clear, but the words were spoken softly. An understated power, that made me itch to turn around and see the person it belonged to, but I continued to the classroom. Their conversation becoming less and less clear as the distance grew. After all, I only had human ears and my gift was wearing off fast as I got further from them.

Richard had warned me that there would be dogs at the school. I knew that if I called my family, they would all get here within minutes to protect me. They wouldn't have left the city yet. But I was prepared for this and I didn't need anyone to fight my battles for me. My dad is the top dog of the biggest pack in the country. I could certainly hold my own against this bunch. Dad had made me strong and confident, even if I was the mistake that came from a fling he'd had before he settled down to lead the pack. A fling with a witch of all things. At this very school. Bah!

My mother, well, she gave birth to me and that was it. She could see the lack of magic from the moment I was born so they presumed that I would take after dad. Technically I was an impossibility, cross breeding barely ever managed to conceive. Dad took me in, with his wife who treated me as her own pup, and my birth mother never looked back. Just like that, she'd dumped me, disclaimed her knowledge of me, her dirty little secret, and got on with her life. Dad told me, after a severe breakdown on my part, when I was about five, that he'd always known I wasn't a proper Dingo. I, however, finally found out that my mom wasn't my real mother. The kids that had been teasing me confirmed what all the adults had been hiding. Neither Witch nor Were. But my family loved me anyway and I grew up as part of the pack. I was faster than a human, more graceful too and could see pretty well in the dark. My sense of smell left something to be desired compared to the dogs and I never shifted. Nobody expected me to shift but we all hoped I might just be a late bloomer. My half-brothers and sister, and the other kids in our generation got along well. I played the games, got the same education and training, I was even allowed to hunt with them. Dad never let me off easy and I ran patrol on the boundary as a human while the others ran as dogs. Big beautiful, scary Dingo dogs. Native Australian Weres.

And now I would be surrounded by different packs in a school with all different species. I could hold my own, certainly, but I'd have to work hard to hide my secret.

Chapter 2

School. Every pack, every group of any kind, except the old vampires, had people that came to this school to learn. It was the best medical school in the southern hemisphere. Every race and species was accepted here. Even though almost everyone that came here had a position to go to in their own community, we learned about all species down to the molecular level. We would be taught to heal and kill everything with science. Obviously, we weren't supposed to kill with what we knew but, it was an open secret that the best mercenaries had also attended this school, not just the best doctors.

I was going to be training for pack doctor. I wanted it, but even if I hadn't wanted to, I would have been made to go. Our pack send a student every year sometimes two or three. I was the obvious, second, choice for this year to be sent to Med school. But dad only let me go because the one that had started at the beginning of term had left the school to be with his mate, she wasn't in school and already expecting their first child. Next year there would be another person coming too, we all had a pretty good idea of who that would be but this time it was me. A pack human, the first human to study as replacement for pack doctor. There were other humans that lived with our pack, wives and husbands too, but they didn't have my abilities and so I was sided with the dogs by them. My abilities, a bit witch, a bit dog, a lot dangerous and entirely secret. People had been killed to keep my secret. Dad was proud of how dangerous I could be, he only intervened one time, when I had a fight with a human student on our on-air lesson. It wouldn't have been a problem if I hadn't explained just how I would kill him on our next 'in school' day. I had gone into the gruesome details of a dog kill and how I would accomplish that. My brothers had been proudly sitting back and were grinning from ear to ear while I was doing it, but Maddie had gone to get dad because her favourite teacher had been sobbing hysterically, unable to shut me up.

Needless to say, I was punished. Meditation and more self-defence, a nice way of saying time to shut up and not move a muscle, while self-defence consisted of being a punching bag for everyone during training. I learned a lot, most importantly I learned how to be a bit more subtle with my threats. I don't think that's what my dad had hoped to achieve with the punishment, but with my dad one could never be sure.

The reason this strange pack was calling me a chew toy was because of how good the predators of the supernatural variety looked. I realized this and admitted all the boys in our pack, even the older men, looked great. What humans didn't understand was that unhealthy or unfit meant that there would be a good chance to get killed. There were people, humans, which willingly offered themselves to several partners at once to get the protection of a pack. We didn't have them, thankfully dad forbade it. The only humans, accepted into our pack, were mates and their immediate family.

So here I was, first day of new school, trying to pass as human. I stalked into the classroom where my first lesson would be and planted myself in the back where there was still a large group of empty tables. Other students, the dogs, arrived right after me and went to the other side of the classroom. There were whispers and looks. One girl frantically motioned me to come sit with her at the front of the class, but before I could get up a small group of arrogant boys and girls surrounded me. They had swarmed into the classroom like they owned it and one of the boys had cut of my escape route with a cocky grin.

My sense of smell wasn't good enough to tell what they were yet, but they had to be some sort of Weres. I needed them closer to be sure. And I needed to touch one to get their senses.

"Well hello, little girl, have you been playing with the puppies? Did they hurt you, is that why you're sitting here?"

"Dude she's someone else's chew-toy, we don't take cast offs." The kid whose hand I'd broken, from the pack in the hall, answered for me.

I looked around the boy that had spoken to me just now and grinned wickedly at the other one, a dog, with his big mouth. I heard the door close but ignored it to say. "I do believe we established that I'm nobody's chew-toy and if you'd like me to come over there and break some more bones to prove my point, please tell me now. I would like to make sure we understand my position on this." There were a few gasps and 'Oooohs' around the room but everyone remained remarkably quiet as I turned to the boy that had gotten in my face.

"And you, nobody hurts me and walks away... I have *not* been playing with those pups, I hang out with the big dogs...

and they come when I whistle. Now, I'm sorry for sitting in your turf but I didn't know there were seating arrangements. So, if you could just move, I'll get out of your way."

The guy grinned broadly. "Nah, stay. I like you." His friends didn't seem too happy with his statement and the girls hissed.

"Seriously, you're hissing?" I asked, looking at the girl sitting behind the still grinning arrogant, blond guy. It had to be her seat that I was in. I looked back at him. "The rest of your pack doesn't seem to agree with that, Goldilocks."

"Flock." he answered.

"What?"

"We're not a pack. We are a flock."

"Whatareya geese?" I frowned, pretending I didn't know anything. I knew that they had to be some sort of predator, they had to be native and they were obviously pissed at the suggestion I'd made.

"Try something different, bigger, more dangerous and native." The blond boy stated calmly.

"Oh, Pelicans, that's cool." I smiled sweetly.

My words were getting to him and I noticed a shiver of anger run across his features. "Predators!!! You should know all Weres are predators. WE are predators, little girl."

"Oooh, I know, you're kites, and they're native, flying predators! Cute, little, flying predators." I grinned broadly. There was a scatter of chuckles around the classroom but I kept my eyes firmly on the blond guy.

"Wedgetail Eagles." He ground out.

I stood up straighter as he was talking. "That's nice, dear." I patted his head very lightly, making sure not to have full skin contact. "Now be a good little birdy and let me pass, would ya."

"Wedgetail Eagles with a wingspan of at least four meters for even the smallest members!" He growled through clenched teeth. He was looking me straight in the eyes, trying to stare me down; when it didn't work, he slowly got up from the chair that had been blocking my escape. He was standing way too close and I saw that he was way taller than me. He was built well, muscular but not solid like my brothers. His hair was almost white and looked beautiful as it fell over his forehead in lovely waves. His eyes were almost black with a hint of blue and I was fascinated. A new voice interrupted our stare down. The voice was full of power and sounded slightly amused.

"Mr. Blackmere, please let the new student pass. I would like to start my lessons."

Without breaking eye contact he moved his chair in the table. Then he held out his hand and looked at it. I followed his gaze and saw he had it out for a shake. How old-fashioned. I looked back at his face and ignored the hand. "I can't say it was a pleasure but you have made the first day of school even more interesting." I told him. He grabbed my hand.

The cocky smirk was back on his face as he refused to let my hand go when I tried to draw it back. "I look forward to seeing more of you." There was a predatory gleam in his eyes, I'd seen the look in his eyes so many times on my brothers. He was interested, great. He barely moved enough to let me brush past. I ignored the shiver that affected us both when our bodies touched and walked calmly down to the girl that had tried to warn me. I saw every hair on her head individually, I could almost see the breath as it left her mouth. The twitch of her lip was close enough to make my brain believe I was almost on top of her. Everything was magnified by the sight of a predatory bird. I tried to focus on looking calm, I'd had plenty of practise pretending to be normal. I made it to the chair next to the girl and sat down gracefully.

"Class, this is Julia. Julia, you'll get a chance to meet all these lovely creatures during study time. This will be your pack for the next four to six years, get used to them. We had our dropouts the first two terms. The lovely, little human at your side is Molly, I hereby assign her to be your guide for this first week. You should get along just fine."

"Why is she here?" Someone asked loudly, it sounded like a girl from the flock I'd left behind.

I kept looking at the teacher and he answered smoothly. "To learn, same as you lot."

"She'll be behind, why accept her in our class now?"

"She is not your problem, Lisbeth." He said sternly. "She is in my classes and that's all you need to know. We will keep going where we left of last semester. And she will be part of this pack."

Chapter 3

I saw a few dubious glances in my direction when the teacher didn't elaborate on why I was allowed in halfway through the year. The first year was the hardest. A year of testing saw the student population drop by more than a quarter before the start of the second year. Spec Med Qld was the name of the school. Officially it was The Medical Institute for all Species, the place where the future doctors and assassins, were shaped to perfection. It was divided in classes and the classes were bonded with the teacher for the full term of the education. Four to six years depending on subjects chosen. Only the brightest mortal students became teachers and they only served to teach one class. The Vampire and other immortal teachers were a different story altogether, but they had most of the human population in their classes. Other supernaturals didn't want to be bonded with them. For our class to be called a pack this teacher was most likely a dog or a wolf. Wolves aren't native but they immigrated Before Anarchy also known as BA. They had established in Australia since before the magic of the world was revealed when the veil disappeared, Before Anarchy.

The teacher introduced himself to me as Dylan Hunter, dad hadn't told me much about him, just that he should be manageable as a teacher for me. The class schedule was handed out for the coming term, his version included the PE classes, so I replaced the schedule I had. PE was needed to keep the animal counterparts of the Weres under control. PE was basically running and fighting. The humans wouldn't be allowed to run with the pack, they'd slow everybody down. Fighting was compulsory though, Molly gulped when she noticed that it would be before theory classes every other day this term.

The school tried to make units and form bonds between different races by having this intense regime. Sometimes it worked, sometimes it didn't. I thought it all depended on the teachers. To create better teams there were inter-class competitions at the end of each term, compulsory. They were another reason that the humans usually requested Vampire teachers, bonding with them meant sharing blood and humans got great benefits from that, they didn't even seem to mind the fact that it gave a vampire control over them.

The first two terms there would have been some shuffling of students, some student-teacher mixes would never work and the teachers had to be dominant to every student they had in their class. My position in the pack at home and the level of knowledge I already had on some of the subjects had been the reason I was allowed to enter late. Apparently, this class was the best one for me. Maybe someone had tried to be nice when they assigned me to a class with a pack of dingos, maybe it was my father's idea of a joke. Obviously, they had miscalculated, though I suspected my father's influence. Great! My years here would be interesting, far more interesting than I would have liked. They'd dumped a majority of the Dingoes in one class from the look of this and they had formed their own sub pack, my guess that the same thing had happened with the birds in this class. A few days of observation and a few well-placed questions would enlighten me.

As the day dragged on, I kept my head down. Mostly I ignored my classmates to the best of my abilities and hoped that my siblings hadn't left town. I didn't think they would leave for the first few days but I had stated that I wanted to do this alone. It'd be my luck that they'd finally decided to listen to what I wanted. Lord help me, day one and I was already homesick.

The classroom was too big. People smelled funny and there were far too many people here. I stayed in the classroom when everybody filed out for lunch. Mr Hunter had all but ordered me to stay, so that he could create the bonding. As soon as I was part of his pack, he would be able to protect me. Molly had blushed ferociously when he stated he'd be bonding me over lunch. A few of the other girls had giggled and the blokes had let a few growls slip. I'd never been through this process before. I was born into the pack I was in because I had a blood link with my father.

When the class was empty, Mr Hunter closed the door and locked it. At my look he explained that it would be dangerous for anyone if they interrupted the process.

"Relax, it won't be that bad." He smiled gently as he walked back to me.

"Uhuh." Was my smart reply, I suspect he saw uncertainty in my expression.

"How are you part of a pack, if you don't know this process?" He mumbled as he came closer.

"Birth!.. I mean, euh, well, my dad is the top dog. I sorta moved there right after I was born, they thought I'd be like him. And he made me part of the pack by being my dad and, . . . blood and all that, you know..." I trailed into silence at his look.

"Well, that explains why the smell of dogs on you, you must have brought some to help you settle in. I knew that you came from a pack. Chanel Country, wasn't it?"

"Yes. Yes, that's where I lived. That's where we are from." I trailed off. He smiled gently.

"Don't be nervous, I'll do my best not to hurt you." Anger sparked inside me and I snapped at him.

"I'm not nervous. I'm pissed off because it doesn't feel right to become part of another pack. It's unnatural to be part of two packs."

"Actually, you should know this, a lot of women stay part of their old pack as they join with men from another one."

"Yeah well, that's because they follow their mate. You are not my mate."

"Stranger things have happened." He mumbled under his breath before saying out loud. "I am wolf and I am Alpha blood. I left my old pack instead of fighting for dominance. Unlike dogs, we can't resist the urge to fight for leadership. There are three litter mates from my old pack teaching here because we love our old man." He sounded sad and without thinking I asked.

"Do you still get to go home to see the rest your family?"

He looked surprised at the question and nodded yes.

"I will have to familiarise myself with your smell, touch you and then mark you. Do you understand what that means for a wolf?"

"Kinda. Just do it. If I refuse you, the shit I had to put up with today was all for nothing and I'll get planted in a new class. The school board made the choice and my father approved of you. They chose you for some reason and if I refuse on the first day, they might even kick me out. So, let's just get this over with."

He looked surprised at my outburst and a slow smile crept up his lips. "You know most human women would kill for a chance like this. You are the third human female in my class that made me feel like a leper."

"What!?"

"Molly, the girl you sit next to and Amy, she sits in front of the birdies with her partner Rolf, both girls acted like bonding with me was a punishment."

"Well maybe they are just independent, like me."

"You are raised pack, you'd never be independent." He immediately replied. I burred up instantly and put my face really close to his as I growled.

"I think for myself, unlike wolves, we are capable and allowed to do so. Pack is family and family take care of each other. You are not family. So let us be really clear about this. NO, I am not comfortable being in your pack just so I can study here but I understand the necessity of the system. And YES, I am independent and you being our Alpha will not change that. I have no intention of fighting your authority or anyone else... but I will not my bare my throat to anyone."

"You smell good under the smell of dogs. And I do like a challenge as much as the next bloke." He grinned wickedly. "You are lucky you are a student here or I might have taken the challenge! Be careful. Now, shall we start?"

I raised my hands in defeat and dropped into a chair. He was right, I should have known better than talking like that to a dominant Were male. "Fine, do what you have to."

And there was the part I dreaded. I knew he would have to touch me and there was a chance I would not be able to hide my gift, my secret. I took a deep breath to calm myself and closed my eyes focusing on clearing my mind and grounding myself in my body.

I felt his breath caress my neck. He inhaled deeply and suddenly put his lips against my neck. I gasped and started to pull away but stopped as he growled softly and grabbed my arms to keep me from moving. Oh bugger, I was so deep in trouble. My senses went into overdrive, he smelled like cold damp soil and maple syrup. I tried to focus on the smell and squeezed my eyes shut. I concentrated on the thought pancakes on a cold winter morning, pancakes on a cold morning. I kept repeating it over and over as I felt his every hair that drifted over my cheek and shoulder. His scent was overwhelming and I moaned as his skin caressed my jaw. This was too intimate; he had no idea that I could smell him now. My abilities working full force now that he was touching me. I could smell his arousal as he pulled his face back and said. "I know your smell now."

He sounded husky and he didn't let go of my arms. We were now that close my legs were between his and our faces were so very close, I could feel his breath on my eyelids. He was sitting on the edge of his chair. Oh, he had no idea how much I was feeling, I tried to keep my thoughts on pancakes to ensure I wouldn't link to him.

"Where do you want to be marked? It's minor and I'll make sure you won't scar badly but because you are human it will need to be in sight. You will not be safe in this school if you aren't marked by a teacher. Shoulder is most common."

I knew that it was coming but the sensations were overloading my ability to think. I didn't answer.

"Where?" He asked again. I snapped out of it and without thinking opened my eyes. His eyes were right in front of mine and they were an orangey yellow colour. His wolf was right there in his eyes and I could feel his impatience. 'Pancakes and maple syrup' I thought as I quickly closed my eyes again. "Shoulder, right one please, I'm left-handed. Place it low, I promise that I'll wear singlets to school."

A sexy image flitted across my mind and I shut it down with pancakes on a cold winter morning, with maple syrup. "Pancakes?" I heard him mumble. Oh-oh, I hope he didn't understand the concept that those were my thoughts in his head. My abilities didn't need a formal link to access someone's thoughts, just touch.

"Oh, for goddess's sake, just mark me! Get it over with." I snapped.

With a loud growl his head dipped to my shoulder as his hand roughly tore my t-shirt to the side.

Chapter 4

Stupid Alpha male pride. His scent was filling my now sensitive nostrils and his thoughts were possessive as he bit down on my tender skin. There was nothing playful about it and his teeth broke through the skin. I felt his pleasure. It only hurt briefly, it was just a bite, no venom. His thoughts overwhelming mine, I did what I could to go with it, hiding my own thoughts and feelings. When his teeth released my shoulder, he started kissing the sore spot he'd created, licking the wound to make it heal. I was used to people licking a wound, it was a Were thing, they had healing properties in their saliva. My siblings had done that heaps of times while we were growing up because I was so much easier to hurt. It had never felt this intimate. Pancakes, maple syrup, wood fires, cold ground under bare feet, maple syrup pancakes.

He let go and I slowly opened my eyes, still too close. I backed away and my senses returned to manageable, now that he had released me and had backed away from me as well. My extreme sensitivity never lasted too long when they stopped touching me. I always missed it. At home there was always someone within hand-reach and I always felt so much more thanks to them.

It was a family secret, a pack secret, one person that had known and tried to leave our pack had been killed because of it. I didn't feel bad about it because it made me a freak, but my dad had explained that it also made me a very good commodity because by all appearances I was human. I had practised with my siblings and was capable of mind linking with the whole pack when I touched one pack member. That was strange enough but I could do it to any Were in any pack without being part of it.

Other than that, I could calm upset animals and turn Weres back to their human form if they were too upset or hurt to do so themselves. In short, I was a danger to others and a gift to my pack. I'd spend a lot of time with the pack doctor and already knew heaps, hence the reason I could start late. The risk of going to this school, with the pack system was a well discussed one and it was decided that I was indeed the best choice for doctor this year. The one from our pack who had started at the beginning of the year had dropped out because she had found her mate. They had moved back to his pack wanting to start a family immediately. My dad made no secret that he valued my development of killing skills as equally important. Me, coming here, was a calculated risk.

I felt lightheaded as we stood up, my teacher stepped back to give me some more space. I looked at Dylan Hunter, my new alpha, my teacher for the next few years. The urge to run from the yellow wolf eyes that stared at me from his beautiful human face became too much and I started to move, to escape, it was instinct. My feet turned and I tensed to bolt.

"DON'T!" He growled. Softer he added. "Don't move. My wolf will treat you as prey, you are too new." I froze, unable to look away. He was breathing deeply, calming himself. After what seemed like hours his eyes were normal again. Deep, emerald, green. He chuckled as he shook his head in disbelieve.

"Well, that was new."

"W_What was?" I stuttered, I was praying he hadn't figured my secret out already.

"I've felt sexual tension and bloodlust, the urge to kill the prick I marked and lots of other things with this class as I made them all mine. I, however, have never felt the urge to eat pancakes with maple syrup before, not while marking someone."

He had been looking at my face and mistook the look of horror for something else as he quickly added. "Hey, it's alright. I like pancakes, I really do! I just didn't know a person could make me feel like I needed a fresh stack of pancakes, with maple syrup of all things, I normally have mine with honey. You learn something new every day."

I stood there like a stunned mullet. He started grinning broadly. "I'll have to tell the old man about this! He likes freak events."

That snapped me out of my stupor. "Great, so now I'm a *Freak Event*. You will be a great teacher, I'm sure."

He laughed loudly. When, finally, I cracked a grin at his uncontrolled laughter, I asked. "So, what's the pack name?"

"You are now the newest and final edition of the Red Hunter Pack. Welcome aboard, Julie." With a bow he handed me a card and I made sure not to touch him as I took it. "This has all my details on it. Memorize it, put it on your speed-dial and call me if anything happens while you are here in town. Doesn't matter if it's after hours or middle of the night. I am now, by all accounts and purposes, your Alpha. While you are here in the city of Brisbane you belong to my pack only and I will protect you as such."

I shivered lightly and put my hand up to the mark. I pulled my shirt up over it and he growled softly. "You will show my mark! You chose that spot!" It was said with authority.

"I can't today, I'm not wearing a singlet under this shirt."

"Then go home. You won't need notes for tomorrow, you are more than up to date with Were laws according to your file, and after that will be PE anyway. Humans are excused for those afternoon sessions."

I didn't move, surprise must have been clear on my face as he grumbled the next few words. "I am your teacher but as a wolf I need to see the mark. Please. I'm sorry."

It didn't make sense why he was saying please and apologizing in the same breath, but I nodded and moved carefully. His wolf was obviously still not too far away. I went to get my bag and as I moved to the door, he was suddenly there blocking me. I didn't move; he was too close, his eyes were glowing with his wolf. Slowly, carefully, his hand moved to my shirt, he pulled it aside without touching my skin but already I felt the gift begin to work again. I had to get out of here fast!

"Permission to leave class, Alpha, Sir." I asked softly while making sure not to breathe in too deeply.

Thankfully he withdrew his hand and stepped aside. "See you in class tomorrow morning, Miss Westlander."

I opened the door and the crowd of my, now pack mates, moved to let me pass without a word. Smartest thing they'd done all day. I held my head high and didn't look anywhere but to my way out. Lunch was over, classes had started again. I moved down the deserted corridors with escape in mind and almost made it to the front exit. A Vampire stepped into my way. "Lost, little human? How convenient, I was just feeling peckish."

I didn't immediately reply just pulled my shirt further to the side before saying. "Student, Sir. Red Hunter Pack."

"No, I am sure that I would have remembered you from the last tournament. I know all the students. You were not in that Hunter's pack." With that he tried to grab me. I turned back to where I'd come from and ran, yelling at the top of my lungs. "HUNTER, GET YOUR ASS OUT HERE!"

I heard the pounding of footsteps from every direction but I had been almost at the entrance of the school and my class was well down the long corridor. Then the vampire was suddenly before me again. So fast! I stopped on a dime, yelling "HUNTER!", pulling away as the vampire grabbed for me again. Anger clouded my better judgement as he his hand came at me yet again. I grabbed his wrist instead and suddenly had a question answered, one that our pack had had forever. I could feel him. It was cold, dark and remarkably quiet in his head. My gift gave me the strength he had though and I used it to block his attempt. I danced under the wrist, lifting his arm, and ended behind him with his arm uncomfortably high on his back. "Stuff you, you unnatural piece of shit, I am a student from the Red Hunter Pack! I told you! *I am not your snack!*" I proclaimed loudly, right in his ear.

The hallway had filled up with students and other teachers, great, I just made a name for myself. I had so hoped that I could fly under the radar. The vampire jerked loose and turned around to grab my throat, he lifted me off my feet.

"You're not a snack anymore. You are dead!" He stated calmly and remarkably clear despite his fangs giving him a slight lisp. I didn't struggle but tried instead to find out in his mind just who the hell he was, to get away with this scene and clearly threatening a student. His mind however was taken by a haze of red, anger, pure rage, all for little, old me.

"MINE!" A loud growl had everyone part and the vampire slowly set me down. "She told you she is mine. You are attacking a student. More to the point! YOU are attacking MY student!"

I coughed and caught my breath.

"She defied me!" The vampire boldly stated, his hand still loosely on my collar bone. He sounded angry but his mind settled remarkably fast.

"Like hell I did!" I snapped, pushing his hand off me. He looked surprised at my input as I drew back my arm and punched him with all my might. The moment my skin touched his cheek, his strength flowed into me and it gave me a bit more oomph. But it was still like hitting a brick wall. I never did know when to quit and I pulled back to hit him again. Then I was pulled up against my teacher, which was full body contact. He took two steps back with me in his arms. I could smell the vampire, musky, dry and unnaturally full of life but even more, my now sensitive nose could smell the wolf that held me. Pancakes with maple syrup, cold mornings at the wood stove with pancakes, cold ground under bare feet on an early morning run, big trees covered in frost. I started to repeat my new mantra to myself to keep from entering his head and giving myself away on day one.

My shirt was still over my shoulder and the mark was clear. Then my teacher, the gorgeous Dylan Hunter, my new pack leader, a guy only a few years older than I was and a wolf to boot, did something that made my breath catch in my throat. He kissed the mark. "Mine! My pack!"

I felt the others of the pack close in, dogs closest. I also felt something strange, other wolves. We had no wolves in class, I was sure of that, how could I feel them via my teacher? Unless he was still part of his old pack too. Very unusual for a man to be part of more than one pack.

Chapter 5

The smells were too overwhelming to sort out and I whimpered as my teacher continued to hold me tightly against his strong body. I'd never been around this many species without my family, without my own pack to protect me.

"Funny Hunter, she's looking more scared now that you are holding her than she did when she was fighting with me."

I could see where this would go and opened my eyes. Everything was so clear as I saw things with wolf sight. I focused solely on the vampire and my maple syrup mantra, then found my voice.

"I clearly stated that I am a student and who my pack is. You started about tournaments and having a bad memory. I 'spose that happens when you get really, *really*, old but your hearing must be gone too because I didn't say anything more than that. So, *Blood Sucker*, I didn't defy you."

The Vampire looked fit to burst as Dylan and my new pack burst out laughing. Dylan released me. But I wasn't finished, I was beyond angry at myself for getting into this situation, everyone knows you don't run from a predator. I was angry because I felt Dylan's anger about the vampire having touched me. I was angry because the bastard had held me in the air by the throat and that had hurt me. I was angry because scared would make me a victim. Roughly, I pulled away from the man that had plastered himself to my back and pointed a finger at the angry Vampire.

"I am in this school, I told you my pack name and you

tried to treat me like a damned juice box. What the hell is wrong with you! Of course I look more scared when my damned teacher is holding me back. You are a fricking Vampire and you were going to eat me, I should kick your ass just for that! This is my first day of school here. My brothers kept me out till early this morning, so I hardly had any sleep and when I got here I got hassled by some idiot, who turned out to be a class mate. Then I get hassled by a freaking bird in my class for sitting in the wrong chair. But wait, it gets better, I then got bit by my teacher, to get marked just so I can have the pleasure of an education here. Following that I missed lunch altogether just to be dismissed because I'm not wearing a singlet and we have PE. *And for your information*, I loved PE in my last school AND THEN just to make my first day even worse, YOU treat me like I'm your freaking LUNCH! I'm not afraid of you because I'm too pissed off and if I looked afraid when he held me, it's because I thought I'd get kicked out for fighting. But you know what?! I don't even care anymore!!" I stomped my foot for good measure.

I looked around at the crowd that had gathered and snarled. "If any of you *freaks* have anything to add to my crappy first day here, *by all means*, don't hold back now!"

To everyone's surprise the silence that had descended after my little rant was broken by the lovely laughter of the vampire who had tried to eat me. "Oh man, D! I could almost feel sorry for you, she's big box of dynamite with a tiny fuse! If you want her out of your class do send her my way."

I didn't give my teacher, my new alpha, a chance to respond.

"Seriously?! You think this is funny?" I snapped as I stepped closer to the laughing vampire and I poked my finger at his chest. He bowed gracefully and with a deadly smile. Now all I felt was a deadly calm, no more rage from my teacher. No thought or noise in his head at all. It was actually quite nice when the vampire wasn't angry.

"Julien, at your service, milady." He said sweetly with a hint of an accent slipping through. "I would like to apologize for being the bad ending to your crappy first day. Allow me to make it up to you?"

He looked sincere and slightly amused but I asked dubiously. "How?" Vampires weren't as bad a the fey folk but it couldn't hurt to be careful with his offer.

"Whatever you wish, milady. I would be happy to show you pleasures beyond your wildest dreams to make up for the bad start of your day." Several members of my pack growled at that suggestion but I ignored them. I felt Dylan take a protective step closer when I answered. "No thank you, Julien, how about you just owe me one and get the hell out of my way for now."

He laughed again and stepped to the side with another graceful bow. "As you wish. I shall *owe you one*, my dear." I didn't look up or sideways or even back, I just walked out of the school calm as you please.

Oh sure, my dear heart was racing and I knew that everyone with good ears had heard. I was scared and pissed off in equal amounts and everyone with supernatural senses would have smelled that too. But I still had my pride, my blood and my game face on. The only thing I could think was that if my siblings had left town... I would have to hunt them down and kill them for deserting me!

I had thought that one of the great things about the school was that the neighbourhoods around it were all owned by the school for the students. I therefore managed to snatch a place within two blocks of the school for a decent rent. It was the place our previous pack member had rented before me. There was a huge, green park for Weres close by and the restaurants in the area all catered to carnivores. Raised on a cattle station in the Outback by a pack of dogs, I am a carnivore in every sense of the word. I love meat. Any meal without it is called a snack. I picked up some food on my way to the apartment and prayed that my family was waiting for me.

As I climbed the stairs my heart sank, there was no noise greeting me from my floor. No way could they be that quiet. I opened the door and found the living room as I left it, swags everywhere. I grinned to myself despite the emptiness. They hadn't left yet. There was a part of my gift that would make me a perfect assassin. I grinned as I walked into the kitchen and made myself a sandwich. Then I put on the oven and cut a heap of vegetable into a dish, added water, meat and herbs and put the pot in the oven to cook for a few hours. They had stocked my fridge yesterday when we moved in. I took a cold drink from the fridge then I put on a clean set of clothes and slapped a nice load of antiseptic and a big bandage over the new mark. I'd touched too many people today but I wouldn't shower until tonight. This was going to be messy. I grinned happily as I grabbed a potato from the kitchen bench where I'd left it before.

Jeans, check. Good running shoes, check. Loads of

antiseptic on fresh wound, check. Closing in on siblings with potato, check. I giggled in anticipation as I focused on finding my family. Due to the years with them I had an uncanny ability to find any pack member when I was alone. Nobody in our pack could hide from me. Nobody played hide and seek with me anymore, there was no distance great enough to hide from me for the members from my pack. And right now, I was seeking.

Meditation had side effects. When dad had punished me for threatening the boy at school and upsetting the teacher, I had to learn meditation. Dad thought it would teach me to calm myself doen. I had to learn to sit down and shut up! That was how he put it, control, but we then found out it had side effects. I had drawn all my siblings to me on the second day I was made to meditate. I'd only wanted to play. I'd been relieved of my boredom by dad's howl. His voice a roar coming closer fast. The door to my classroom had burst open when a furious dad had walked in. Without a word he'd dragged me outside and there, all my siblings had been straining against the adults of the pack. I'd called them and because of this they had been able to openly ignore dad's command. It had taken two months, under supervision of dad, to learn to turn it around. That was many years ago, I'd perfected the process. Anticipation of my hunt had my senses sharpen. I felt the gift tingle under my skin. If I focused on my pack and kept in mind that I wanted the members who were close to me, I'd feel the pull.

I felt something else pull on my subconscious but discarded it as I realized where to go. I didn't have far to go, they were near the park, even better. My guess was that Zack and Zoë, the twins and youngest of mum's kids, were already running and they created the separate pull I'd felt. I felt a remarkably strong pull that way but ignored them, I wanted the others. Richard was my focus. It was always easiest to identify my big brother. When dad wasn't around, he was the top dog. I stood still and focused on him. Calling on my gift I started walking, still in the direction of the park but near the entrance of the green paradise that the city cultivated for Weres, I veered left. Restaurants, well that made sense, they were always hungry and they would have done the other shopping this morning while I was going through hell at school. It didn't take long to spot them. Perfect, they were sitting on a terrace. I grinned cockily at Maddie, she always spotted me first, she had the best nose of all of them. She linked with the rest because they all looked in my direction as one, so I waved.

Chapter 6

Now here is what you need to know about my siblings. The oldest children of my father are Richard, Nathan and Harold, he prefers Harry. They were born four years before I was born to dad. Then dad's dirty laundry came back to bite him in the ass, one crazy night with a witch. A bad decision, in the shape of a baby girl, me.

My mother and father had met during school, they had been in a pack like I was now. They weren't even in a relationship, they'd had a fling just before graduation. Different species generally didn't conceive so they hadn't thought about the risk of a child. When I was born she found out I had no magic. Worse, I was blind to it, and so she deduced that I would be a Were like my father and dropped me in his pack. She disowned me. Lucky for me because I've since found out that most interspecies children are killed by either the mother or the father. Two months after I joined the family dad's next litter was born, Mark, Matt and Mick. Mum always said she picked those names so that it would be easier for yell at them come puberty.

Andy was the litter born after the M & Ms. He was two years younger than me and the M&Ms. There were problems and he was the only one that survived. He was stronger and more cunning during a hunt than any dog in the pack. Dad said it was survival instinct that drove him.

And last of all there were the twins. Like with Andy's litter, mum had trouble. To make sure that the kids had a better chance of survival, she shifted to her Dingo and refused to go human the whole time she was pregnant. The twins were born as pups. If a Were is born as an animal there is a chance that they don't turn back. It's a big chance and if they turn human, they are always different. Normally women try not to shift during pregnancy, the only time in their life they can do that. The twins hooked up with the pack faster and stronger than anyone before them and they refused to let their human side out. They refused to go near dad, he could force the change but he wouldn't because they were so small. They steered clear of me too, like I had the plague, they instinctively understood I could force them to change, even at such a young age. It wasn't until they were almost three that Zoë came to me. She ran into my arms during school. She normally never came near me so for her to run straight at me worried everyone. As a pack we felt anguish and hurt but she couldn't communicate why. When she jumped into my arms, she cried one thing through the pack link. "Change!"

Harder than ever before I forced the dog down. A stark-naked little girl we had never seen before clung to my neck for a brief second before jumping off and yelling "Help him!". Then she ran for the back of the property. By then everyone had already assembled, bikes, cars and dogs were waiting to be led by the tiny, little, now human, girl. She got Andy's shirt as we drove to her directions. There at a turkey nest, which is an open water tank on a small hill, we found Zack in dad's arms. The pup was barely alive when dad passed him to us on the side of the tank. For the second time in my short life, I forced a change. The pup had never changed and was close to dead. Dad hadn't been able to force their change but Zoe had already gone to get me. I was eight and that was the day it was decided I was a danger and would be kept a secret.

When I was nine there was trouble up north. I never did find out or even wanted to know what exactly happened, a pack was attacked and most of them were killed. The survivors were spread out to the family packs. An aunt on mum's side had died and her kids moved in with us. Maddie, Ronnie and Donnie, that's what they wanted to be called. They didn't want to hear their real names, names their parents had given them, and we all respected that choice. They were almost a year older than me. Because of my gift and the nightmares that haunted them, they slept with me. I kept them calm and helped them deal with the trauma by making sure that they could change back if they got too upset.

When Maddie and I reached the tender age of twelve it was decided that the boys had to sleep with the other boys, there were no excuses left for them to sleep with Mads and myself. Richard had been ordered to keep the boys from sneaking out to our room after dad found out that it had been happening. It took dad three weeks to figure out that Richard had done as told and us girls were sneaking into their room instead. We slept in one big puppy pile, even the twins and Andy were there every night.

Most nights we still sleep as a small pack, none of my brothers have mated yet. Maybe the fates will put them in the path of their mates while they are here in the city with me. For now though, they were my unwitting prey.

I walked closer to my pack, unable to keep the grin from

my face.

"Good first day?" Richard asked suspiciously. He knew me so well, some days I honestly thought he could read my mind.

"Nope, day from hell."

"What happened?" He asked as Ronnie pulled another chair to their table. I dropped into the chair between him and Nathan then grabbed Nathan's drink. He always got iced coffee and I love that stuff. None of the others liked that poison, as they called it. Nate grinned at me as I leaned into Ronnie because he had put his arm around me.

"What didn't happen?" I sighed dramatically into the mind link. "I really just wanna relax before going over all that."

Ronnie put his nose in my neck, I could hear the frown in his voice as he asked. "What is that smell on you?"

Maddie answered for me. "She's soaked in antiseptic. Just give her a minute, she'll tell us bro." Ronnie growled and I shot out of his embrace.

"I don't need shit from you too!" I growled back as I jumped off the chair. Richard sighed dramatically, like I had only a moment before. "Now you done it, we'll have to calm her down before she'll tell us anything. It'll take forever."

I struck a pose and snuck my hand in my pocket. "Yeah, now you have done it." I repeated and stuck my tongue out at Ronnie then yelled. "Hot potato!" I threw the potato at his head, spun on my heel and took off for the park. It was a huge park and I had plenty of places to run too. Behind me I heard the shouts of 'hot potato' as it got passed between my siblings and people got tackled.

The game hot potato had started when one of us heard about it from some human kids in town. We had given the game our own spin. It always involved a real potato to start with. One of us would throw it to someone. Then the game took on a whole new twist from the original. The person with the potato turned into the potato and everybody would try to get the potato. The strength they had, and I got from being with them, meant that the 'hot potato' would get thrown around while the potato tried to pass the real one on to someone else. Usually by stuffing it into their clothes. Hence the reason I had to run. I felt them close in and I heard their howls split the afternoon air. I looked back long enough to see Donnie closing in, he was the fastest of our pack. Matt wasn't far behind him and Nathan was keeping pace too. The others were still well away. Donnie howled again and Nate picked it up. Goosebumps ran over my arms and I screamed when I felt Donnie right behind me. I didn't stop and Donnie yelled, not even out of breath. "Go faster or the bad potato will chew on you!"

Ronnie, that was who he was talking about and I grinned, knowing that he was right. Ronnie was a bad potato. I veered left, the pull drew me to the twins, who always played along and liked this game when they were in their human shape. Donnie put a hand on my shoulder, I ran faster and we ran in sync like we always did when he made contact with me. Nathan was still a few steps behind with Matt and they pretended to be angry as they yelled. "Cheaters! We'll get you!" Yeah, we were cheating, a human could never run this fast but they'd catch up in no time.

And they did. Matt tackled us and Nate jumped into

the mix trying to pin me to the ground as the other boys rolled, laughing and fighting, besides us. I kicked and bucked and heard the tearing of fabric as we fought. I am a great fighter, but my brothers are better. Nate pinned me down sitting triumphantly on my waist with my wrists caught over my head. His shirt was ripped down the front and I tried to sound angry. "Hey, you shit, what are you thinking? Do I look like I want your attention?"

Nathan put his face really close to mine and grinned. "You were asking for it!" He sounded angry but it didn't go with his face.

A new voice interrupted as Nate was roughly dragged off me. "If you like your throat where it is, I suggest you start running and don't stop till you're well away from the city!"

I looked and saw that all three of my brothers were held by several angry looking Weres.

"RICHARD!" I yelled at the top of my lungs as I wildly looked around for the rest of our pack. "RICH__" I stopped as I realized that I knew theses Weres. They were my new class mates, my new pack! And the very angry wolf that was holding Nate by the throat was none other than my teacher. "Shit! Shit, double shit!"

I turned just in time to almost get thrown to the ground by Mads and Ronnie as they took up a protective stance around me. Richard calmly walked right up to Hunter and held up his hands. "It'd be good if you let go of our brother." He drawled.

Dylan Hunter never moved a muscle but my classmates moved closer to surround my family. "It'd make it easier to talk." Richard calmly added. I could feel him in my mind as he weighed up the options for a fight. We were a very well-trained unit of fighters.

"Westlanders" I heard the recognition in my new pack and there was an uneasy shuffle as the top dog from my class stepped up to Dylan and mumbled something in his ear.

"Stay away from her!" My teacher growled dangerously as my brothers now all moved closer to me.

"Guys meet my new class." I grinned cheekily. "Class, meet my family. Richard, Nathan, Harry, Matt, Mick, Mark, Donnie, Ronnie, Maddie, Andy, Oh and there are Zoë and Zack." I said as two huge dogs burst from the undergrowth, silent as death and just as scary. I was very proud and let everyone hear it as I finished with. "Children of Cameron and Louise Westlander. The Westlander pack. Sorry guys, can't tell you what all my classmates are called but the guy that growled at you was my new teacher. Dylan Hunter. Alpha wolf of Red Hunter pack, the pack that will be my second pack for the duration of my lovely education."

Chapter 7

Ronnie was the first to speak following my revelation and epic introduction. "Like hell you will be part of his pack! You are coming home." I didn't reply as he got in my face instead, I looked at Richard. Ronnie had been unreasonable about me joining a pack for school so I would let 'The Boss' handle it.

"Back off, Ro." Richard growled lightly in his dominant voice.

"Not with her looking like this in front of strangers!" He growled right back glaring at me. I looked down and saw that my shirt had ripped at the front just like Nathan's and my bra was showing. I glanced at Donnie and Richard, Richard nodded to us both. Maddie piped up happily focussing everybody on her standing beside me. "This is going to be good."

She stepped back, obviously aware of our silent communication. Donnie got right in front of me pushing his brother out of the road, then he slowly stripped off his shirt. He looked great but I only saw him as a brother. I felt Richard's hands on my waist and lifted my arms as he stripped me of the remains of my shirt. My arms stayed in the air and they were both practically plastered to me. This way I was barely visible between them, protecting my decency. I grinned as I heard several growls. Dylan and some of my new pack were having issues, together with Ronnie. I hadn't expected that but we had done this before, so I knew that Ronnie had a problem with this. Donnie slipped his shirt over my arms and head and gave me a quick light kiss before stepping away. Richard wrapped his arms around me and I heard a strange girl voice gasp. "I had heard they had a human sister, obviously she isn't related."

One remark and Richard was holding me back instead of just holding me. I saw red, I was going to kill her.

"My sister is very sensitive about her status in our pack. I suggest you keep your class in line."

"She is part of my pack, just like Bethany, and make no mistake it is a pack, not just a class."

Richard asked me in my mind and I told them what had happened at school. We were quiet a long time as I recounted events. Richard moved my shirt to the side and looked at the bandage. Dylan growled and stalked over. Without a word he ripped off the bandage. "MINE!" He growled for the second time that day. Maddie tapped him on the shoulder to get his attention, when he looked at her with his yellow wolfy eyes, she grinned. "Dude, I'm going to let you in on a little secret." She paused and he cocked his head to indicate that she had his attention. Hell, she had the attention of the whole class as she continued. "That is my sister, not by blood but by pack. We were adopted but, please pay attention, she wasn't. She can't change but she does not think like a human. If you want to live, I suggest you listen carefully... The last person that tried to claim that they owned my sister, well, they died. She killed them, we helped. You marked her. We understand that you have to, to keep her safe in that dumb school, but she is NOT yours."

The same dumb, unknown girl gasped loudly. "Jesus, I heard that about them, they apparently wiped out a whole pack because one guy tried to kiss a Westlander girl."

Richard held me tight when I growled in the back of my throat and Zoë and Zack started circling our legs. "With that particular incident the sons of their Top Dog tried to rape me. Their dad tried to tell my whole pack that I'd wanted it and was playing hard to get human. That I'd run off when they were ready to get down with me. Others of his pack claimed the same for my sisters, my youngest sister was twelve. They asked for our blood! They got blood, just not ours! If you are going to listen to stories, make sure you get the right details. Capice?!"

Whoever she was might have been dumb but she had guts as she asked. "So is it true, that you guys did it without your whole pack? Is it true that you are a pack within your father's pack?"

I relaxed and smiled because Richard answered. "You have a lot of nerve asking that. I like it. Dad breeds true, so all my brothers, sister and I are Top dogs. We have a lot of territory which means we don't need to divide the pack. Cameron Westlander rules." He used his dominant voice and I saw some of the girls swoon. Bitches. I'd thought that through the link and Mads burst out laughing, loudly. "Great all sorted, let's eat. It was not that nice meeting you all, but we'll see you around. Be nice to our little sister."

"Good idea. Class dismissed. Richard, Julie. Stay... "As an afterthought Dylan added. "Please."

Richard kept a hold of me, the twins didn't leave and everyone else left reluctantly. Our pack only left because Richard told them to wait at the clearing's edge using the pack link. The Top dog and two others from my class stayed as well. They probably stayed because of the twin dingoes at our feet. It didn't matter if the leader of the pack was called a top dog, alpha or whatever. Pack would always protect the leader.

As soon as it was clear who was staying and everyone else was out of earshot, Dylan started. "Please let her go."

"Wolf, the only reason I am listening is because she needs your protection in that school." Richard said, his voice like ice. He released me slowly.

"Understood and accepted. Thank you." The twins settled, still as dogs, against my sides. Hunter glanced at them but didn't say anything about it as he continued.

"I was informed by your father that there would be no problems with your. . . pack. There would be no problems with your pack while your sister was in this city. I was made to believe she would be left to my pack and her class for the duration of her education. It is bad enough to get someone halfway through the year. Cameron assured me that if I allowed her to remain distant from her new pack mates on everyday interactions, Julie would be a team player for the interschool competitions. More importantly, she would behave like this pack is *her pack* at all times. He assured me she understands the dynamics of pack."

He looked pointedly at Richard. "That little display, from the lot of you, just now, made a mockery of all that."

Richard didn't look embarrassed or angry. Much to my surprise he was grinning like the proverbial cat that got the canary. "Look I can understand that you got your knickers in a knot about this, but my little sister has been in fights before, with us and with others, we always make sure we dress our sisters. Suck it up wolf."

In the mind link I asked him why he was antagonizing Dylan but outwardly I shrugged when Dylan and my class mates looked at me. "He's right. None of us mind walking around without decent clothes but in public we make sure all the enticing bits are covered."

Richard mentally high fived me and I could feel his laughter in my head. I could also feel the amusement of the twins. Zack licked my hand and I looked down at him. '*Do you want me to kill him? Richard and the others don't like him either.*' I patted his head and thought back. '*No baby, I need him.*'

A new voice interrupted my conversation and I focused only to hear Richard laugh at whatever was said and answer. "Nah, they're not my enforcers, they are hers and they do the occasional job for dad." Somebody had asked about the twins.

The Top dog from my class looked at me and asked. "How does a human get the Westlander enforcers? They have quite a rep and I'm sure it's these two because the descriptions I heard are perfectly matched. Can they change or are they pets?"

Zack growled. Zoë cocked her head and thought. '*I'm sure I can take him out in seconds.*' I put my other hand on her head and smiled down at her serious doggie face. '*I'm sure you can but you're not allowed.*'

The air shimmered and a beautiful teenager appeared beside me. Dressed in a loose long shirt, a clear sign that she was Top dog. She hated clothes but understood the need as human. Zack followed suit. He was wearing jeans with a t-shirt and looked at the other dogs and my teacher. "Touch her and die." He said in an emotionless voice as one of the boys took a step forward. I didn't think he'd done it on purpose, he snapped out of it at Zack's voice. Zoë was hugging me closely and she sounded husky as she asked. "Why not kill them?" Following the conversation that she'd started in our head. I understood why she had changed to ask me as Ronnie had started telling her that she probably should kill the lot of them, starting with my teacher.

"I need them, sweetie."

"Ronnie said you only need us."

"Ronnie doesn't realize that a vampire almost bit me today. Dylan Hunter is a good Alpha, he made sure I didn't get snacked on. You know Ronnie can be an idiot."

"Matt and Mark agreed with him and Maddie only told me not to touch the dogs."

"Sweetheart, please remember what dad said about idiots?"

"Everybody is an idiot at some point during the day. Some people more than others. If you suspect that someone is being an idiot don't listen to them. If you are unsure ask your sister. You can't kill every idiot you meet." She quoted to me in an emotionless voice and then a smile lit up her face. "They are being idiots. Dad also said you need to spend time in this school away from us."

"That's right, sweet stuff, they are being idiots."

"Why didn't you kill the vampire yourself?"

"What?"

"You said that the wolf saved you from a vampire. I want to know why you didn't kill him yourself."

"Oh that. I'm pretty sure it was a teacher. Nobody killed anyone, he was going to snack on me because he didn't know I am a student."

She grinned cheekily. "Wolf's useless. I'm not a student, I can kill the vamp for you."

I never knew when she was serious or when she was joking, so I smiled back and explained. "Nah, they might replace him with a complete idiot! Now, at least I know what I'm dealing with. And he owes me."

"What does he owe you?" Zack asked. "And why? Is it because of the marks around your throat?"

Richard moved fast as he gently moved my head up and finally spotted the handprint right under my chin and jawline where I'd been held by Julien. His eyes changed colour and I quickly wrapped my arms around him in a tight hug whispering *'I'm okay, I'm okay.'* Steadily until he hugged me back and repeated me. He let go and asked the exact same thing Zoë had. "Do you want me to kill him for you?"

"No Richard, the vampire owes me. Open favour, Zack. It's worth a few bruises and just so you know, I did my best to bruise his ego." Zack nodded while Richard chuckled lightly and he was about to respond when...

"Come to me. Please." Dylan Hunter, my teacher and Alpha said in a dangerously soft voice.

In the blink of an eye the twins returned to their favourite form. Lethal Dingoes.

Chapter 8

I vaguely heard a faraway conversation and strained to listen. It was strange but my family didn't question me, they had always been eerily in tune with me. My sibling went quiet when they felt my mind focus. *'Man, they are the stories that are told to young dingoes to keep them in line. If you don't behave the Westlanders will find you. You don't freaking boss any of them around.'* I glanced at Richard and he nodded, he'd heard through me. That was the mark that made me part of their pack. Humans only got marked to show they were part of a class, there was no mind link for humans so these guys didn't know I could hear them. Sporadically new members would join our pack and for the first few months I would be really quiet in the link so that they could get used to the pack without finding out that a human could link. We, I, focussed on the conversation that my new pack was having in their link. *'I don't give a shit Kayden, she's part of my pack. I AM HER ALPHA!'* He roared through the link and I saw the boys step back in deference to his power. He was very powerful. I got a naughty though and grinned at Richard while walking to my new alpha, careful to keep my mind hidden from his link.

I stepped right into his personal space and he stiffened. *'Oh shoot, my last girlfriend got that look sometimes. Careful man.'* It seemed that the Top dog in my class wasn't as dumb as I had assumed.

I gently put my hand on Teacher's arm and spoke softly. "You know I always thought that wolves were unnatural in our country." He looked suitably disgusted but remained quiet. "I really appreciate you having such lovely manners, sir. I didn't expect that. I thought your kind was much more. . . primitive." I hesitated and whispered the last word before continuing. "You know, I kinda expected you to be yelling by now that you are the Alpha and all that." Kayden coughed to hide his laughter and Richard played along beautifully by saying. "Glad to see he has those primitive urges under control, sis. It has however made me decide that we will stay in the city for a while longer than planned. He might be too soft to protect you as pack. You are merely human to the wolf in him, probably prey."

Richard pulled it off with a straight face and I let go of my teacher as if burned. Turned and yelled at Richard. "You made him do it didn't you? Shit, shit, double shit! That bastard promised me I would have a decent teacher. I'll kill dad myself, he listened to you and he picked a freaking wimp. I'm happy there are dogs in class at least I should be safe on the school grounds with them knowing I'm a Westlander, they wouldn't wanna get on the bad side of our pack."

The mind link of my teacher roared to life with three men talking at once and Dylan yelling in a powerful voice. He was very powerful and I shuddered in delight at the strength of my new pack leader. It was instinct. It was also instinct to act like a human and back away as his cold, yellow eyes honed in on me. '*I am you teacher, your alpha and you best damned friend while you are at this institute! And I am the only one you will ever need to protect you! YOU ARE MINE!*' He roared this at me in the link not knowing I could hear him. Out loud he spoke softly. Carefully, as he gently ran a finger over the mark on my shoulder.

"I am quite capable of protecting you. My wolf does not see you as prey." He looked me straight in the eyes. "You will not need your old pack here." Zack growled and suddenly the wolf came out to play in my teacher. He growled menacingly at both the twins. His teeth shone in the late afternoon sun and they were sharper too. "Do not threaten me, pups! You might be someone else nightmare but you are not mine! She was willingly marked. She IS my pack and you can choose to deal with it or leave." Then he looked at Richard. "Same goes for you. And just for your information I am the strongest Were teacher in the school with exception of my brother who is equal to me. She is safe."

"Wow, nice eyes. That is really cool." I had to say something as the dominant male in Richard bristled at the implied threat in Dylan's words. His pack link buzzed. '*Hunter man, you just threatened the Westlanders and she is clearly taking the piss now, we really should go. Can't you tell she has no fear, her smells didn't match her expression or her words.*'

'*I know Kayden but she belongs with us now and this needs to be established. For her as well, she grew up pack she knows the rules.*'

He grabbed my hand then. Maple syrup pancakes, maple syrup pancakes and frosty ground. "Let's go and have a coffee, Julia. I'm sure your family will be waiting when you get home. You obviously need to meet some more of this pack." His voice was like ice and left no room for arguments, he was the boss and he was going to prove it. I wasn't sure how to get out of it when.

"We need to be with her." A soft, dangerous voice stated. "We will stay out of your way. It's too new!" Zack had materialized again, Zoë stayed in her dingo shape as much as possible. Dylan seemed to consider the statement. His pack seemed scared and they informed him that the twins were dangerous. Through our touch I could smell fear on them as Zoë also appeared. "We need her." She said. "It's simple, wolf. She is our humanity."

Zack was angry and he let us know in the link, on the outside he never showed a thing. Kayden put his hand up and coughed to get everyone's attention, it was a very sweet gesture and strange seeing it on a Top dog. "I'm sorry but could I say something here?"

I giggled and replied before anyone had a chance, while carefully backing away from the teacher and taking the twins back to where Richard was. "That's very sweet. I appreciate the manners, with the amount of testosterone in the air, I didn't think anyone would be capable of being nice about anything. Do tell, what's on your mind?"

He blushed, probably unsure if I was taking the mick outta him. He cleared his throat turned to Dylan and said. "Well, euh, it's like this. We heard about them. See Hunter, the Westlanders are the biggest and strongest pack in Australia. There are stories out there about their human daughter that runs with the pack. And I don't know about wolves, man, but with us dogs it isn't done."

He looked uncomfortable but continued. "The thing is that survivors talk. They talk about a human girl who raised her siblings and got them into their human shape at an age when most dogs go feral. Firsthand accounts say that they kill for her. The only reason there are survivors is because some people are let go. Westlanders don't kill randomly. It's even said that they take her orders over their dad's. That means they are both, what you would call alpha, in their own right. And we saw that just now, they can change with clothes, that's a lotta magic man. They don't have to listen to anyone. They are more dog than human and they protect her. I think what they are trying to say is that she is the only reason they go human at all. It's the same for all Weres. If you have a taste for killing, bigger prey is better. If you can't go human, you go feral. Feral gets hunted and killed. They need her, Hunter. It's pretty damned scary if, using your terms, an *alpha* goes feral. It's even scarier to think that two would do so as a unit. And if the two in question are Westlanders, that makes it a freaking nightmare. Not just for dogs. I'll make sure the dogs in the school steer clear if they come around, just let them be, man."

"Kayden, that is the most I've ever heard you say." Dylan said with a cocky grin. "I did understand when their father informed me but your perspective is interesting. Also, those two might look cool but I'm sure that, other than Julie, we can all smell the rage on the boy." He walked over and stood right in front of Zack with his hand out. "I am Dylan Hunter, Red Hunters Pack and Alpha to your sister. I will protect her while she is in the city but as you asked politely, I will accept your presence. If she is under threat my pack and I will protect her, you have already seen our need to do so. All I ask of you is that you stay away from the school grounds. I cannot protect you there as you are not of any school pack."

Zack didn't hesitate, he took the hand and nodded.

Hunter held his hand out to Zoë and she shook it with vigour. She even smiled. The twins turned to dogs without another word and both rubbed against his legs before stalking over to Kayden and the other boy. Only Zoë went right up to them, she bumped their legs with her head playfully nipped at the other boy's hand and then Zoë took off on a dead run with Zack at her tail, chasing each other and tumbling out of sight. Like wild pups. Kids.

"I'll go tell the rest what's up. See you for dinner in an hour." Richard said to me as he grabbed my arm in passing and though. *'Be careful sis, if he finds out, we might have to go to war.'* It wouldn't really be war but there would be a lot of people dying. The whole red hunter pack to be precise. If they found out what I could do. I grabbed his arm and turned into him for a hug. My big brother was my rock. *'As long as I can keep them from touching me too much, I should be fine.'*

Out loud I said. "You better keep Ronnie outta the kitchen 'cause I don't feel like take-out again. He stuffed up a perfectly good meal yesterday. Oh, and call the twins for dinner would you. I want to see them before we go out tonight."

My big brother and I split apart and he was grinning, it didn't reach his eyes but he faked it pretty good as he replied. "Tomorrow is a school day, Sis, you don't wanna get in trouble do you."

I batted my eyelids at my brother ignoring the overwhelming scent of my new pack closing ranks around me and replied. "I'll be a good girl."

"Euhuh"

"I'll buy all your drinks."

"Keep going."

"We'll wreck the apartment if we don't go out before bed and then we have to run in the dead hours."

"Twins will take care of you while we do." He lightly stressed the word we and I realized that supposedly I couldn't keep up with them.

"They don't like being inside and get grumpy or they'll wanna play and they might bite me too hard again."

Richard growled playfully. "Still don't see what's in it for me, the old man told me to make sure you settle in and behave."

I laughed loudly and answered. "I'll make you crème Brule for breakfast. Come on, babe you know you want my sweets, take me out."

Richard saw something on the guys behind me as he pulled me to him rather roughly and linked while snarling. "Get your freaking mind out of the gutter, it's my sister, stupid!" In the link he said. '*Be careful with that dog, he wants you.*'

Chapter 9

I knew Richard had to leave me with my new pack but I wanted to hold on to him and he could feel it in our link. With difficulty on both our sides, he gave me a kiss on the forehead and we let each other go. As he walked away from us, he said over his shoulder. "I'll get the twins, make Maddie dress Zo and we'll go to dancing tonight. We could all use it. BUT YOU *owe me* crème Brule for breakfast and enough for the others too. I don't have to fight for a spoonful like last time."

"Spoil sport!" I yelled at his back.

Not being able to put it off any longer, I turned to the alpha. My alpha and teacher. He was closer than I'd thought and my senses stayed in Were-mode despite the growing distance between my brother and me. I fell into an argument as I focused on their linked conversation. *'Well, you remember the old dog that came and sat in for a day?'*

'Yeah, so you're saying that was daddy Westlander? Wow!'

'Yup, and after he checked all four of us, he called us in and told us he would let his human daughter come here. He was pretty blunt. Sky is too nice, he doesn't think his child needs a new friend. Patrick and Aaron are too close to the wolf mating age, which is ridiculous because it is possible to find a mate later or sporadically even sooner but he wouldn't budge so he picked me because I'm younger and still as strong.'

'But,. . . .'

'There is no but Kayden, we had to sign a confidentiality agreement with blood before he even spoke to us. The only thing

I know is that they are all just as protective of her, including their father.'

'Still could've warned us that we were getting a West-freaking-Lander in the pack. I didn't realise she was directly related when you said her name in class earlier.'

'Have you paid attention to anything I said, she's their precious human, so there will be no ties for you to worry about, she's off limits.'

The other guy entered the conversation, I'd almost forgotten about him. *'Euh, guys, she's looking at us funny. If I couldn't smell the human on her I would have sworn she was listening to us.'*

I kept my face blank, years of experience, when all three suddenly looked at me. I made an effort to sound bored but it came out sarcastic when I told them. "Oh goody, you remembered I'm here. You made me stay with you and then you proceed to ignore me. If you boys are single, I can understand why. I assume you were discussing where to have coffee? And for future reference don't link with me around, I know you are doing it and it makes me feel left out when I can't join the conversation."

'Holy Mother, mate, I seriously felt like she was listening!'

'Knock it off idiot, she lives in a pack, it makes sense that she knows when someone is talking in a link.'

I ignored the conversation between the dogs and focused on Hunter. "You are buying." I said to him. "I mean, if I'm going to have to spend time with you boys after school and I'm not allowed to say no to your company, the least you can do is buy the coffee."

"That's fine. Shall we?" He held out an arm and I looked

at it. It was a nice, well-muscled arm, my gaze travelled to his shoulders, he had a great body and I liked what I saw. I took it all in and continued to boldly check him out, down his body before going back up finally reaching his face. He looked amused. "Miss Westlander, are you checking me out?"

The boys went quiet in the link and looked at us. I made sure to look bored. He was totally hot!

"Yep, I was just trying to decide how bad the smell from you will be for my family. I'll be fine walking alone, doesn't take more than a human nose to tell that you smell."

The amused look was gone and all three blokes looked shocked. The third extra had taken off when the twins did. The look on the remaining guys was priceless. STTT-RIKE and she scores! I turned and started walking away from them, they followed. I went to where my family had been and sat at the same table. They all sniffed delicately but didn't say anything about it. I knew for a fact that they would be able to smell my family strongly. I waited to order and asked for a menu instead. When the waitress came back, she hardly looked my way. They all refused to order as she looked at them while they pointedly looked at me. She got the hint and I got a glare for it. I suppose I could see why she wanted to spend more time on them, they did look amazing. Shorts and singlets, mussed hair and still slightly sweaty looking, they had obviously been working out.

I had to know, curiously and without making it noticeable I rubbed my hand against hers as she took the menu from me when I handed over. Witch, good to know. I ordered a large chicken and bacon burger with extra cheese, fries and a large Asian beef salad. I was rude enough to also order a big slice of pecan pie with cream and a large hazelnut coffee frappe. I sat back with a contented grin on my face. Much to my surprise the boys all ordered the same. The witch didn't look very happy with the order. When she walked off, they grinned at each other and then me. "You realize we just saved your ass, right?" Kayden asked me. The other dog added. "I'm just happy you eat like a Were, at least we won't starve eating the same as you."

I was confused. "What's your name and why do you need to eat what I eat, some strange pack ritual I need to know about?"

"Name's Grub, make jokes about my name and die painfully... as for the waitress, she looked fit to poison you and if we all have the same the risk for her is huge."

"Why would she poison me?"

"Just food poisoning, nothing lethal. It's a witch and she's not in a coven if she works here. Too many Weres near the park, they normally don't come here, they have the little park at the north of town. We're hot. We come here every day after school." He answered.

"What he's trying to say is... She liiiiikes us!" Kayden sang. Dylan remained quiet and was looking at the counter the whole time. When the waitress returned, he gave her a big, beautiful smile and she melted at the attention. She also, quiet pointedly, ignored me. He took the plates from her and distributed them. He set the last plate before himself and she paled visibly. She bowed at the waist, showing off her ample bosom at Dylan and moved his plate in my direction, then she touched his face and whispered something in his ear. He pulled her closer and shifted to the side, so she could sit in his lap. Then he grabbed the back of her head and pulled her face to his. I didn't want to look but I was also fascinated. Vaguely I heard a whisper in the link, they hadn't used it since I asked them not to, when I tried to turn away Kayden pushed my face back in their direction. "Keep looking." He said softly.

The witch boldly sat in his lap as she looked at me in triumph. I glanced at Kayden and Grub and they smirked watching the show, she was rubbing herself over Hunter like a bitch on heat. He put his face beside her ear again and sniffed, she still thought it was sexual but we could now see the deadly gleam in his animal eyes. He started whispering in her ear and suddenly she tried to pull away, he had his hand in her hair and pulled her back. She went white at what he said and when he finally let go, she scrambled off his lap in a rush. She grabbed the two plates in front of me when she left, looking shaken and scared. I looked at Hunter and his face was calm and collected, only a slight smile played on his lips.

"So, what'd ya say to her man?" Kayden asked what we all wanted to know, being surrounded by Weres I still never hear more than a mumble, he'd spoken so softly.

"I just told her I am Wolf, we are pack and Julie is ours. I told her that I would enjoy the thrill of taking *my whole pack* for an urban hunt if anyone ever hurt what's mine. Then I told her that her smell is an interesting one. I might have added a few minor details but I'd never discuss those in front of a woman."

Kayden and Grub burst out laughing, I couldn't help a

little smile but noticed he'd said mine, again. And I so wasn't his! I would have to keep my distance from our teacher. Great. Somehow, I didn't think it would be that easy after this day. I'd put myself on the radar with my little outburst in the hall. To change the subject, I asked no one in particular. "What's the story with Julian?"

It had the effect of a bucket of cold water. They all looked at me as one, disgusted now.

"Well teach, seen as he's your colleague, how's about you do the honours of 'splaining that one." Grub grimaced at Dylan. Dylan glanced at both the other guys and Kayden put his hands in the air. "Don't look at me, mate."

"Fine!" Dylan grumbled. "Julien is a Vampire, he's old, he's been at the school since it started and he only teaches the unplaceables. Immortals, the fey and the vamps. Won't allow any mortal race in his class. Oh, and he's an ass."

"And. . . .?" I prompted.

"We beat his class in the inter class competitions last term. His class of immortals got beaten by the most diverse Were and human cross class. There are more different species in our class than in any other, ever. And we topped the competition with teamwork." Dylan smiled proudly.

"Yeah, we had to work together or he would have had us run laps for lunch all this term." Grub said with a shiver. Dylan just smiled. "Threat worked well, we have the most diverse class in the history of school packs and we used that to our advantage. Ah, food's here."

The waitress carefully placed four new plates on the table and bowed to us before turning quickly and almost running off with the two she'd left before. I looked at the four plates and frowned, they'd been eating off the two plates she'd left earlier. Kayden explained. "We all eat together. She stuffed up the order, well, she stuffed up full stop. So now we all eat together." She brought our drinks and left in the same fashion, scared. Kayden swapped his plate with mine and we started eating. "Why would you do that?" I asked him.

"What?"

"Swap our plates. Mr. Hunter scared bejeezez outta her. Surely she wouldn't do anything."

"I know, but why risk it. If there is anything in it at least I have a better chance at survival." He grinned around a mouth full of chicken and bacon. "You are our newest little human. We must, at least, take care of you until we decide whether we like you or not."

Strangely enough Dylan growled. Kayden burst out laughing and added. "Well, guess my man D here likes you already."

"My wolf is protective of pack." He snarled defensively.

"Uhuh!" Mumbled Grub with a grin. The hair on my neck rose as I smelt the approach of a mixed mob of Weres. I couldn't see in that direction and didn't recognise them by smell.

I stiffened and the boys noticed, they would have noticed the smell at the same time as I did so I snapped. "I have a pack and I can protect myself just fine. Your wolf can suck eggs, as far as I care. Just remember that you ordered me here. I could be spending this time with my family but instead I'm here with you three trying not to get poisoned just because I'm here with you."

I'd distracted them from my real reaction with a true

lie. Lying to Weres doesn't work, it doesn't work with many sups. Telling the truth and getting angry, about something to distract from what they want or suspect, does. I learned this trick very young.

Someone closed into my personal space and Dylan didn't look pleased as a face parked itself on my shoulder. I couldn't turn to see who it was but I knew it was a stranger to me. I felt the wolf in this man and smelled the original pack of my teacher. Family then. He put his lips closer to my ear and inhaled deeply. "Look at this, you are the feisty little human that made a mockery of our Julien?"

"Hmmm." I responded lightly.

"Get off her, Patrick." Our teacher growled.

"She doesn't seem to mind."

"Mine." Was the low growled response. Good Lord Almighty this man just didn't understand that I was my own person. The other guy laughed huskily in my ear. "Don't send her to Julien if she gets too much for you, I'd love to tame this one. Her anger smells sweet even with the stink of strange dogs and antiseptic. You were right to mark her so fast." Then he made his biggest mistake. He licked my ear. Dylan growled and I winked at him. He frowned but settled back in his chair.

I put my hands up slowly and proceeded to put them in the stranger's hair, much to the shock of my other pack mates, even my Alpha looked hesitant as I asked softly. "Name?"

"Patrick Hunter. At your service, hot stuff." I tightened my hands in his hair, shifted forward in my chair and janked his head down against the back of the chair. I heard a satisfying crunch as I spun off the chair while it crashed to the ground with Patrick. I swiped a fork from the table, then grabbed his arm and proceeded to drop myself on his back. His arm raised to the point of pain and the fork embedded under his jaw. I looked up to see my pack members sitting back with pleased grins and the rest of the Weres around me fit to kill.

Chapter 10

I grinned brightly at the angry faces. "I am Julia Westlander of the Westlander and Red Hunter Packs. I know the universal laws of Pack, regarding all Races, and I am within my rights to extract revenge. My Alpha told him I wasn't to be touched and he admitted he knew of my bonding to my pack despite my race. So, unless my Alpha tells me otherwise... I am going to have a little chat with this charming fellow and you will all Back Off!"

I looked at Dylan and he raised his hands. "Hey be my guest, saves me doing it. Go for gold." He was looking like he was trying not to laugh. I grinned back. "Thank you, Alpha."

There was a tangle of links in my head now with so many Weres and I shifted through like a ghost unseen and unheard. I focused on Kayden and Dylan. '*If he bucks her, you'll need to step in man, he'll kill her.*' Kayden said in their link.

Dylan sounded happy as he replied. '*Let see what our girl can do shall we.*'

Grub sounded worried. '*He's as strong as you, if she doesn't make her point properly he's within his rights to kill her, do you think she is aware of that?*' I knew that but then I felt Patrick shift, tensing his muscles to make a move. I raised his arm until I heard a satisfying crack of bone breaking and jammed the fork into the skin. I waited for a few seconds and with the Were hearing I could hear the drops of blood hitting the tiles. Even the links went quiet.

"Don't move pet. I really need to talk to you." I said

softly. Then I leaned on his broken arm and put my face next to his ear like he had with me. It had to hurt but he never made a sound. "I grew up with my pack. And was raised my father's daughter. You know why my family isn't worried about me here? It's because they know I can take care of myself. . . If you ever tangle with me again, I will kill you and I won't have any trouble sleeping at night. You knew I am pack. You knew that I'm off limits, you acknowledged the bond I have with my Alpha and yet you continued to touch me anyway. You were warned and the laws that give me the right to hurt you leave a lot open. I could cut your balls off with a blunt knife and your pack could do nothing about it if I don't give you a chance to retaliate. These laws are older than dirt and I know them all. You are very lucky I'm a nice girl. I'm going to let you up and then we are going to be polite and start over." I lowered my voice to a menacing whisper. "Do you understand, pet?"

"I understand." He said without emotion. I twisted my wrist slightly to make my point just as I got off his back and then held out my hand to help him up. There was respect in his eyes now as he looked at me. We didn't let go and there was no power play while he held my hand.

"Julia Westlander. We good?" I asked looking straight in his eyes. The eyes turned to wolf but I never looked down, staring at his wolf as it tried to cower me to his Alpha status and power. Finally, after a few tense and remarkably quiet minutes, I felt the wolf back down.

"Yeah, we're good." He said then added. "And my name is Patrick, not pet."

"I'll stick with Pet, it suits you."

"Explain."

"You remind me a beautiful, Brumby stallion we caught once. He almost killed some of our best riders and broke a fair few bones. They called him Hellfire. After a few months he broke more of our pack than anything ever had so finally dad gave him to me for my birthday. I called him Pet. That's what he is now. My pet and if he hadn't made the choice he did, I would have killed him myself." The implication was clear and yet he smiled as he asked.

"Do you take good care of him or is it respect by fear only?"

I didn't think as I answered. "I don't hurt him, I love him; he's beautiful! His respect is based on trust, he knows he'll be taken care of." I saw the smirk on his face and realized what he was thinking so I quickly added. "Well, respect and a mutual understanding of who is in charge." The smirk died down completely as I continued. "Now that I'll be living here the kids will care for him and he's good with all the kids. He knows I'll come home and kill him myself if he misbehaves. Slowly and painfully."

I smirked as I looked straight at my new 'pet'. Then, to make sure they all knew how I felt about them I didn't look at anyone other than my new pack members that were still sitting where I'd left them and sat on the chair that Kayden had kindly put upright for me.

Someone pushed the chair in a bit as I sat, what a gentleman, I'd smelled and felt him right behind me and wasn't surprised. Their respective links were very busy as they all discussed my actions. I started eating the Asian beef salad and ignored the chairs and tables that were pulled over to join ours. My Alpha remained quiet and when Grub tried to use the link, both Dylan and Kayden refused to answer in the mind link. Kayden answered out loud. "Grub my man, I do believe that the rest of our time at Spec Med just became so much more interesting. Never thought I'd be in a pack with a Westlander."

I grinned, couldn't help it, he respected me as a Westlander. Not for my name but for my actions.

Grub High Fived him and said. "Mate, we now have bragging rights, a Westlander in the pack. One with her own enforcers and we've seen her in action. She took on a grown wolf without getting a scratch on her." I felt all the wolves burr up at the comment, even our own Alpha, so I quickly said. "Yeah sound good, Grub, but we all know that he could have torn strips of me if he wasn't bound by laws older than dirt. I'm just glad that he's not human."

"Why?" Grub asked, but I knew everyone was listening for my answer.

"Because he obviously respects the law and understand the necessity for violence. I've found that humans just don't have the same honour code. That and they just don't heal as fast. Pet obviously is a strong wolf in his own right because I didn't give him a clean break, yet he is healing well and fast. Also have to give him kudos for not whinging like a little girl when I broke him..., I mean his arm." I'd purposely hesitated and Kayden high-fived me as he laughed at the intentional stumble.

"You really are a righteous bi. . "

I interrupted the new voice. "Think before you finish that sentence, is getting a few laughs worth the pain I'll give you in return?"

I now knew who'd spoken, as a nerdy looking guy with sunnies went bright red while at least six people burst out laughing. Three of them were here with me. "Damned, she got you scared. Big baddie like you, scared of a little human girl."

The nerdy guy didn't look like any Were I knew and certainly not like a big baddie. He was tall and lanky, I couldn't even see if he sported a decent set of muscles because he was wearing a collared shirt and, I kid you not, a tie. He was quick to respond to, what I could only assume was Dylan's other brother, Aaron. "Let's see. There are four of you wolves here from your daddy's pack. You are the third brother and known to be less strong than the other two. That means that 'The little human girl' just took on an Alpha that is stronger than you. Now following down that line of thought, if she knows the laws of Weres she would have been aware that, had he been able to get free she could have ended up dead. I didn't see any worry on her face at any time. Did you? Never mind, don't answer that. Now, if she wasn't afraid of your brother what the hell makes you think she is making empty threats to me, a Beta. I'm not scared Aaron, I'm practical and I know how to pick my battles."

I laughed. "Wow, you might be as smart as you look. What are you?"

He grinned. "Guess."

"Smartass?"

"Wow, she got it right first try!" Said Aaron grinning brightly.

"Owl." The nerd said, ignoring the snickers and Aaron's

remark.

"Barn owl, Boobrook, Barking, Pacific, Grass, Masked Owl, Frogmouth?" He shook his head with every species of owl I named. "What sort then, Rufous?"

He didn't get a chance to respond as Aaron butted in again. "She guessed it right, admit it, Doofus."

Ignoring Aaron, he said. "Powerful Owl." He was obviously proud of the fact and added. "Coonabarabran. How come you didn't know what sort of Owls are also Were species?"

I shrugged. "Never met one before, never been relevant. There are none as Guarders. Only Weres that work as Guarders are allowed through our territory, so I know a bit more about them. And I know natural owls, I learned about them at home. What's with the sunnies?"

"Too bright, even in our human form we are better equipped to handle nights."

"Sorry, I didn't realize. Dogs don't have that problem. What's your name?"

"Brains."

"Seriously? Brains?" He nodded with a big grin as I added.

"Wow, I really wasn't far off with Smartass."

He burst out laughing. "I like you." Everybody looked surprised.

"What?" I snapped at Kayden, he just stared at me.

"Close your mouth Kayden and can someone explain why everyone is looking like I grew another head?"

Brains laughed again and answered. "I don't talk much on an average day and I don't like many people. You surprised them with your. . . pet situation. And now I'M talking to you as well. In full sentences."

I sank lower in my chair and felt my face flush. '*I think Brains has our girl flustered. Make a note, D. She deals with violence very well but she can't deal with people talking about their feelings. You better buy Brains a round, my man.*' I heard Grub in the mind link. I almost lost my cool and responded in the link but I was thankfully distracted by Hunter's response. '*I think she might have a few more surprises in store for us, Grub. And I'm not sure if it is for the better that we have her in our pack.*' Kayden sounded thoughtful as he added his two bits worth softly. I had to pay attention because there were other links intruding on my mind. '*I like her. I am glad we got her.*'

Chapter 11

I looked closer at Kayden. He was cute in a rugged sort of way. He carried his Status as Top dog without showing off but the power radiated off him like the heat of a bitumen road in summer. He was strong and quiet and willing to be second to Hunter just to get an education. I decided I liked him for that.

"Hey Kayden, what's the time?"

"Almost four thirty, why."

I turned to look at Dylan. To make sure that I showed him the proper respect I didn't look him in the eye and asked softly. "We had coffee Alpha, sir, may I please be excused to go home now?"

Dylan looked angry, I didn't understand until I picked up on a new link, the link between himself and the other wolves, his family. *'She hasn't even met us all yet, D.'*

'Yeah well, there was an altercation before Patrick touched her. She's held out very well, all things considering.'

'You're gonna let her walk away without meeting us properly?'

Dylan never stopped looking at me while he was talking to his siblings. *'Tomorrow, Sky.'* He said to the female wolf in the link. To me, out loud, he said. "Permission granted. Tomorrow at four thirty after we are done with PE you will be here to meet us."

I knew that there was no way I could go against him if I wanted to make sure that the others knew I respected his leadership, so I nodded. "Yes, sir." Keeping my voice soft and polite while I wanted to rip his face off for ordering me around.

"She smells of rage and yet she sounds so sweet. Sure you're gonna keep her? Offer stands bro." Patrick said it lightly but there was a dangerous undertone to his words.

Dylan grinned dangerously. "Yeah, wouldn't want you to get hurt, pet."

Brain winked as Grub and Kayden looked at him in disgust when he said. "See ya tomorrow, babe."

I couldn't help but calm down and smile. "That would be nice, Brainy." I replied, suddenly feeling shy. I quickly scooted out of my chair and made for home, never looking back, knowing that everybody at the tables behind me was looking at me go. Before their links faded in my head and the senses they woke, through my gift, settled down, I felt a familiar presence. I couldn't help but feel relieved as Andy appeared beside me. Opening the familiar link to my family. I felt the anger in the Weres I left behind. I thought I was home free, how wrong I was.

"Hey!" I turned to see Dylan standing at the table. His hands balled in tight fists at his side. "What the hell are you doing here?" Andy turned slowly as if he hadn't realized that Dylan was talking to him. "What me?" He asked with a cheeky grin and then put his arm around my shoulder and pulled me flush against his body, being comfortable with my brother I put my arm around his waist and looked up at him instead of looking at my new Alpha. It was the wrong thing to do. Dylan stalked over with a thunderous face but before he could say anything Andy spoke.

"I'm walking home with my big sister." He held up his

hand and showed us a big bag from a shop two doors down. "Saw her leave as I left the shop, why make her walk home alone when I was here anyway." He looked like a little boy, so innocent and I could feel the anger drain from Dylan.

Dylan held out his hand and Andy shook it without hesitating. "Nice to see you care man." He said sweetly to Dylan. Andy was the most cunning hunter we had in our pack, as a human he could present himself as anything. We always joked that he was more chameleon than Dog. He was a Top Dog in his own right but unless he would get angry, there was no way to tell, his power was perfectly contained. "I lost the draw to get more food. Ronnie stuffed things up and we were hoping to fix it before she got home." He grinned stupidly.

If I hadn't known any better, I would have believed it too. Dylan did.

"Guess I'm glad I'm not in your shoes, mate." He said to Andy as he turned back to the table with the other Weres. I gave a little wave to everyone and turned with my baby brother still holding me.

When we reached home, we looked at each other and burst out laughing.

"Holy Shit, Juuls! You named an Alpha wolf, Pet, and they didn't kill you. I love you! Did you work him?"

"Just how long were you waiting for me?"

"Never left, got to the shop before you got to the café. But that's beside the point, did you work him?"

He meant: did I use my gift like I had on Hellfire? I could tame any animal. Rogue Weres, normal animals, ferals of any description. We'd tried my gift on anything that we could catch. Obviously, we mostly just killed the Weres if they were trespassing but they were normally terrible people that were set on destroying lives. I managed to calm anything. Some of the Feral Weres we'd caught had even joined our pack and they weren't all Dingoes either, but that was a very well-kept secret. I'd always done it with dad there so that they didn't just bond with me. Dad didn't need the twins as enforcers because he had heaps, thanks to my gift.

"Nah, didn't have to use the gift on him. Don't need a pet alpha wolf to compete with the Alpha of my pack. We had an ordinary stare-down and I think I surprised his wolf. No challenge, yet no back-down they don't know how to handle that.

We got into my building and I stalled. "Is Richard really thinking it's needed to keep an eye on me?"

"Spoke to dad the moment we left you with them. Dad said he'd picked the teacher most capable of teaching you and most unlikely to be interested in doing more. He proceeded to say that he should have known you'd stuff up his plans and told Richard to stay put for a few weeks."

"Just Richard?" I asked hopeful for more. Andy grinned broadly. "Nope, whole pack, seen as the twins didn't wanne leave you anyway. He also arranged to have our stuff picked you. Ronnie is being made to go with Mark. We all know that Ronnie mightn't be coming back so we are gonne party hard tonight. Just don't let them know I told you. Ronnie wants to be a martyr." I laughed sadly. "Yeah, sounds like him. And we'll have to say goodbye again."

We slowly walked up to my floor and could hear the rest of our siblings before we even got there. The moment we got to the floor my apartment was on, the noise from our place stopped and the door banged open as Zoë ran to greet us as a human. She hugged me like her life depended on it. Then she surprised us all by saying. "I like your new dog, can we have him?" I linked with her and saw a picture of Grub.

"What?" She snapped as I laughed loudly. "He is strong, he isn't related and Zack doesn't feel the need to kill him. I want him. We can get more territory if that's what he wants, he should fit in. You like him, don't you?"

"Yes, sweetie, I do like him. He talked sense to the wolf too, just like the other dog." I grinned.

"The wolf isn't nice and I don't like how he talks about you." She mimicked Dylan perfectly. "She is mine!" We were all laughing as we walked into the apartment and shut the door behind us. Dinner was already at the table. Nachos and pasta salad, coleslaw and sandwiches, burgers and a huge dish of steaming hot lasagne plus the stew I'd made earlier. They had the kitchen bench full of drinks and plates. We all loaded up and went to hang out in the living room. After I gave them a full rundown on the day I'd had, right up until I met Andy just now, the conversation turned light. Nobody told me what to do about the situation I was in and Zack kept poking Ronnie in the ribs without saying anything. I knew he was purposely distracting Ronnie, we all knew. I closed my eyes and opened my mind to just loose myself in the link I had with my siblings when the strangest thing happened.

Despite the incredible amount of food that had been prepared it was all gone. I had a Were metabolism and I ate almost just as much as they did. We were having a chill out before going out, letting dinner settle. I was at that point between sleeping and awake when I suddenly felt others. Not my family. These were in a different location. There were Kayden, Grub and Dylan but I also felt Brain and the others that had been at the café earlier. Again, Grub seemed to notice but this time I was shocked as he said. *'Dude, even now I can feel her. It's like she is still listening in. I mean the situation you guys created by interlinking packs is highly unusual and it should, by rights, not be possible for us to communicate like this. What if she is more dog than they are letting on.'*

'Grub, you are insane. She smells human and the doggiest part of her is that family. She can't link.'

'She's freaking hot man! I wouldn't mind a piece of that.' I didn't know this bloke but he was with Aaron's pack. It felt strange to be able to distinguish that so easily. Kayden snarled into the link. *'If she doesn't kill you, we will. She is off limits!'*

And there went my hope to any normal dating opportunities, if Kayden was gonna scare off any potential boyfriends before I even met them, I was screwed. That's what my brothers had been doing for years now. I reached over twenty without much excitement in the love department because my brothers did exactly what he did.

'Where are they going? Do we know?'

There were a few negatives when Sky entered the conversation. *'We can just follow them.'*

Dylan sounded annoyed. *'Great! You are suggesting we stalk my new student because you all want to know what her family is like.'* He groaned into the link. *'Why me?'*

'*Because you refuse to use your status as her Alpha to find her.*' Patrick replied smartly.

'*It's called decency bro. Remember, it's basically what she accused you off earlier when she was saving your ego.*' Just like that my opinion of my new teacher went up, way up.

'*Shut up D! I could have taken her easy.*' He snapped.

'*Uhuh, whatever ya say. How's the arm?*'

Suddenly I felt something hone in on me. I pulled back on instinct as the fading voice of Grub lingered in my mind while I gasped back to a fully wakeful state with adrenaline pumping hard. The last thing I'd heard was. '*I think I found her. She's here. I'm sure of it guys!*' Obviously, Grub was smarter and more dangerous than I had given him credit for.

Chapter 12

Nathan and Donnie had been sitting beside me and felt, plus smelt, my terror first. They growled at the unseen threat and held me protectively while everyone else looked on in confusion. "Settle boys, it was just the links. SHIT. I don't even know how it happened. . . . I was spotted."

It had happened before, we practiced my gift on everyone that passed through our territory. Thankfully we didn't have any problems because nobody understood what I could do. It was new. When it became clear what I could do, the adults had done a lot of research and found exactly nothing, nada, zip, zilch, not a damned hint of anything like me. Dad, being the awesome father he is, made sure to test every option and help me develop every part of my gift. If that meant on others, he had no problems making it happen. Now we had a problem, because the last person that had traced me in a link had been killed. He'd been made to tell exactly how he'd done it and what he'd felt, under pressure. I'd been the one to use my gift to pressure him and I'd broken him, it had taken me four days and by then I'd developed feelings for him, I was sixteen at the time. Richard had killed him, quick and clean, the moment he'd found out. You can't be in someone's head, find out he's a nice bloke and not develop feelings. That had been my excuse. But you can't have feelings for someone that could potentially give away your secrets; that was the reason he had been killed.

What my family never knew was that I'd been with him in his head when he'd died. He told me he forgave my family and me just before the life drained from him and the connection between us faded. And now it looked like Grub could do the same. Feel me, the ghost in the links, and find me there.

Zoë was the first to link and figure out my jumbled thoughts. Her body flickered between dingo and human. Everyone held their breath. She had to control this herself. If needed I could help her but she needed to learn control herself. Or else she would end up feral and that was a death sentence. She was dingo and howled. Nobody moved, the link was dead silent. She jumped on my lap, a big, heavy, dangerous and angry dingo. She growled in my face, baring her gleaming, razor-sharp teeth. I gave her a sad smile. A girl collapsed on my lap and started sobbing. I held her while everyone looked on in amazement. Zoë was in love. With Grub. Poor boy, I thought and couldn't help but grin. We would never leave dad's pack, he would have to join the dreaded Westlanders.

"You think he will?" Zoë sobbed.

She'd obviously stayed in my thoughts and followed my reasoning. Zack answered. "He will if he knows what's good for him."

"I'm good for him." She snapped. There were a lot of versions from all of us as we agreed that she was too good for any boy.

"Let him know we are going to The Pitt, Juuls. We'll see what he thinks." Richard wasn't worried about her being only sixteen. She was more dog than human, she knew what she needed and Zack was only slightly better at being human, dad always said he could just fake it better.

The link went quiet again and this time Zoë stayed with me as I focused on the other pack. The Alpha. Pancakes. I found him. Quickly I went to search past him to Kayden and Grub. The moment I found their life-force I thought '*They'll probably go to The Pitt.*' And then I disappeared from their link.

Zoë, Maddie and I dressed up to the nines. Provocative and elegant, sexy on the verge of slutty. It was a fine line and we walked it well. We all had our hair up in tight high ponytails, subtle makeup highlighting eyes and lips. Chunky necklace to draw the eyes down to bare neck and cleavage. Yeah, we were hot and we knew it. The moment we stepped out Ronnie growled angrily. "NO. They are not going out like that. They look like bait." Nathan laughed and Donnie sidled up to me. He started rubbing his hands down my arms and over my exposed skin. I shivered, he was my brother but something in me knew that he wasn't blood. I smacked his hand lightly. "Knock it off."

Then he did something that made me gasp and all hell broke loose. He nipped my neck on the other side from the mark that Hunter had made. Next thing I knew he was on the floor fighting with Ronnie and Matt. Richard broke them apart with one word. "ENOUGH!" It rattled through the room and we all froze, he had let all his power soak into that one word. "Ronnie and Matt, you will go home."

"But Mark. . " Richard didn't let Matt finish. "NO, YOU are going with him!! NOW!"

They walked out the door without another word, we didn't move until we heard the squeal of tires as his truck tore away. Then Richard turned his angry eyes on Donnie.

"You had to do it, didn't you?! You knew how he'd respond."

I tried to stick up for Donnie. "Ronnie is behaving ridiculous. Ever since I was given a date to leave, he's been acting like an Idiot."

His anger turned on me. "You are an idiot, Juuls. He isn't your brother and you forget! You always_" I interrupted. "He is so!" I snapped.

"NO!" He snapped right back. "And more to the point Donnie and Maddie aren't blood either. Ronnie isn't an idiot, he wants to claim you and dad has forbade it."

"WHAT THE __?? NO!" I looked at the others, they nodded. "How long?" I asked, still in shock. "Always." Maddie answered softly. "You're the reason we survived, he said he'd claim you the first month after we moved in."

My legs gave out and I sat on the floor, stunned.

"Remember how dad ordered a light mark the first time we went to the city to go out, how that would keep you safe."

"Yeah, Richard marked me. It was gone within two days." I looked at Richard.

He was still angry but continued where Maddie left off. "The next time we went out, remember what happened then?" He asked.

And I started to remember. Ronnie had come to my room and said that Richard was still getting ready. He said he'd mark me and he'd grabbed me from behind. I'd laughed as he growled in my ear and then I'd exploded in pain, I was seventeen. He'd bit me. The pain had been insane. I woke up more than a week later in the infirmary with my dad beside me. The first thing he had asked me was who I wanted to see. I'd asked where mum was and he'd smiled, telling me I was a strong girl, then called out my mother's name. There had been some commotion outside and mum had come in shortly after. I'd been sent to school, with my teacher, in town for almost a month. To let me know it wasn't punishment Richard, Nathan and Harry had been with me.

He saw me remember and started talking again. "Ronnie marked you with a mate bond that day. You passed out and the doctor put you in an induced coma to give dad a chance to break the bond. It took him a week. If Ronny would have succeeded in marking you, he would have been killed. You never asked, YOU NEVER EVEN FREAKING ASKED, JUULS!" Richard took a deep breath, and another one. "Dad said you didn't understand and we weren't allowed to talk about it. Ronnie is getting stronger, if he reaches Top Dog status, he will be free of dad's orders and we are all pretty sure that day will be the day he marks you again. You on the other hand are freaking clueless. And his own brother, the only one he has, our Donnie dearest, does his best to provoke and harass. Because you, being the idiot you are, let Donnie mark you every time before we go out."

"YOU SAID!" I got up and screamed at Richard. "YOU, you are the one that said it was wrong for you to mark me and you didn't want to do it."

"You're my sister and a beautiful woman at that. IT IS WRONG! I don't want you to go out at all! We all want someone to properly mark you because that would make you safe! But only to make you safe! And now you are walking around smelling like breakfast because of that stupid school and that stupid wolf and we don't even want you to be here!

Dad's dumb enough to think you can pass for human but you are a freak. You draw us and dad thinks it's just our pack, he is so wrong! You draw all Weres, Juuls! Dad didn't believe us but you do." His voice broke.

Maddie put her arm around me. "You draw us to you like a moth to the flame, you calm my dog when you touch me. Donnie is the only one that doesn't feel the need to bite you hard when he marks you. Temporary marks are just nibbles for us, chick, something that says that this human is ours for the duration of the night, a light back off. Temporary marks are for sexual partners."

"WHAT!"

Richard got angry again. "IDIOT, freaking, dumbass idiot, how could you not put two and two together on that. You grew up with us, you've seen us do it to dates. Why the Hell do you think that no Weres go near you when we go out."

I hid in the embrace Maddie had me in and felt my face go bright red. How could I not have ever put that together. He was right, I am an idiot. Then I put four and four together too and looked at Donnie in shock. "That's why the Weres won't date you! It's my fault." He didn't reply but walked over and kissed my head gently. "Now we're getting somewhere." He mumbled. Then he yelled into the link. *'LET'S PARTY LIKE THE ANIMALS WE ARE!'*

Without another word we went out the door and to The Pitt.

Chapter 13

A mixed club and the biggest damned club in town. We mobbed the bar, got three shots and a beer, each, and hit the dance floor. None of my brothers other than Richard and Donnie had spoken to me. Zoë hadn't left my side, even on the dance floor. There were a lot of Weres here and I dealt with it the like I always had. By touching my family and Zoë made it easy. '*I got her.*' I heard in the link as I felt a set of hands grab my waist. Zoë moved away from where she'd been dancing practically plastered against my front. I'm sure that we looked like a pair of hussies when we danced like that but I needed the contact, they knew. Donnie slipped his arms around me and as we continued to grind to the music. For the first time ever, I felt uncomfortable. I turned in his arms and he pulled me flush against his body then he dropped his head against mine and linked. '*I actually like that you finally know. I used to think it was better when you thought of us as brothers but I like the way you feel and now I can say it. I can dance with you like I want, not like I should.*'

'*Shut up Donnie.*' I heard Nathan growl in the link and Donnie grinned.

His hips were moving against mine and even in the link his voice sounded husky. I looked into his eyes as he kept my body moving, his dog was close to the surface and suddenly he didn't look like my brother anymore. Someone sandwiched me from behind, seamlessly joining our moves. I smelt Nathan, my real brother and sighed in relief. Without thinking I put my head back against his shoulder and lifted my arms so that he could slip his arms under to put his hands on my shoulders in a backward hug. I put my hands on his while Donnie still held my hips glued to his body with his embrace.

'I think it might all be a bit much for her right now bro.' Nathan joined our conversation. *'You need to give her time, we talked about this.'*

'You talked about this? When?' They didn't respond to my question.

'Nate? Donnie? When?'

Richard grabbed my hand, Maddie was beside him as he dislodged me from the other two. They dragged me to the bar and Zack was already there with a whole row of shots lined up before him. I grinned. *'Now THAT I understand!'*

'I'll race you to the middle!' Maddie grinned as she challenged me in the link. I didn't reply but toasted her with the shot I grabbed. Zack and Zo grabbed the two in the middle and started drinking as fast as Maddie and myself, working to our end. Richard stood by to pick up the pieces. And there would be pieces. I would be in pieces. I didn't want to think anymore, I was going to get totally wasted and for that I would need a sober family member because they had to make sure I didn't intrude on other Weres with my gift. Maddie and I reached the twins at the same time. Zack waved to the bartender and all the glasses we'd slammed down got refilled. I felt the approach of Donnie and Nathan. Micky and Mark were partying hard on the dance floor with some lovely looking girls, they weren't coming home tonight from the look of that. The twins blocked Donnie. I felt his frustration but right now he wasn't my brother, he was a

problem I didn't need. We cleared another line of shots between the four of us. The bartender put a Bloody Mary in front of me and pointed to the end of the bar. Kayden waved looking amused, I groaned when I saw him get up to move over to us. I'd forgotten. If he was here, Hunter and Grub would be too and if they were here there would be others from the table incident. Shit, shit, double shit. I drank the Bloody Mary in one long gulp.

'*We need to go!*' I thought to the rest. But Richard vetoed the remark with a calm. '*Too late for that, sis. Andy, you better clear the ally and take the high-ground. Finish your shots and centre yourself in our link.*' What he meant was that I had to feel for every member of our pack that was within range and pick one to hide behind. Richard was impatient as Kayden staggered closer through the crowd. '*The twins!*' I snapped just as Richard started to say something else. Whatever he had been wanting to say turned into '*Fine. But it'll have to be Zoë and Donnie because you have his mark and you reek of him. If they see how we use the mark on you there could be some really bad consequences for all of us.*'

Zack stepped aside as Kayden reached us and he shouted to be heard over the music. "Good to see you can hold your alcohol, new girl. Wanne dance?"

Donnie pushed him aside and put his arms around Zoë and me. "Back off man. We're having some quality time here."

"I'm only asking for one dance." Kayden said as he stepped closer and sniffed. He was rude enough to move my head to the side and he did it gently while ignoring the anger of my pack.

A new voice cut through the music. "Go outside you lot! There will be no fighting in here!" The bartender had taken note of the situation and looked at Kayden in sympathy. "Why don't you go find your own toy, everyone can see this one is taken."

"I just asked for a dance man, I'm not looking for a fight."

"In that case, all of you OUT!" the bartender snapped. Kayden grinned cockily and got right in my face. "Our Alpha has requested the pleasure of your company, not to interrupt your night, so do take your family." It wasn't a question, it was a command. Technically he couldn't do this to me, it was after school. But lines were blurry because, as I had so aptly proven, the laws of pack were older than dirt.

'Shit guys, pancakes is calling me as Alpha and you're all invited.' I said in the link. I looked at Richard and he nodded. Kayden was watching like a hawk and I yelled for good measure. "We're gonna have a beer with the teach." Kayden nodded but looked thoughtful, then he shook head, probably thinking that Richard had heard him already. I was too drunk to try getting into his head without giving myself away so I kept a death grip on Donnie and Zoë as I yelled over the music that he should lead the way.

We went to the back, private lounges, should have guessed. He passed some open smaller rooms and led us to the door next to the back-exit. We entered a large private lounge area filled with softer music and loads of Weres of all sorts. The biggest surprise was that Mark, Andy and Mickey were already there. They looked relaxed but there was a tension in their shoulders that showed to us. Surprisingly they kept the link quiet. Donnie let go as Zoë pulled me to the boys. She linked briefly. '*No mind talk, Juuls, you are our human.*' I had too much to drink if Zoë understood what was happening before I did. There was a reason why they weren't using the link and it was me. Their metabolism was better than mine, even if my metabolism was better than human.

"What are you doing here?"

"Got invited to a private party, how could we refuse? They told us you would be coming too." The implication was clear.

"I drank too much for this shit." I groaned. There was a soft laughter from my left and I finally looked around. The wolves were sitting, spread out on some couches, looking hot and in control.

"Come here." Dylan growled in a sexy voice. "Please." I shuddered and clung to Zoë as I obeyed my new Alpha. She looked happy and relaxed, unusual for her but then I noticed that Grub was sitting with the wolves and so was Brain. He winked at me.

"Whaddayawantnow?" I grumbled.

Patrick grinned. "THAT's no way to greet your Alpha."

"Oh, hello Pet, didn't see ya there." I said in a bored tone, just to annoy him because I'd seen everyone and I could feel them clearly.

"Bitch." He snarled.

"Born and bred, Pet. And what's your excuse for being an ass, I was told you were born wolf." I grinned right back. My family, spread out around the room, laughed, but Zoë squeezed my hand in warning.

"You didn't want to meet my family this afternoon so

when we spotted you here, we thought it would be nice to have a drink with you." Dylan said in a dangerously soft voice. "Why don't you sit down?" Richard used the link *'Donnie!'* was all he said but I got the hint. I turned around to see where he was, I saw them already sitting on one of the sofas behind me. "Sure." I smiled at my Alpha, ignoring the space beside him and walking a few steps to my family. I was going to sit beside Donnie but again Richard piped up in the link. *'On his lap, sis, he nipped you for the night, you are claimed.'* Donnie grinned and suggestively wiggled his eyebrows. I plopped in his lap and Zoë sat beside him grabbing my hand again. She was still looking at Grub. Zack stood behind the sofa like a body guard and I saw that the rest had spread themselves strategically around. Donnie wasn't super quiet as he lowered his head to my ear and said. "Don't like the interruption, babe." The growl in his voice and the possessive tone he used made me shudder in his arms. The feelings he created reminded me that he didn't see me as a sister, apparently my body agreed. I was too drunk for this. Hell, this was the reason I was drinking tonight.

The silence that descended on the room when I'd sat in Donnie lap was deafening. *'Aaaah, the sweet sound of progress.'* Richard mumbled into the link. It was a saying that dad used when we were in trouble and squirming because we'd been caught. As one we all burst out laughing. Thankfully I was in Donnie's lap because he took that moment to graze his teeth over his mark hard enough that I looked at him in shock instead of joining the laughter. He gave me a kiss and grinned. *'You can't hear us remember. Now kiss me back or they'll know something's up.'*

He deserved a taste of his own medicine and the alcohol made me bold. I slowly ran one hand down his chest and the other up his neck. I tugged his head to the side and kissed the spot where I would have marked him had I been a Were. He groaned. I nipped it with my teeth. He shuddered and I felt his response. Grinning in victory I kissed the tip of his nose and said. "Be a good boy. Tell me what was so funny."

"If you're a good girl, I might tell you later." He replied in a low, playful voice.

"Oi, Human! Could you be a bit more respectful of your hosts."

Chapter 14

I heard the murmured 'oh oh's' from my family as I shot up. Zoë had the smarts to turn and the great dog was stuck to my side as I stalked over to the bloke that had spoken. "Get up!" I snapped standing before him.

"What for?"

"Get! Up!" I ground out through clenched teeth. I did hear Richard and Donnie telling me to calm down and I knew they were right but the alcohol made me careless. All my frustrations poured into my fist as he got up. I knocked him right back down again. There was a loud crack of his nose breaking and I smiled grimly.

"First! Don't ever 'Oi human' me!" I counted off on my fingers as he looked fit to kill me. "Second! I was ordered to come here, not invited, so that makes the wolves something other than hosts, DOESN'T IT? Thirdly! I'm pretty sure there are just Weres here and touching is part of what we are." He moved to get up again and Brains put his hand against the guy's chest saying. "Let's let the little lady finish, shall we? She makes some interesting points." The authority was strong in his voice and I shivered as his power dripped down my skin. The whole room seemed filled with top of the food chain Weres and I felt them all. "Thanks, Brainy. Where was I? Thirdly,. .NO! Fourthly! I was having fun and after the day I had I should have been able to do that in peace with my own p_" Zoë bumped me just in time and I adjusted what I had been wanting to say "people. I've been wanting to go to Spec Med since I found out about it and it's all just crap

90

so far, it was supposed to be awesome!"

I started crying, alcohol and frustration getting the better of me. Zoë turned back to her human form and hugged me. I lowered my head to her neck and kept mumbling to her between sobs. "I need more shots. This still all sucks. I want the others back. I hate this school already." I felt someone take my hand and softly rub circles in my palm. "Poor little human." Brains said when I looked down to see who it was. "Too many Weres, not enough you."

I laughed through my sobs and replied. "Too many dominant Weres, Brains. I thought there would be more structure. I also thought I could have my own life and this is day freaking one and already he's trying to get me to assimilate like a good little wolf and there's four of them and they're all so freaking bossy. I mean did you look at them this afternoon? So bossy. I thought they'd ignore me like the human I am."

"You don't behave like a human. How much have you had to drink?"

"We did two rows." I replied proudly. "And Madds didn't beat me to the Twins this time." He looked behind me and Donnie answered some unspoken question. "Shots, 'bout thirty per row, the girls and Zack were doing shots, she needed it. They run the rows to the middle!"

"Ooh don't forget, that dog got her a Bloody Mary and we had a few beers before we started." Maddie helpfully added.

Brains kept rubbing thoughtful circles in my palm and I was fascinated with his face. The contact made my eyes so sharp, so much sharper even than a dog. He looked away and I realized he wasn't wearing sunnies. He actually looked really good now, not so nerdy and definitely hot. I felt him as I kept looking and Zoë kept a strong presence in my mind, humming in the link of moonlit runs and border patrol, fights and hunts. We'd found out that I could hide my gift behind something like that as I felt other Weres. And boy did I feel Brains. Contemplation and sadness with a steel core, he felt like the twins in the respect that he might at one point have been close to feral.

"Take her home." He suddenly said. Nobody argued with him, Dylan growled softly and I smelt his distinct maple and cold forest smell. I couldn't help my mouth as it ran off before my brain could put the brakes on. "Hey Brains?"

"Yes?"

"Know a place that serves good pancakes for breakfast 'round school?"

I winked at Dylan and he groaned. Brains grinned, pulled himself up on my hand and said, "Try Fat Freddie it's on the other side of the park to where we were today."

"Do you go there for breakfast?"

"I do, I'm telling you, it's the best place for breakfast anywhere."

"I might see ya there." I smiled.

"Like hell you will." Richard snapped. "You OWE me crème Brule sis."

I turned to Richard with a wicked grin. "Only if you can catch me. You up for it?" Zoë laughed as I dashed for the door with her, leaving our heels behind, we were in sync. Zack had the door open and off we were. Donnie's laughter followed us out combined with the sounds of a shuffle. Nate and Donnie would hold Richard as long as they could, they always helped me when I caused trouble with Richard. We took the backdoor out the ally and ran. I ran with the twins at my side in human form. At some point I thought I might have heard a 'Woo-hoo' overhead while we raced through the deserted streets but I didn't care, I was finally free.

I woke up to seven alarms. I was in Zack's arms and holding Zoë, Maddie was piled over our legs and Donnie and the others had slept as dogs after a late run. My head was pounding but I smiled anyway. Richard hadn't caught us last night, we made it home before him and laughed at his disgusted face. Out of sympathy I promised to make the dessert for dinner time, even leaving a list with the ingredients I'd need. I got out of breakfast cooking but was scolded for leaving like we did. I'd have to apologize to the teacher.

First things first however, I took a long hot shower, long enough to steam up the bathroom nicely. I heard the door open but wasn't worried. We always walked in and out on each other, as I expected a towel was slung over the shower curtain rail. I took the hint and wrapped it around myself as I got out of the shower. This what we did at home too if there was a rush on the showers. Donnie was leaning against the door.

"We need to talk, Juuls."

"Nah, we're good. Ronnie and I will have a few words I'm sure, but we're good." He didn't respond. "Aren't we?" I asked softly. He just kept staring at me. Just when it started to become uncomfortable, he spoke.

"I don't know how you couldn't tell, how you couldn't even remember what he did."

I didn't know what to say and he continued. "He has always said he'd claim you again one day, as soon as he can go against your father."

"Our father."

"No Juuls, it's your dad not ours, only Maddie ever thought of him as dad. But even Madds doesn't think of you guys as siblings. She likes Nathan too much for that."

"What? No! When? How long?"

Donnie smiled, still leaning against the door. "Since the nightmares stopped."

"But? But...that's like...years!"

"Yep. And that's how long we've been arguing about you." I knew Donnie and Ronnie had some fierce competition going on but I'd always thought it was just sibling rivalry. I blushed, flustered, while I thought about how many times I'd been nearly naked with them around. Donnie nodded, looking pleased as I was desperately trying to think of how I never noticed.

"Good girl, now you're getting it." His voice sounded rough.

I gripped the top of the towel. His eyes following my hands. I suddenly noticed things about him I had never let myself think. I noticed how the muscles moved as he uncrossed his arms, how his eyes were darker than my brothers. I thought of all the times we'd run together his hand in mine. When he changed, he was so fast I always felt like I was close to flying if I ran with him, my hand behind his head if he ran in his other shape. He'd always pushed me to my limits when I ran with him, when we fought and he always had a shirt ready for me. That was how we'd gotten in the habit of changing like we had in the park. I felt the blood rush hotly to my face.

"You have no idea how long I've waited for this." His voice husky, he'd moved to the sink but he never closed the gap between us. The door burst open. Maddie looked between us and settled on Donnie.

"Sorry bro, sounded like you were taking it further. Richard will kill me too when he finds out if that happens."

"It's alright sis, I think she's heard enough for now. I'll give her time to come to grips with this new reality." He turned and walked out past Maddie, closing the door softly behind him.

"Maddie?"

"I'm sorry. I am so sorry, he needed to tell you. Unlike Ronnie, he has always respected you. I had to give him some time with you." She turned the shower back on and started to undress. I was still gaping at her. "You never notice that they don't treat you like a sister. Or that your brothers don't touch me like mine touch you. I've. . . .I'm. . .I. .I'm sorry." With that she stepped out of the last of her clothes and into the shower. I got dressed slowly as she was showering. Suddenly I didn't feel like breakfast. I tossed a towel over the rail for her when the water turned off and heard her laugh. "Coward." I sat down with my back against the door and my eyes closed. "Yep." Was all I said.

The boys were already done when we got out and even Zoë was dressed to be human. With her that meant she had more than just a shirt on, and even wore shoes. My real brothers looked suspiciously between Donnie and me. Nobody spoke. I stood for a little while looking at them all. They were all very handsome yet when I looked at Donnie, I didn't see him like I used to.

"This is going to take some getting used to. Take it everyone knew?" They nodded affirmatively. "Well thanks for the heads-up, boys." Then I grinned at Richard. "I know you said that you would kill any boy that came near me but don't kill this one, he practically family."

"Depends on how he treats you.." Richard didn't sound like he was joking.

"So, does dad know too?"

"Your dad is the reason Ronnie never bit you again. Ronnie spent even longer than you recovering after he bit you, in his case from the punishment he received. Cameron knows how we feel, he's always known." Donnie said softly.

"Okay, back to basics. Let's go eat." I didn't want to deal with anything else, I grabbed my bag, checked that I had lunch and went to the door. Everyone snapped out of their daze as one. "Yeah, food."

Chapter 15

Knowing that most of the Weres from last night would be at the diner that Brains had suggested, we still decided to go. Well, Richard decided and he vetoed our protests in no uncertain terms. I had to agree that it would be better to face the music with my family instead of waiting for class. When we got to Fat Freddie, it was already full. This place had to be good. Brains had an eye on the door because he welcomed us the moment we set foot through the door. He took us to the back and into another dining area. You guessed it, the whole load that had been in the private room the night before was there and then some. Brains introduced everyone to us and I quickly rattled off the names of my family.

Much to my surprise there were spots, per two, reserved for us. I got to drag Zoë with me. Richard had decided that she would be the best one to stay with me because, as a human, she looked harmless and she'd already stated her need for me to my new Alpha. That way it wouldn't look like I needed them more. And she played it well, clinging to my arm like the little sister she was, never once looking like the dangerous predator she could be.

She smiled shyly at Grub and Kayden but pointedly scowled at Dylan. Much to everyone's surprise she also stated. "This is my sister. MINE! You only got to mark her for school! WE belong to her AND she belongs to us. So how about YOU stop looking at her like she actually belongs to you. As a teacher you have no lasting claim and you should remember that!! I'll be watching you, wolf, and if you set one foot wrong, we'll rip you to shreds. This is the only and last time you get to dictate her schedule outside of school." She gave me a kiss on the cheek and told me. "I'm sorry Juuls but we all know he only got to mark you for that stupid school, he is only to keep you safe. Daddy promised he had no real claim. You promised he couldn't change things and this is only your second day and he's already trying to change everything. Please don't be angry with me."

"It's alright sweetie, I could never be angry with you." Before I could continue, she interrupted. "Yes, you could, remember when I killed that boy that tried to kiss you. You were angry then." There was a gasp of shock from some of the other Weres there and even Brains looked disgusted. But worse Grub looked upset. That was something we didn't want that because she liked him so I said. "He tried to rape me, I was only slightly upset with you because I wanted to kill him myself."

"I remember. You yelled at me for a long time and__"
I stopped her mid-sentence and pushed her into the chair. "Right, Zo, enough."

"So, do you want pancakes?" Asked an amused voice beside me.

"Whatever, as long as it doesn't take too long. Wouldn't wanne be late for class on my second day."

He laughed and softly stroked my skin where he's marked me only the day before. "You heal fast and very well, for a human. I might have to redo the mark if it doesn't scar properly."

My head snapped around to Dylan, he was smirking broadly. Zoë was snarling lowly beside me. I squeezed her hand and linked. *'He's doing it to prove he's The Man. He's Alpha and wolf, they are more primitive Zoë. Calm down.'* I glanced at her and saw Brains watching with interest but I ignored it. To Dylan I said. "I'm sorry Mr. Hunter, Sir. I was under the impression that the marking would be a onetime thing, as long as it created a light scar, and that you would make sure that it didn't scar like a Mate Mark. My family assures me that I smell like you already due to what you did. Surely that is enough."

His arm shot out and he grabbed my head, much like he had done to the waitress the day before. His mouth was on my ear causing my body to shiver as I felt the hot breath fan my face and then he whispered. "What if I want you? My wolf likes you and he likes a challenge, if you run too fast, I might decide to chase you. You certainly make things. . . interesting."

I waited until he let me go and looked at Richard, I shook my head just once to let him know that my death grip on Zoë had meant that he hadn't felt my gift. It tended to react strangely to stress and my siblings all knew what to do to calm me. Once, a Guarder on his way to Longreach to report in at the end of his shift, had tried to get fresh with me. I'd gotten stressed, sadly that was because I'd liked him. I'd been trying to hide from my link, trying to hide what was happening from my family. I'd ended up in his head, he couldn't move. Later he told of how he was a passenger in his own body and how he'd felt me there. Dad poisoned him and as he lay delirious for days, they'd created a whole set of false memories to go with his real one. He wasn't allowed near me after that. I never saw him again.

There had been other responses and other incidents, not all so easily solved, more to the point not all so kindly solved. Death had probably been easier than the poison. Once again Zoë created a nice diversion as she said. "I'll need maple syrup, people, can't have pancakes without them." I saw the trays loaded with pancakes and toast and bacon and eggs being brought in and had to agree with her.

Light conversation started up around us as people ate breakfast, my family kept the link humming with information they gathered and the whole time I did my best to ignore the man beside me. It took me a while to realize that someone was talking to me. Brains again. "Earth to Julie. Babe, where you at?" Zoë pinched me and it dawned on me that he had been talking to me repeating the same thing over and over. "What?" I snapped and immediately felt bad so added. "What do you want and now that we're talking, don't you have a real name?"

"I don't like my real name nearly as much as my nickname, makes me sound smart."

'*He is like Donnie, Maddie and Ronnie. They won't use their real names. Dad told me when we were little that that is their way of separating the past from who they are. He is closer to his nature too. He's like Zack and me.*' Zoë whispered in my link. I cocked my head at him to indicate that I was listening.

"I was asking if you'd like to meet with me at lunch today."

"Nope, sorry Brains but I am spending time with my classmates." I could almost hear my teacher purring beside me when I said that, but I fixed that with the next sentence. "Molly seems like a very nice girl and I'd like to get to know her better." Ha, I was going to hang with the humans, take that.

Zoë leaned in close. "I'll wait for you after school. You better go now or you'll be late."

There was a scattering of laughter and Patrick replied to her. "Sweetheart, it doesn't matter if she's late as long as she doesn't arrive later than her Alpha. Most of our classes and all the Alphas of the school are here."

"I am not your sweetheart, *wolf*. Behave yourself or I'll make you." Zoë sounded disgusted and most of us laughed, including some of the other Weres there.

"Well, guess your sister isn't one of a kind after all." He laughed.

"She is too!" Zoë argued.

"Zoë, he means you are amazing, beautiful and tough, just like me." I grinned boldly. "Is that what you meant, Pet?"

"Close enough." He grinned back with a wink.

"I still think you need to go, Juuls." Zoë said seriously. I didn't argue, as if we'd prearranged it all my family and I got up as one.

"Thanks for the invite, Brains, the pancakes were great. Might see you in school."

"Oh, we'll see each other again, babe."

"Hey! How come she doesn't chew his head off for calling her babe, that ain't fair." Some smart mouth said. Brain was quick to reply. "I'm cute and innocent."

We walked out without another word as the discussion broke out about how innocent Brains really wasn't. Their laughter followed us as insults flew freely. I tried to pay but the lady behind the counter said it was taken care of. Donnie wormed his way past Mark on my side and slung an arm around me. I shivered at his touch and when he kissed my cheek at the school gate, I'm sure I blushed. My brothers and Zoë looked speculative though they let him do so without a word. I'm sure I wasn't the only one that noticed Maddie glance longingly at Nathan. Everything was changing.

Chapter 16

Dogs at the front on the far side of the class, two shifters behind them and then six humans. Wedgetails on the side of the door in the back, one human girl, Amy, and a human boy before them and then two snake Weres, pythons! It was indeed a very diverse class. In the middle there were more humans and behind us were some crocodiles. Dylan was indeed a strong Were to control such a diverse mob of super naturals. I was impressed as Molly softly tried to tell me who was who in our class. She obviously didn't realize that most of them could hear her, or she didn't care, I wasn't sure. She looked innocent but she had to be tougher than she looked being here in this school and make it past the first two terms.

The pace that Dylan Hunter set for our class was fairly fast, he was a good teacher and we didn't get a chance to get bored. P&A was now my favourite subject, poison and antidotes, it was extremely in-depth. We got to see slides with symptoms, effects and end results wherever possible. We also got to see the antidotes, if there were any, and that also included slides of how they worked and where to get them. This subject would be taught very intensively for the full four years, there were a lot of poisons out there, man-made and natural. There were also a lot of things that worked as a poison for one race but not another.

My second favourite subject had to be anatomy A. It was all about the differences between one shape and another for every species that had more than one. For the races that only had one shape we had the subject anatomy B but it was not nearly as interesting as anatomy for those that could change, I can't wait to get to the subject of shifters but that wouldn't be this year. Obviously, we also learned when they were at their most vulnerable. Good for the killers in training. CPM was the subject that dealt with the Common Problems for Mortals and IHP dealt with the Immortal Health Problems, a lousy subject as hardly anything affected them. It was about what happened if a Vampire didn't get fresh blood and if a Fae got exposed to cold steel for an extended period of time, that sort of stuff. Wound Management was interesting because healing is so different for every race and so much faster than human. Killers in training could use this for torture.

Dylan didn't hold back on homework but he didn't go overboard, thankfully. I sat with Molly, Amy and Rolf, her shadow for lunches. They wouldn't tell us what they were to each other, speculation was that they were training to become hunters. As long as nobody could pinpoint what their special interest was, or prove that that was why they were at Spec Med, they were safe and ignored. A break times our table had a few other humans at it from class but they didn't speak directly to me. When I finally got sick of it, after more than three weeks, they informed me that it was safer for them. Kayden had informed the whole class of my status in my own pack and assured everyone that I was dangerous to be around, 'specially for the boys.

Teachers stalked the lunch areas because there were regular brawls. That day it was me who started one. I'd stalked up to where Kayden sat with his buddies and told him. "Get up!"

"Nice to see you too, Westlander, to what do I owe this pleasure."

"Get. Up. Kayden. Don't make me kick you while you are down."

"I don't know, Julia, you seem rather unreasonable and I wouldn't want you to regret anything later."

A new voice interrupted but I was too angry to turn around. "Problems?"

"Yes!" I'd snapped. "No." Kayden had said at the same time. But he'd stood up when our Alpha had arrived and I used that to my advantage, I punched him in the jaw.

"That's it, both of you, gym now." It was how fights were solved here. Others started to get up but Dylan snapped at them. "No, just these two, all of you, sit!"

It wasn't unusual that there were spectators if there was a fight but sometimes the teachers dealt with the fights alone. I didn't care either way. I was already stalking to the gym and they were unaware that I could hear them behind me as they spoke softly. "Shit, Kayden, whatyadotoher?" I heard Dylan mumble.

"Not sure what she's upset with yet, but I'm sure she'll tell me." I could hear the grin in his voice as he spoke and it made me even more angry. We got to the gym and Dylan unlocked the doors, pointing to the mats he said. "Right, same rules as training, no assault when the other party is down. Kayden tone down the strength to keep from bruising her too badly."

I interrupted, "I'm not gonne get bruised, he is!... And I have no intention of toning it down either." With that I stalked to the mats. Without thinking I pulled off my shirt to keep it from ripping, I had a halter top over my bra, so I wasn't worried. I didn't take any notice of the groans behind me, looking back I probably should have. Kayden wasn't far behind me as I got to the mat.

"Look D, she's cheating already."

I growled and punched. He ducked and tugged his shirt over his head. WOW. I stopped moving for a second. I hadn't had the pleasure seeing him half naked, then he reminded me that I was angry by saying. "Goddess be blessed, you look hot when you're angry." I faked a punch and kicked from the same side. The kick landed in his ribs and there was a satisfying Oomph.

"Miss Westlander, how about you tell us why you are so set on hurting Kayden." Dylan said in a dangerously soft voice. I didn't respond but instead tried to kick Kayden again, he dodged the kick and avoided my rapid blows that followed. I just got more angry. I couldn't use everything I was capable of, or they'd figure out my gift and that just made me angrier. I stopped to glare at Dylan because Kayden made no move to counter attack. "He told every class member, every damned member of YOUR pack, that they shouldn't talk to me because they would get hurt on account of who I am. There isn't a single person willing to even have a simple conversation with me. Only Molly, Amy and Rolf talk to me." I turned to Kayden and started in a rapid series of blows, fist, fist, elbow, knee, other knee, fist. He blocked every one of my moves with ease. I was stronger than this but I couldn't show it and the grin on his face never left its place.

"You know that your brothers or your boyfriend will kill them if they try anything with you, I did everyone a favour and simply told them how it is."

I growled in the back of my throat and kept attacking him, he finally started to make mistakes and I got another good kick in on the same side. "We are not like that, we don't just go around killing people!" I yelled at him. I felt his dog rise at the continued assault and couldn't help myself. "You are just pissed that every single member of my family could take you! Including me. We scare you!"

He hit back then, his pride was under attack now. I dodged and we started fighting properly. Our pack taught every member to fight from the moment they could walk, girls are no exception and the dogs are not made to hold back like Dylan had told Kayden to do, so I kept managing to, mostly, dodge him and got some hits in. As we danced around each other, looking for an opening, I saw our teacher relaxing against a wall. He was however still keeping a close eye on our fight.

"You know the reputation of your own pack, I just made sure that nobody will get hurt by your mob. We all know they're still here. You reek of them."

"You are going to get hurt! By me! Maybe that will teach you to keep your mouth shut, you mongrel." His speed was phenomenal as he suddenly hit me in the diaphragm. Oomph, the air rushed out of me, he was on me before I could recover. He swiped my legs out from under me. He'd used his Were strength and speed while I wasn't focused. He was on top of me, my hands pinned beside my head while straddling my hips. "Careful, you might be used to playing with the big dogs but you don't seem to realize that you are still human." He said dangerously.

I remained passive but lifted my head just a fraction as I whispered very softly. "You know what, Kayden?" He shifted his weight to hear me because I'd spoken so softly, he was interested. "You are clearly not used to playing with the big dogs, like me." I said. His face was close enough to kiss and I dropped back, as expected he instinctively moved with me and when he shifted his weight that last bit, I flipped him over. He was still holding my wrists but now I was on top. I felt a strange tingle of excitement running through my body as I looked down on him. Then I pushed up on my hands and flipped over him to stand at his head I twirled to face his way, he had to let go. Slowly he turned around on his belly and started lifting himself up, his eyes on mine the whole time.

"Don't worry, I won't kick you while you're down, boy. I can take you!" I didn't break eye contact, sweat ran down my forehead and as I wiped it away, he jumped me. I dropped back, going with his momentum and pushed him right over the top of me. We both flipped fast and were crouched down now, looking at each other trying to spot a weakness. "I don't see why you'd wanne talk to any guys in our class, you're obviously taken. You're marked." He growled at me.

"The only permanent mark I have is the one that our Alpha gave us for school. And if I'm not mistaken you got one of them somewhere too." I snarled back. He lifted his wrist slowly to show a bite mark. I barely glanced at it. "So?"

"That pack member of yours, the one that isn't related, the one that you sleep with. His claim is pretty obvious most mornings." It didn't register. I slept with all my siblings in one big puppy pile and I only had a mark if we went out. He saw my confusion and scowled. "The one that gives you his shirts and looks at you like he can't wait to undress you again. If he is your actual brother, there is something totally fucked with your family."

It dawned on me, it was all still rather new to me as our relationship had changed. Donnie was trying to court me, according to Richard, he was taking it slow. And dad had given him permission. I was still getting used to seeing him as a guy instead of a brother. "You mean Donnie? I grew up with him. He's wouldn't kill anyone. He might not be my brother but he still is one of my best friends."

He attacked me and I dodged his kicks and punches, but he was going so fast, I had no time to do more than that. "Kayden!" Came a warning growl from the sidelines.

"Leave him go, Hunter, I'll still hand him his ass!" I snarled. Dylan laughed and Kayden pulled back.

"Do you seriously think you can take me?"

"Do you seriously think you can just tell people not to even talk to me?"

"I can and I did." He replied with a nasty smirk.

"In that case: yes, I can and I will take you!" As I finished saying it, I launched myself at him taking him down at the waist in a footy tackle, it was childish and unexpected, so it worked. With my hands on his throat and one leg between his legs our position was incredibly intimate. My other leg was pinning his hip to the mat. I didn't realize all this when I cut off his air and growled in his face. "I learned from better dogs than you!" But there wasn't much steam in my voice anymore, I had worn myself out.

He raised a hand and gently stroked some stray hair from my cheek, his voice suddenly husky as he replied. "You fight well for a human, it's a great turn on." I gasped at his words I suddenly noticed the smell of arousal on him, thick and strong. I realised our position and tried to jump off but his other arm had wrapped around my waist. "Stay, I haven't had a chance to apologize yet."

Now I had my hand beside his head and the other on his chest, trying to push away and he had his hand on my waist and another on my head. Keeping me locked in position. I also noticed his bare chest and how one leg had wrapped itself around mine. "You feel good." Panic kicked in and I struggled but my body betrayed me, his hard body plastered against mine felt good. He took a deep breath. "Fear and a hint of arousal." He grinned. "We can do something fun with that."

"ENOUGH!"

I'd forgotten about our teacher and he sounded pissed. Kayden grinned, pulled himself up as I was still holding myself away from him, and kissed me straight on the mouth. Then he released me as Dylan stalked over and grinned, still on his back while I got up quickly. "There, now we've kissed and made up."

I wanted to kick him in the family jewels but settled for dropping back down with my knee in his chest. He wasn't fast enough to tense and I heard a rib break, good!

"Sorry lost my balance there, are you alright?" I asked sweetly.

"No, wanne kiss it better?" He asked, clearly in pain yet grinning like an idiot.

'Knock it off or I'll break something too.' Dylan growled in the link.

Kayden was quick to reply. *'Jealousy's a bitch isn't it, D. Take a good deep breath of her now that you're beside her and tell me you don't want some of that.'* He taunted Dylan. *'I dare you!'*

Dylan didn't realize I could hear them in the link and more to the point with them this close I heard Dylan as he took a deep breath just behind me. He groaned. Even if I hadn't had the pleasure of their senses I would have heard him, so I turned around and looked at him, snapping. "What?" I stepped back as I looked up at his face. It was instinct, there was raw lust written in his eyes as he looked me up and down slowly. In the link I heard Kayden taunt him some more. *'Term one! We'll have her for at least four more years, D. I know you want her, hell, she now knows you want her. But I already kissed her and I'm the species she's grown up with.'*

'Mine!' He replied. *'This one is mine, Kayden! You kiss her again and I will rip you apart!'*

'Chill D, she's got a boyfriend remember, the one that marks her every time they go out. It's only a matter of time before he claims her properly. Mind you, if she wants to kiss me again, I won't argue and if you do anything then, she'll probably protect me anyway.' He laughed in the link when he got up.

"I know you are talking in the link. It's rude!" I snapped.

"Go shower and change." Dylan said softly. "You stink."

I tried to make sure he could read the look on my face as I thought 'Yeah right' before I rushed off.

The boys in class still wouldn't talk to me but some of the others I met at the same time as Brains had no such trouble.

They invited me to sit with them on a daily basis, just like Kayden. I stubbornly remained at the human table of my classmates.

Chapter 17

A few more weeks passed and Richard settled the rest into a routine. The boys were working in one of the guarders buildings in town. Dad and the witches had created them so it was easy for my brothers to get a position there that suited them. Four nights a week we went out, dancing, to let off steam. The rest of the nights he'd run with the others. Zoë always had her hair loose and wore clothes like mine. After more than a month Richard finally said the words I had been desperate for. "Your turn to run tonight, Juuls. The routine is strong and they've stopped following us more than a week ago. Wear Zoë's stuff and behave as planned. We'll take you to the bottom of the river for a game of tag."

He'd kept me from running with the pack, leaving someone to babysit every night they went out. One night I almost got Donnie to go running with me but we were caught by Richard himself. Stressful feelings of Donnie, at the decision to let me run, had reached Richard and he'd know what I'd been up to. Spoilsport. Being part of a pack had disadvantages if you wanted to keep a secret.

Tonight, I would go in Zoë's clothes and run, as she had, with Donnie or Zack. She'd been staying in her human shape for every run they went on as pack. For me. Richard said it was good training for her to learn to control herself better, so I didn't feel quite as bad. Zoë assured me she didn't mind.

I kept my head down as I clung to Zack on the way to the car, slouching to look shorter like Zoë. In the car I kept my face hidden behind my hair and by the time we got to the river I was humming with anticipation. We piled out of the car at close to nine that night, I stuck with Donnie and he seemed pleased.

"Every night we've been using items of yours to confuse them, the first few times they actually thought you were here and hunted for them. We think that it was the dogs from your class. Then there were a few others that checked out the items when we used them, and we caught one, so we explained the game and he joined for the night, he was in your pet wolf's class. We haven't caught any tails, pun intended, since last week."

Tag is played like this. Everybody get an item of clothing from one particular person from our pack. Now it was always me, to confuse the people that kept an eye on our little family pack. We paired up and tried to keep from being tagged. But it would be too easy just like that so we also had to try and catch another pair and tag them by giving them the items we had, before they could do it to us. A run past and dump was the best thing for that. Donnie was that fast, that he was always paired with me, the handicap was that if we didn't touch, I'd be slow enough to catch and tag, but touching meant being more careful when we ran so that slowed us down a bit. For my gift to work I had to be close to someone, touching was easiest and strongest. This game was played in total silence for up to four hours. We set our watches, the pair with the most items at the deadline lost and had to cook the following night.

You could hide, stalk, hunt down, attack, mislead, cheat and trick the other teams in any way you could think off. But teams were not allowed to be, give or take, more than two meters apart. We all got our items and took off. I relished in the freedom of running hand in hand with Donnie. Even in this shape he made me feel like I was running with the wind. The game was progressing nicely and we'd tagged, and been tagged, several times now. We'd just dumped our items on Richard and Maddie and ran for cover. They'd been just about ready to drop their stuff on Nathan and Zack so we'd surprised them now we were running for cover. There was an old, abandoned toilet building in a stand of trees that we were headed for. We were laughing softly as we rounded the corner, hiding from the others for a little while, while getting a fix on where the next threat would come from.

I was not allowed to use my gift to locate anyone while we played.

"I 'spose it's my turn to climb for lookout?" Donnie grinned.

I didn't get a chance to answer him as a voice from above said. "Allow me to inform you that there is nobody headed your way, they all went South."

A dark figure jumped from the roof and landed before us, continuing like we were having a conversation. "You masked your smell well and I do like how you look running with your hair loose. I almost would have believed it was your sister if you hadn't come too close."

I was stunned and Donnie was snarling. I kept him back with one hand. "Whatdayawant?" I asked lightly.

"Just to talk, I'm curious. What are you exactly?"

"Human."

"Like hell you are. I saw you. Several times now. Oomph." He was pinned down by a huge very dark Dingo,

Zack, my baby brother. His fangs were gentle around the throat of his prey and his eyes were on me only. The rest of the pack had arrived on a whisper. Zack had been advance guard and the boy between his fangs was lucky that Zoë wasn't here, she killed first and asked questions later. At least Zack had more control.

"Are you in contact with your pack?" I asked calmly. I could cut him off but he'd taken us by surprise so he could have already called for help.

"Nope, just me. Nobody coming to the rescue."

"You gonna leave if we let you loose?"

"Nope, too curious."

"Let him up, Zack." Zack replied without a word, even in the link he didn't argue or even acknowledge the others when they tried to tell him not to listen.

"So, Brains, want to tell us what you know?"

"I know you smell human, act mostly like a human raised by dogs and have a problem with the fact that you are part of the same pack as Kayden. I know Kayden and you had a fight and Dylan ended it by breaking up the fight, but I also know he wasn't fast enough to stop Kayden from getting fresh with you." He winked at Donnie. "I know for a fact that she replied to this by breaking three ribs and D is still pissed with him. I actually know loads of things, more than you'd want to hear right now but what bugs me is that I don't have a freaking clue as to what you are."

"Tell us what else you know."

"I followed you out that night at the club and I saw you run, faster than any human could. I told the others and they all tried to get a look but they are now convinced that it was the little one, Zoë, and that I made a mistake. They stopped looking, I decided to wait." He smiled sadly. "Any chance I'll survive this encounter?"

"I like you Brains, so I want you to answer four questions for me. One. What is your status in the school pack and your own flock?"

"I'm second to the Alpha of my class, Patrick, and I have no flock just two siblings."

"Two. Can you keep your thoughts to yourself in the pack link?"

"Perfectly." He answered shortly.

"Three. How badly do you want to live?"

"Very. I will swear in blood to keep your secret. I will let you bind me if that's what it takes." He looked serious, that was a good answer and I listened quietly as the rest of my pack discussed his statements, they could smell no lies.

"In that case, question number four. Real name?"

"Seriously. You want my real name? No!"

"Your choice, die then, to protect your name." My voice was like ice and Brains flinched.

"You're serious? You'd kill me because I won't say what my birth name is?"

"You know what? You're right. That would be ludicrous." His face brightened and I continued after taking a thoughtful breath. "We'll kill you if you don't tell us your name AND why you don't wanne share it."

The silence that followed was deafening until Zack grinned cruelly. "Aaagh, the sweet sound of progress". We all chuckled but Brains paled at his tone.

He sounded defeated when he finally started talking.

"Once upon a time there were a lot of Were owls. There are no flocks, just families where the parents stay together. The kids leave when they are old enough, like with our natural counterpart. There is a central rule, the council. The councillors were of the oldest families only. They are arrogant. My father is one of them. At one particular gathering he spotted a woman, barely old enough to mate, he wanted her. In his arrogance he forced himself on her. She fled her family and her life when she found out that she was in child and went to ground in her animal shape.

She hatched four eggs and kept them in their owl form until the first one changed by accident. She tried to stop them but they all started changing on a regular basis and finally she told them the horrors of our rulers when they were human. She showed them the cruelty of humans in so many different ways that the children started to hate their other shape. They all stayed in the animal shape. The children promised never to go human again, like their mother, and they were happy. Then one morning one of the children couldn't sleep. He found his mother, in her human shape, on the phone and he overheard her. She said: 'They are close to going feral and when they do, I will make him be the one to hunt down his bastards and kill them. He will know my revenge. Until then I will have to wait 'till they sleep before going human. I've made them hate, they love nothing more than me. *Nothing but me.*' "

Brains sat down, looking defeated. He took a deep breath and his eyes glazed over, looking into a past we couldn't ever fully comprehend. He continued his story with an emotionless voice.

"The other person said something and the child heard her reply. 'I'd rather die than raise them like I should, they are tools only.' The child woke the others and showed them what she was doing but they heard nothing incriminating. So, every morning they'd pretend to sleep and then changed to check on her, every time was the same. She argued with someone on the phone on a regular basis and the other three started to understand that she didn't love them at all. When they started to understand one of the children refused to return to his human shape, to him it was more proof that she'd been right about the human society. They were the product of hate. Living proof. To cut a long story short. His father was made to hunt him down and kill him, just like she'd planned. The others left and went into hiding. Three, alone. They were seven years old. They heard stories of their father as he still hunted for them. They heard stories of their mother who'd remarried but refused to ever have kids again, of how she'd left the country. Of how she'd brought a councillor to his knees and left. A legend. The legend says she had one child from the rape and he killed it when it went feral.

The remaining children stuck together though. They made a city their home, they made do in their human shape, they used what they had. The first boy was Perseverance, he never gave up. When the others felt like dying would be better, he pushed, pulled and prodded until they kept going. Their sister was light on her feet as a human and had fast fingers, she stole the food and snuck into windows to open houses for them to sleep in without ever getting caught. She had Stealth. The third sibling was the one to figure out where to steal the food, where to break in and how to get out if anything happened. He was the one that got them officially registered in the city with new identities. He made the contacts to sell their stolen goods and he built the life they wanted. They called him Brains."

Brains took a deep breath closed his eyes and whispered. "Franklin, Kaitlin and Leonard is what their mother had called them. But they were new people now so they went with Percy, Stella and Brian. And they only had one goal. Kill the man that made and ruined them for one moment of pleasure against the will of their mother."

His features changed, he looked dangerous and cold. "And then they'll find the spiteful bitch that caused the death of their brother."

"Holy shit!" Donnie exclaimed when Brains looked up at us. "And I thought we had it bad Madds. At least we were taken into a pack." Donnie knelt down beside Brains and held out his hand. He gave Maddie a strange look and she put her hand on his shoulder as she nodded in some silent communication that didn't even use the link. "My name is Derrick and this here is my sister, Adele." He ignored our shocked gasps at his declaration and continued. "The rest of these guys are the ones that took us in after our pack was wiped out. The bastard that did it was killed by their dad. I'm known as Donnie and my sister is Maddie now. We lost two of our litter and the other one that survived with us is still broken. If you ever need a hand with your 'goals' call us." Maddie nodded at Brains as he looked up with tears in his eyes. She smiled sadly and said. "We went for knowledge, speed and brute force."

It now made sense, Maddie heard everything and made a point of always knowing what was happening, with whom and where. Donnie was faster than anyone else in our whole pack and Ronnie was ruthless in a fight, he fought hard, very mean and did whatever it took to win. He was brutal to the point of cruel and he'd hardly ever gotten in trouble over it by dad. I guess dad knew their story firsthand.

Chapter 18

There was nothing in the link as my brothers and I turned away from the three on the ground. We didn't look back. We didn't wait at the car. When we got home Zack told Zoë and we didn't say another word as we all crawled into the swags that seemed almost permanent on the living room floor by now. There was nothing to say. We woke at the sound of the door opening and several people entering. None of us moved. There was the sound of clothes rustling and a few other preparations for bed then Maddie softly asked. "Can they join us tonight? Please?" Richard growled softly and I stretched past Nathan to touch him, to calm him. The link of our pack remained quiet, we couldn't use it with the strangers we had among us. Again, we moved as one as we all turned and sat up to look at the new arrivals.

"Well, that is eerie." Said a soft unfamiliar, male voice. "I'm not one to give up easily but you lot are actually more daunting than anything we've ever faced. I think I'd prefer yelling or fighting."

"I don't know you." I said softly, breaking the uncomfortable silence that stretched between us.

"I'm Percy, you know Brian also known as Brains and this is my sister Stella." He rightfully assumed we could all see him.

I shook my head, negative. "I don't know any of you."

Maddie made a strangled sound and I felt Nathan tense beside me, guess he might feel protective over her. I didn't want her in pain. They all waited for my response. Richard was our leader when dad wasn't there, but I was their conscious right now, because this was started by me. I slowly got up and shook hands with the new people. It was two am in the morning and I had school in the morning. "I'm tired. We'll do proper introductions in the morning. You better not snore." I said as I walked back to the swags and my brothers and sister, curling into Zoë with Nathan behind me.

I woke up feeling blessed, the sound of my family making breakfast, someone singing rather badly in the shower. I could smell bacon cooking, I focused on that because that was by far my favourite smell for breakfast but today the smell was better. I tried to decide what it was as my mind was still wrapped in the lingering effects of a deep sleep. Eucalypt trees after rain came to mind. Fresh air. Oh, it mingled beautifully with the smell of Donnie. For me he was freedom, running that fast I felt like flying. I moaned in pleasure. His arm was over mine and his body was behind me spooning me. My arm was over a well sculptured chest and my leg was pinning that body down. I snuggled against the body while putting my head back against Donnie and mumbled 'morning'. He took a deep breath against my neck and mumbled something incoherent. My body had happily accepted that he wasn't family and shuddered in pleasure at the feel of his lips on my neck.

With a mind of its own my hand left the chest it was on and went to Donnie. But my leg raised on the body I was plastered against. There was a groan and my mouth moved stupidly before thinking. "Did I hurt you?" I started to remove my leg but a firm hand gripped my thigh, long fingers moved down to my knee and pulled it up just a bit more. Finally, I registered the reason for the groan. Oh lord, I stiffened. Someone was happy with me. I realized that the smell of eucalyptus and rain came from the body under my leg. Childishly I shut my eyes tightly, unsure what to do. The body turned into me at the same time as Donnie moved even closer to my back. I felt the heat rise to my face and tried to keep from moaning. They were, well, they were awake. Awake and in a good mood too.

"Too much?" Asked Brains softly.

I nodded, afraid to speak. There was a husky chuckle in my ear. "Enjoy this moment, she's not speechless very often."

"Righto, enough already. You lot are stinking up the room." Mark growled, but he had a chuckle in his voice. Weres just aren't as uptight about sexuality as humans but we were not raised to be overly public about it either. I ducked my head into Brains' chest and hid my face as I realized that the air around us was thick with the smell of arousal, mine included. But then the weirdest thing happened. Donnie said. "We'll have to continue this some other time." Which wasn't the weird part, the weird part was that Brains happily replied. "Yes, when we have a bit more privacy."

I giggled. Donnie sounded suspicious as he asked. "What's so funny?"

"I feel like I'm in the middle of something here. Do you boys want some privacy now? I can move."

Brains burst out laughing, much to my surprise, and Donnie responded by tickling me. Zoë jumped in, to protect me, and Zack wasn't far behind. It was all in good fun but I was still slightly surprised when the two other owls waded into the now wrestling mess of bodies. Someone grabbed my feet and dragged me out from the pile. Obviously, I went, kicking and screaming.

"Don't fight me, I have bacon."

"In that case, lead the way!" I giggled as Nathan helped me out of the pileup and we stalked, arm in arm, to the kitchen area. There was a table and six chairs at the table and I promptly grabbed the dish with bacon, added some eggs and sat on the far chair next to the wall. Nathan laughed and picked a few rashers from the dish in front of me, then he loaded the last six eggs from the pan on his own plate. There were loads of things on the table, vegemite, peanut butter, jams and a few loafs of bread fought for space with milk, a few different sorts of cereal and a huge plate full of maple syrup pancakes. The reason that the pancakes were made with maple syrup in them was that we all loved the stuff and mom had said it was too hard to get in the quantities that we devoured the stuff. It was a good compromise and as I put a few pancakes on the dish in front of me. Richard walked in.

"Why the hell do you let her do this, every damned time you make breakfast, she ends up with the whole lot and we have to fight to get any."

He was referring to the situation that the serving dish of bacon was in, I was utilising it as my plate. In return for the heads up on the bacon I always made sure Nathan got the dish with the pancakes when I made them. Richard always complained and as per usual we just laughed. Nathan would have had most of his breakfast while he was cooking so there were pancakes enough today.

"FOOD!" Richard yelled after he loaded a plate and sat at the table. He made sure that he had a chair, first come first serve is our rule.

Maddie ran in, fresh from the shower and we heard Mark yell at her as she had shoved him out of her road to get to the kitchen. Maddie, Zack and Harry made it to the table in time to get a chair. The newcomers were the last to enter the kitchen area, guided by Donnie. He told them to help themselves as he loaded a plate and casually approached me. He leant against the wall beside me and I kept a watchful eye, so, when he made his move to snatch some bacon, I swatted him and missed Zack as he grabbed a handful instead. The second time they both attacked the bacon at the same time and both had a win. Brains and his siblings looked on in silence. Finally, Stealth asked sweetly. "Could I have some bacon please?"

"Are you coming here more often?" I asked in reply.

"If we are allowed. Der_euh, I mean Donnie said we could, if the rest of you have no problem with it. Maddie didn't think you would mind."

"In that case, NO! No bacon for you!" I snapped in jest and stuffed another piece in my mouth. She looked shocked but my family laughed. Maddie however was looking slightly upset.

"Great Juuls, let's make them feel welcome!" She snapped.

"Lighten up, sis. This is my bacon she was asking about, I treated her like pack, you should be happy!"

"I AM NOT YOUR SISTER!" Maddie yelled.

Silence fell hard. I was hurt by what she said and grabbed the link in my mind. *'Either you explain yourself very clearly or we'll take this one step further.'* My voice in the link was a cold as I'd felt when she'd yelled at me.

'I am not your sister, Julia, I never was. We are pack, that's all.' One of my brothers tried to interject and I snapped out loud. "Keep out of it!"

'Have you always felt like this?' I asked softly in the link.

'Both my brothers want you, how would that be if you were my sister too? Grow up Julia, I have. We are part of your father's pack and for that I am grateful. Growing up with THE Westlander children had certain benefits too but when you guys aren't there everyone is quick to remind us that we aren't Cameron's kids.'

'And you never thought to share this before?'

'Why Julia, you Julie, good old Juuls. As long as you are happy, that is all that matters.'

I found my voice then and I softly started speaking out loud. "I love you, Maddie. As much as I love Zoë and all my brothers. It's hard enough to see Donnie as a guy, I've always made sure I didn't see them as anything more than brothers. I didn't want to make you uncomfortable when I first noticed them as guys, so I never told you. Both your brothers are hot Madds and I made sure that I only looked at them as brothers. Not for the damned pack or even dad. I did that for you! But you are right... You aren't my sister are you!? I never even knew your real name. I was never important enough to tell!"

I let my hurt and anger seep into my voice and continued. "I loved you so much I always made sure not to pry and you know damned well I could have. Instead, I used it to see which boys at school, from other packs, liked you. I used it to find out where everyone was to help you sneak out.

I used my damned gift to make you happy! Thanks for finally telling me how you feel and how stupid I've been. Thank you for letting me know you were just using me because I am a Westlander."

I got up from my chair with the dish of bacon and put it on the counter beside her. "We always fight over the bacon, *Adele*." I stressed her name, the name I'd never known and turned away from her saying. "But don't worry. I don't want it anymore. My appetite seems to have shrivelled up."

I felt someone move. "Don't bother, I am going to school. Richard?"

"Juuls?" He replied.

"Just the twins. I want the rest of you all gone by the time I get back. Give dad a hug for me and tell him I love him."

"Julia please, don't do this."

"I was supposed to do this education alone, Richard. It's been months and obviously it's been too long. I'll see you soon anyway, I'll still come home for the holidays. A few days at the end of them, probably wouldn't be good to stay home too long."

"Juuls. . ." He pleaded.

I walked into the bathroom and for the first time in my life I locked the door behind me while my family was on the other side. The sound was very final in the silence of the apartment. The link remained blissfully quiet as I showered. I rushed everything and when I got out of the bathroom I didn't look at anyone. "Want to go to the river tonight?" Zack asked as I grabbed my bag. I looked up at him with my bag in my one hand and the doorhandle in the other.

"That would be lovely, Zacky, we could do some

training."

"I'm sorry she hurt you."

"It's alright Zack, loving people means you can get hurt by them. Maybe it's better this way. Being all human, all the time, is exhausting. It'll be easier when it's just us. At least I always know how you two feel about me and everything else."

Zoë was clinging to him, obviously stressed. "I don't know how to fix this, Julia. I don't know what to do. What do you want me to do?"

I broke away from my exit, dropped my bag beside the door and engulfed them both in a hug. "Run, little sister, it'll make you feel better. Make the bed, it's big enough now that there will be just three of us and prep an early dinner so that we can leave on dark to let off some steam."

"But what about them?"

"Say goodbye when they leave, that's all you need to do. Richard will take care of the rest."

"I don't like this." Zoë mumbled. I gave her a kiss on the nose and Zack a kiss on the cheeks and walked out without looking back. By the time I got outside tears were streaming down my face. I still had almost an hour before school started, breakfast had been a lot faster than usual. The small amount of food I had consumed churned in my stomach.

Chapter 19

I didn't have any idea of where to go so I headed to the park. My vision was blurry and my head felt like a bomb had gone off in my life. First her brothers and now Maddie. My whole life had been turned upside down. I cried harder and ducked into an alleyway. I made it halfway before my legs gave out and I sank to the ground. Vaguely, the smell of garbage registered through the fog in my head but I didn't care. The hard cold stones of the ground were probably uncomfortable, I didn't notice right then. Maddie didn't feel like she was family. Holy mother earth and the Goddess combined, how had I never noticed that before. I'd been in the dark about so many things, so many feelings. Even knowing that the twins listened to me before dad, I never thought about what that meant. And it was so true, they did listen to me and they were enforcers, they were my enforcers because if they went a bit wild when we hunted, they stopped for me but for no one else, not even dad.

I felt someone watching me but they didn't come closer and I didn't look up. Faintly, I heard a link being used near me. I didn't care, not anymore. I closed my mind to any noise and focused on myself. I built a wall around my mind. Who would have thought that a girl could break my heart?

Maple syrup pancakes and black soil, cold winter air and red dirt on hot, summer days. They were so different and so alike. I smelt them just before they touched me. Dylan on one side and Kayden on the other. "Julia?" I didn't respond, Dylan put his hand on my shoulder and I turned into him. I grabbed him like my life depended in it and sobbed harder. I needed someone and as my Alpha he had to help me, it was his own damned fault.

"Julie, sweetheart, talk to me. Are you hurt?"

I nodded against his chest. It rumbled in anger beneath my face. "Who hurt you? How are you hurt?"

"She broke my heart, Hunter." I managed through some sobs. "I never knew she felt like that. I never knew any of them felt like that."

"Who sweetheart, I don't understand?"

"My sister, Maddie, Adele, her brothers, the twins. I never knew." I sobbed.

"Shit, D! Trouble with Westlanders. Now what do we do?"

"We figure out what the hell happened first, Kay."

I raised my head just to put my face in Dylan's neck, I snuggled into him and took comfort from his smell. My gift made me Were whenever I was with one. I'd never shifted and never would but I'd grown up with the enhanced senses and took comfort like they did. With the mark he'd made himself my second home. I needed that now. Kayden was part of that home, being second in the pack. They'd never know just how much I needed them. With Dylan's arms tightly around me and Kayden stroking my hair I finally started to calm down.

"Baby, talk to us. We can't help you unless you tell us what you need." Kayden sounded so sweet I just started crying again, then the mind link became clear and I'd calmed down enough to listen. *'How the hell do we fix this? She's breaking me, D, I never thought I'd see this one cry. Whatever happened must have been bad for us to feel her. I'm going to kill whoever did this.'*

And I realized how they'd found me. My stress had translated to a distress call in their pack link. Dylan sounded dangerous when he responded to Kayden. *'I can smell that owl of Patrick's very faintly and her own pack, but nobody else.'*

'I've seen her talk to Brains, but he wouldn't hurt her, D.'

'Is that so?'

'You're right, maybe we need to have a little talk to him.'

I slowly lifted my head, rubbing my face. Kayden produced some tissues from his bag and they both remained silent as I tried to get myself together.

"Can you talk now?"

"Yeah." I sniffed. "I'm sorry I bothered you. I didn't know you'd be able to feel__my_, this_,well, you know. Me. In your pack I mean." I rambled.

"It's alright sweetheart, you must be feeling very badly indeed. It's been known to happen with humans in stress. What happened, Julia?"

"My pack is leaving today. Only the twins will be left here with me, but they won't bother you if you just, you know, just leave me with them after school and stuff." I fell quiet.

"What else happened?" Dylan asked in his controlled voice. I recognized it now. It was the one he used even if he was screaming in the link. Like now, I heard him and he didn't know it. *'Tell me! Who did this! Now!'*

"I had a fight with Maddie, no, she had a fight with me so I gave her all the bacon because she told me stuff they'd never told me before and I saw that they all knew this stuff and so I told them to leave and I told Richard to let the twins stay cause they don't understand that sort of stuff and I told Zoë she wasn't allowed to kill anyone and that would've make her unhappy but if she killed someone then she would have been unhappy too because they are ours, they're pack, so I told her to run and make the bed because it's big enough for three and then I ran away myself. I didn't know where to go so I found this alley and it looked dark enough to cry in." My voice faded into nothing as I finished my rant. I took a deep breath and finally looked at the men beside me. Dylan looked stunned but Kayden actually looked happy. The moment I closed my mouth he started talking in the link.

'Holy crack D, she sent her pack away. That must been one hell of a fight.'

'Don't sound so damned happy about it, Kay. She's pretty damned upset, in case you forgot.'

'Well then maybe you didn't hear her, her bed is big enough for three! I don't mind sharing if you don't!'

'Not the time man. Get your mind outta the gutter. I still want to know why I can smell Brains.'

'Mate, that's my brains burning, the picture of her in her big bed is___'

'Kayden!' Dylan growled in the link, power seeping into his voice and I shivered as it rolled over me. His arms tightened around my shoulder. "You're cold. We've got about fifteen minutes before class, let's get you a coffee or something. Do you drink coffee?"

"Doesn't every human?" I tried to laugh but it came out sounding very sad. Broken.

"Was the fight regarding your being human?" Kayden asked.

"I don't wanne talk about it anymore."

Dylan let me go and held out his hand to help me up. Kayden rose silently beside me and grabbed my other hand. I looked at him, waiting to see what he was going to do. The link was quiet.

"I'm sorry about your sister."

"Don't worry about it, she's not my real sister, just another member of dad's pack from now." Even to my own ears my voice was cold and hard. I dropped his hand and turned to the mouth of the alley. Dylan held on to my other hand as he moved with me. He flinched and Kayden replied to the comment in the link, he didn't know I heard him as he said. *'Man, please remind me not to get on her bad side.'*

'Hmmm, I thought you already were.'

'Nah man, she never cried over me, I just pissed her off, anyone can do that, she has a nasty temper. That's easy.'

They laughed in the link and it took everything I had not to lash out and give myself away.

Dylan let go of my hand only to put an arm around my shoulder. I let him lead me to the café where my family and I came to have breakfast with them, it seemed like years ago instead of weeks. I let him sit me down in a booth and ignored that the waitress tried to convince him to go to the back room. The moment she finally left I looked up at them, glancing between the two.

"Why didn't she want you out here?"

"It's not that she didn't want us here she just wants to make sure that our packs don't take over the diner, that's why the backrooms are there. I promised her that there won't be any others of our pack joining us."

"Yeah, everybody else would be headed to class by now, wouldn't want to be late." Kayden grinned. Dylan looked thoughtful as he listened while looking at where the waitress was bringing us our drinks and two plates loaded with eggs, bacon, hash browns and tomatoes.

"You will have to think about what you want to do Julia. You now smell of Kay and myself. If anyone is close enough they will also be able to smell your pack and some might even recognise Brains on you. Want to explain that?"

"Not really."

"Not really, don't want to go to school smelling like that or not really, don't want to explain the smell of my brother's second on you?"

"Both."

"Can you go home?"

I looked confused as I thought of my dad and how far away home was. Kayden understood because he looked at me with pity in his eyes as he said. "He meant home to your apartment, babe, not running home to daddy and his pack."

I was too tired to take offense. My mind felt like it'd been run over by a truck, dunked in acid and left in the summer sun covered in meat ants, I was officially brain dead. The irony didn't entirely escape me as Brains was the unwitting instigator of this whole mess.

"No, they wouldn't be gone yet."

Dylan tossed something to Kayden and started eating. In the link he said. *'Take her to my place when we're done here.'*

'You sure man, thought you didn't take chicks to your place.'

'I won't be. You will. And she's not a chick, she's our pack and she needs somewhere to go instead of school. I don't want her wandering around the city looking like bait.'

I heard every word but had to act human, so I asked. "What are you talking about?"

'Damned Grub's right, that's kinda eerie how she does that.' Kayden said in the link as Dylan replied to me with a faint smile. "Kayden is going to take you somewhere safe for the day. Have a shower, rest up, sleep. You are far enough along in class that you will be right."

"But I like P & A and I shouldn't miss classes."

"I'll tell you what you missed in P & A this afternoon and you shouldn't go to school like this."

"Yeah, teach is right, you look like shit, babe."

"Jeez, thanks, Kay, you really know how to make a girl feel good about herself." I snapped.

"Aaaand she's back!" Kayden grinned.

They both finished their food. If I hadn't been used to Weres I would have thought they'd get fat eating like they did. Benefits of turning into an animal, great metabolism. But I couldn't complain, I had a similar metabolism without turning into anything, I ate like a Were.

Again, I noticed that they didn't pay as we walked out, so the moment we were out of the diner I asked. "Don't you guys ever pay? She didn't let us pay when we left last time."

"We own the place." Dylan said softly.

"We who?"

"My brothers, sister and I own the place. We made some good investments when we first came to town and now we can take it easy."

Kayden mumbled something but shut up fast as Dylan shot him a look. We got to the corner left went to school and Dylan went that way saying to Kayden. "They all felt the distress call, so you just come to class when you've dropped her off."

"Hey, don't you think I should like show her around the place, settle her in."

"That won't take long."

"If she'll have a shower, I might need to wash her back?" Kayden quipped.

Dylan turned and was in his face before he finished the sentence. His voice was like ice as he asked softly. "Would you like to run that by me again?"

"Drop her off, show her where things are and come to class asap." Kayden said quietly in return.

Dylan walked away without another word. Kayden touched my arm lightly and guided me in the opposite direction.

Chapter 20

We only had to walk for a few minutes when he stopped at a warehouse. He had the key and then he used another key to get us into an elevator.

We went to the top floor where he used third key to open the door from the elevator to the inside. It was a huge loft. There were a few scattered paintings and one wall filled with sketches of animals done in kohl. They drew me over, I couldn't help it, they were so lifelike. There wasn't much furniture and when Kayden coughed to get my attention, I realized that he was waiting to show me around.

"This place is amazing." Despite the huge space it still had a homely feel to it.

"Yeah, yeah!" He grinned. Then he pointed to a corner with a huge bed. "Bedroom." To the left, on the wall I'd been so fascinated with he pointed to a door. "Bathroom. Towels are in the cupboard." Then he pointed to the far wall, more windows than wall, grinned and said. "Kitchen." Then he started back to the elevator and grinned more broadly. "Tour is over, make yourself comfy and don't leave before he comes back because I'm taking the keys and that would mean you can't lock up."

I was too tired to argue his logic and nodded like a good girl. The moment he locked the door behind himself was when I realized that maybe I should have cared but this was the home of my alpha and he had to protect me, so I was going to be fine.

I went to the shower and found some big beautiful fluffy

towels, the bathroom itself was huge, it was made rectangular to take up the whole wall. That was why I hadn't noticed it before. There was a nice big bathtub at the far end and a shower stall with a huge shower head next to it. A thick cloudy glass wall separated the shower as well as the toilet from the bath. They actually made the bath area more cosy. I had a nice long shower and walked out in wrapped in one of the huge black fluffy towels.

I already felt a bit better. Now that I wasn't near any Weres my sense of smell wasn't as pronounced and I enjoyed the subtle hint of aftershave. My brothers used it too. They would spray it in their cupboard when they'd put clean clothes in. That way the smell wouldn't be on their body and wouldn't be as strong as spraying it on themselves. Sensitive smell meant that aftershave would soon be too much. I liked whatever it was that Dylan used and because I knew that I smelled like crap I washed my jeans and undies in the sink and finally my shirt. The alley had been rather disgusting, I found one of his shirts to wear instead. It was way too big and sagged off my shoulder, but I really didn't care, I was completely covered and I'd have my own clothes back on before he'd be back. How he made these t shirts look so snug was something to ponder when I saw him next. The thought made me smile. I was in the house of my teacher and planning to check him out. Oh, the irony.

The bed was tempting but it seemed a bit forward to get in there knowing he would have to put up with being able to smell me, so I took a pillow off the very tempting bed and laid down on the couch. I'd hung my clothes in the bathroom and turned on the heat lights that were in there.

Very flash and currently very handy.

I put the towel over the side of the couch so that my hair wouldn't wet it and laid down. The leather was uncomfortable though, so I got back up and retrieved another towel for the rest of me. I briefly considered the huge entertainment setup but it had three remotes and I didn't feel like sorting through that to find out what was what. I was staring at the ceiling trying not to think about what Maddie had said. I never knew her like I thought I did. How had I never noticed all these things? I had tried so hard not to get into their heads that I'd missed heaps of important things. At least the twins had an excuse for not understanding, they weren't human enough. Me, I was more human than the rest of them.

The ceiling didn't make sense. It was very high above where I was in the entertainment area and half as high over the bathroom and that half of the humongous space. The stairs were cleverly hidden and when I finally spotted them, I couldn't help but be intrigued. I found myself on the move before I could decide against it. I was being rude but then again, I hadn't been told not to go anywhere.

It was a spiral staircase with a closed banner, the banner was painted so that it matched the wall it was very cleverly done. If I ducked on the stairs nobody could see me. Nice trick! Not that it would keep me hidden from a Were but it did give a certain element of surprise. I slowly ascended to the top floor. A wall of all windows was the first thing that caught my eyes. The next thing was that I'd obviously entered a very personal space. I realized that and yet I kept going further into the room. There were four desks. One was full of study books much like the ones I had for school, one was covered in art supplies and drawings, so he was the artist that had made all the sketches on the wall downstairs. Then there was a desk that was remarkably empty but had some major filing cabinets beside it and the last desk was taken up by a very advanced computer setup with all the bells and whistles.

I knew enough not to touch that one but I did look at the sketches, there were some that I recognized as people from our class, our pack. There were also loads of people doing all sorts of things and beautiful sketches of animals. He didn't have any landscapes or objects. I was rather amazed by the quality of his work, he could have easily sold these for a living instead of teaching. But wait, he didn't just teach, he was a part owner in a diner and had clearly implied that they owned more stuff. I turned on my heel, grabbed a P & A book from his study desk and went back to my position on the couch.

We were learning general poisons, stuff that affected most mortals to some painful extent and he'd been right about the fact that I was well up to date, our pack doctor had made sure of that. I still made sure to read up on the material but my mind wasn't in it. Dylan had pegged the situation properly because I would have been useless in class. I closed my eyes and tried hard at not crying again. At some point I fell asleep and I dreamt about Maddie hunting me.

Then the dream changed and I felt a new emotion claim me. I dreamt of strong arms and loving whispers. I felt like I was moving and I felt my body respond, my arms went around his neck. My senses woke up to the heavenly smell of my Alpha. "Oh lord, you smell so good!" I mumbled still partly asleep. I felt a rumble as he chuckled in my arms. "Same to you sweetheart. And you look good enough to eat." This wasn't a dream. My eyes shot open and I was face to face with my teacher.

"You're real!" I said stupidly. He sat down and suddenly I was in his lap with my arms around his neck, he'd been carrying me.

"Don't sound so disappointed." He grinned. I tried to remove my arms but he stopped me by saying. "Not yet." He spoke so softly I barely heard him but my hands stilled on his shoulders. A bit louder he said. "You were having a bad dream and it wasn't nice to watch, also you looked rather uncomfortable on the couch, so I was just moving you to my bed."

His bed. I glanced to the side and saw that we were indeed now on the bed. I was on his lap on his bed with my arms resting on his shoulders like a lover. I felt the situation glowing red on my face and he smiled down at me gently. "I like you here. What do you think of it?"

"Euh, well, euh, I'm not sure how I feel about sitting here. You are my teacher." I mumbled in reply without looking back at his face. Much to my surprise he burst out laughing, tightening his arms around me and burying his face in my neck.

"I meant my house, sweetheart. What do you think of my house?"

"It's big. I mean it's nice, well, it's very open and your bedroom is very well noticeable. I mean that's up to you and all but what if someone comes in? When? Well. .You know?"

"I only have sex on the big table upstairs if that's what

you mean."

I didn't immediately catch the sarcasm, instead I looked up in shock and my face heated again as I imagined him on the table, naked, that was the table that was almost empty. It had to be. Oh lordy, that was. . . "What? Sorry I, . . Euh."

"I was kidding, Julia. But from the look on your face, I assume that you saw my office."

"I'm sorry, I just noticed the ceiling and I didn't know — "

"It's alright. I was kidding, it wasn't fair, you only just woke up."

I was looking at his lips as he talked and stopped hearing him. His lips were full and with his fresh sweet smell tickling my nose I could almost taste him. I thought about how he might taste, would he actually taste like Maple syrup and cold mornings? I licked my own lips just thinking about it and he stopped moving his. The moment I glanced up at his eyes they captured mine. I heard him in the link, like a whisper. *'Just one taste, that's all, sweetheart. I just want to know if you taste as good as you smell. Just one taste, I promise.'*

Instead of pulling away I slid my arms back around his neck. I totally agreed. Just one taste would be all I needed. His head came even closer, it wasn't far and the moment his lips touched mine my eyes fluttered closed with the sensation of his lips. *'Oh Sweet Goddess, girl, you feel amazing.'* They were softer than I'd thought looking at them. He softly moved his lips against mine, an involuntary moan escaped me. *'I'll have to make you make that sound again.'* His tongue darted out against my bottom lip asking for permission to deepen the kiss. Permission was granted by opening my mouth to the gentle pressure. '*You are so beautiful, so soft.*' He kept talking to me in the link as we kissed.

His hands pulling me closer, one moving slowly in my hair. His other hand slid up my leg, to my side and proceeded to my back, he groaned when he did that. I vaguely realised that I was naked under the shirt as his other hand was moving up my back under the shirt without restrictions. '*This is now my favourite shirt, it never looked this good.*' His mouth was expertly exploring mine. I moaned again as his hand brushed the side of my breast. My underwear was still in the bathroom too and I didn't even care. He groaned softly. '*So sexy, nothing but my shirt.*' I started losing grip on my block. I wanted to respond to the sweet things he was whispering in the link. '*You're mine. All mine and mine only!*' He huskily growled into the link as he kissed where he'd marked me for the school pack and that's when I broke away.

It was probably the only thing that he shouldn't have said. What had I been thinking? The situation I'd put myself in was too dangerous. He'd been so close to finding out. My treacherous body had been so close to letting him go a lot further. I backed away, landed on the ground and scrambled backwards from his hands as he tried to assist me. The groan he let out this time was frustrated. "Juuls, sweetheart, Julia, I am so sorry. I just. . . I was out of line. . .I'm sorry."

In the mind link he was also still talking and thankfully he was blissfully unaware I could hear him. '*Baby, you have no idea how hot you look. Your skin, I want you so bad. I need to feel more of you. Come back here!*' His frustration in the link and the calming words he was speaking were so different I felt like an intruder in his mind. He slowly got up. Pancakes and maple syrup, cold morning, frosty ground, maple syrup. I started repeating my mantra for dealing with him. He looked so hot as his muscles moved beneath the shirt when he stretched. He was all predator and there was a raw hunger in his eyes as he slowly came closer. My eyes drifted to his chest. His shirt was showing a hint of tanned skin. The shirt I'd only just had my hands under, feeling those very muscles hot under my hands. I got up as he reached for me and I quickly backed away again. "I better go. I've got to get dressed. I just need to use your bathroom, my clothes, I just. ." I just turned and ran for the bathroom door while he growled in frustration. Thankfully he didn't continue talking to me in the link, his thoughts now his own as I went to hide from my gorgeous Alpha.

Chapter 21

I took a lot longer than needed. Actually, I took another shower because with him this close my senses were wolf and I could smell him all over me. I worked at ignoring the activity that buzzed in the link while under the shower. The smell wasn't much better after the shower because I'd used his soap but at least it wasn't the smell of his body on me.

When I finally got out of the bathroom, I realized I should have paid attention. Kayden, Grub and three other guys from school were sitting on the couch. The moment I walked out they stopped talking and one fool actually said. "Holy crap. Is that our new human? Lucky bastard is doing her too, is he? And you had a piece of that before school, Kay?"

Kayden and Dylan tried to say something but I beat them to the punch. "I'll sort this." They looked on with something resembling respect as I walked right up to the idiot. "Name?" I snapped. They knew by now that I settled things like a Were, in other words I fought for dominance in an argument.

"Jordan."

"Get up, Jordan." I said as I walked to the open area near the door. I was happy that Dylan didn't have a lot of stuff. Jordan followed and the other guys were close behind. He was right behind me when I turned and he'd been looking at my behind. He staggered back as my fist connected with his jaw.

"Jordan. If you want to try and fight back that's fine. But

I am gonna beat bejeeezes outta you regardless of what you do. You see, I had a really bad day. I had to come here because our teacher is also my alpha and he's the only one that could help me this morning."

Jordan shook off my punch and straightened up. I punched him again and he blocked me but not holding back I kicked him in the ribs almost simultaneously, I heard a nice crack. It was the same move I'd used with Kayden several weeks before.

"I did not 'do' our teacher as you so kindly put it. And if it should ever happen that Kayden gets a piece off this. . ." I hit him in a fast series of punches and kicks but he only managed to block half without fighting back. "It'll be over my dead body!"

"Hey bitch, you might have showered but they didn't. Kay came in late with a stupid grin and reeked off you. And teach here had a fair bit of you on him this morning but now he smells of you all over and the whole place smells of heat."

I attacked him again with more vigour but he still didn't fight back. Defending yourself is easier if you can fight back and he was starting to show some wear and tear.

"Guess you didn't smell the dirt from the alley they found me in? What sort of freaking mutt are you? I could even smell the dirt on me. Bit of poodle in the family?" He tried to hit me at the insult and I danced under his arm and around him to kick him in the back. I was using a bit more speed than human but not too much for them to be suspicious. "Our Alpha is a good looking guy. It would make sense to smell some heat, that doesn't mean it's fresh, idiot, unless you know something I don't and you think he's into boys, like you."

There were some growls that I assumed were from our Alpha and a scattered laughter at my implication he was gay.

"Yeah? Bit dumb aren't you human. Smell doesn't work like that. His bed's right there."

"Dude even me, a human, can smell sex in a room. But I grew up pack and learned a few things. Sex in one room can mean the smell of heat in the next room. And I've been told it lingers."

"His bed's right there."

"Yeah well, how would I know, he might prefer sex on the table in his office. The only thing you should have worried about before opening your mouth was if it actually smelled like sex."

There was a cheer. "She told you, man." Kayden grinned. "No sex in the air."

"Yeah well, she also said she'd be dead before she's gonne be with you." Jordan replied tauntingly.

"Hey poodle boy, I wasn't finished with you." I said as I hit him with my fist.

He was about to start fighting back at the insult, I could see it in his eyes. But just as I thought I'd get to let off some steam I was grabbed from behind and Dylan growled in my ear. "Stand down!" Power leaking from his voice. "NOW!"

Softly, so only I could hear, he whispered in my ear. "Nice argument but I never bring women here." A bit louder he asked. "Are you alright?"

I struggled in his arms and replied. "No, I wanted a fight and he was only just going to give me one." My mum's maple syrup pancakes would never be the same again as I used my mantra to counteract the power I felt against me.

Kayden couldn't keep his mouth shut. "I don't care if it's a bed, table, couch or the wall. I could give you a much more fun way to relieve your frustrations, babe."

Maple syrup pancakes, cold mornings, winter runs. With his arms around me, the smell of them became even stronger and the whole pack was open to me. The power of his voice didn't affect me, not the same way it did the Weres in our pack, but it affected me too. '*Stop it! She's pack and human. We need to respect her, not cause her more pain!*' Then again, he didn't know I could hear the link. The boys bowed their head and Jordan apologized to me. Then Grub surprised me again. '*I can feel her and she has that look again.*'

Kayden replied in the link. '*We've been over this, bro. She was raised pack, so she'd know we're talking. And the look on her face is pissed. She. Is. Human!*'

I pulled out of the link and noticed something else. "Oh hell!" And the guys all looked up as one. They'd heard it too but they looked at me. Grub looked triumphant.

"I can feel family. Here!" I said to make up for my mistake. Grubs face fell, he'd thought that my response was to the remarks in the link. I, however, had heard what they had. Yelling and fighting outside, yelling I should not be able to hear.

"How can you hear that?" Grub asked sweetly.

"Hear what?" I asked. "I said I can feel family, it's a bond even humans can feel and that means the twins are here somewhere close, they are probably worried because I should have been home and I left. . ., well, I left things. . in a hurry this morning after the . .incident." I stuttered a bit. I didn't need anyone else to find out about our fight. I just hoped that Brains or Brian or whoever he was could keep his mouth shut. I was already close to the door, the elevator. It was there and Kayden beat me to opening it. Dylan kept a hand on my back. There was no escape from him. I kept my mantra going in the back of my mind so that I wouldn't link. I'd been trained the hard way and for years so it came easy now, but he was a strong presence and I had to be careful.

"Pancakes will be the death of me." Dylan mumbled. The other guys looked a bit mystified but Kayden burst out laughing. "Again?" He asked. I knew but because I couldn't let on, I had to ask.

"What is it with you and pancakes?"

Kayden doubled over in laughter and, other than Grub, we all looked confused. The private link between the Alpha and his second in command opened and I shamelessly listened in. *'Kayden could you just shut the hell up!'* Kayden laughed louder instead. The elevator moved too slow for the rest of us but Dylan actually went into a rant. *'Move, when did this thing get so slow? Move, move and you, Kay! Shut up!'* In the link, which made Kayden's laughter unstoppable.

"So?" I interrupted his link rant at Kayden.

"So nothing, miss Westlander, I have just recently developed an. . unhealthy. . Obsession for pancakes with maple syrup. It might just be the death of me one day."

"Thought you said you preferred honey?" I couldn't help myself. Kayden saved him by replying. "Don't we all?"

The doors opened and Dylan shot out. The entrance was filled by two big wolves and there were a lot of growls outside. I stepped out behind Dylan and Kayden with the rest of the boys behind me. Everyone turned around at our arrival. The Twins looked downright murderous. People cleared the way for Dylan and Kayden while I was right behind them, closed in by the other guys. Dylan had only said one thing in the link before we walked out of the elevator. '*Protect the girl.*' It had been a clear order and all the boys had acknowledged it by taking up position around me.

The smell of blood was overwhelming. I tried to get past the broad backs of Dylan and Kayden before me and the fact that they didn't let me pass was making the Twins even more anxious. I didn't use the link I had with my family even though they were close enough now to do so. "I'm here. I'm fine. It's alright." I spoke clearly without shouting. There were dingo dogs littered on the ground around us and a few wolves and human shapes as well but that was only a first impression. The twins stood proudly in their human shape, they hadn't changed to fight which showed their talents.

"I should have known they were yours." Patrick said with a still busted lip. It was healing fast.

"What's that supposed to mean?" I snapped still trying to move the guys in front of me. Patrick didn't get a chance to reply because Dylan turned around and grabbed me, looking straight in my eyes he asked: "How safe are you with them? They smell feral and more than last time we saw them too."

"I'm fine. It's alright." I repeated. This time as much for him as for the twins. He looked me in the eyes a bit longer and finally stepped aside. I walked over to the twins and the moment I hugged Zoë, she smiled brightly up at my face and made the biggest mistake ever.

"We made sure not to kill anyone but if you want, now that you are here, we could kill the lot! It'd be fun. Just like that other time when that bloke tried to hurt us."

Zack punched one guy that growled near him and the guy dropped like a stone.

"Crap Zo, how many more times do I have to tell you not to talk around others." Zack snapped at her while the testosterone in the air skyrocketed. The feral growls and mumbled threats at what she said made it a dangerous place to be. Nobody moved and everybody looked set to attack. Us. Up until that moment we could have been allowed to walk away without anything else happening. She had attacked their ego so that wasn't going to happen now.

Chapter 22

"Okay." I smiled lightly. "So, this is my little sister and her twin. Guess you all met. They are Westlander enforcers so that should explain the violence thingy. I mean I can see a few other enforcers here." I looked around at the stunned faces around me and continued. "So like, I had a bit of a problem this morning and I had to see my alpha. He kindly let me calm down here." I gestured behind me to the building. "But I'd promised my brother and sister that I'd be home straight after school, so they were worried. Guessing by the looks of things you fellas didn't let them come get me so I can only assume things escalated from there." There wasn't a scratch on the twins and even their clothes were still fine, yet the blood and broken bodies hinted at a huge fight. The twins had made a lot of people look bad. This wasn't good.

"Our father, Cameron Westlander, the Top Dog of our pack ordered them to protect me while in this town, when not at school. I am his only human child. So, you understand that this is just a huge misunderstanding. Right?"

The level of tension had dropped but the anger was still palatable. Then the most amazing thing happened. Patrick spoke up. "Some of what I thought to be my best fighters were put down by that little slip of a girl." I placed my hand firmly on Zoë's mouth and winked at Zack. He relaxed as Patrick continued. "Now this is clearly marked territory owned by not one or two but four packs. Law states that retribution is to be granted. The problem is that they are alpha in their own right." Someone mumbled 'Top Dogs' and Patrick adjusted. "I'm sorry, they are Top Dogs in their own right. I can feel it as clearly as the rest of you." He looked straight at me as he said the next thing. "I want retribution." If he was looking for a response, he wasn't going to get it because I'd been listening to the link that had been buzzing between Dylan and his siblings.

"Fine. Whatever. Why look at me?"

"They are here to keep you safe after school. They obviously don't have to listen to the top dog of your pack so that means that they follow you by choice. That makes you, little human girl, the alpha of those two and that makes you the one I look at. You have already proved to me that you are more than just a harmless, little human."

"Fine. State your proposal."

"I ask for retribution and you call it a proposal. You reminded me that you knew all the laws last time we met so you know it's not the same thing."

I grinned wickedly. "I do know. I know that if the claim of captivity is thought to be real and that it can be sworn in magic that it was truly believed, it wipes retribution laws. Which, with these two, I have no doubt that they could swear to that because they always assume the worst. The right to enter the territory of the other party is automatic. There is no retribution for a captivity claim in the laws... Anywhere, but hey, nice try."

He looked constipated for a second then I heard Dylan in their private link. *'That's my girl! You got to give it to her bro, she's spot on!'* The siblings laughed and Patrick replied with a grin. "Hey, can't blame a guy for trying, you are only human."

"Fine. I'm the poor little human that belongs to your brother's pack and needs protection, oh wait, I'm also the girl that kicked your ass, Pet. Now. State your proposal."

"They help teach our packs to fight."

"For?"

"What do you mean, For?!"

"For how long? For what reason? For how many fighters? For what?"

"Full time, because they can do things we never learned, for every member of our packs and for you." Patrick replied with a cocky grin.

"Three days a week for this school year only, no holidays, for your best three fighters only per pack and for payment for each of them." I replied without hesitation. I knew the twins would use their fighters and their skills to improve themselves in return, that's how we were taught to deal with fights. Learn. Always learn from others.

"What daddy doesn't give you a high enough allowance to feed them?"

"Okay, now listen carefully and don't say anything else until you have thought about it, Pet." I said sarcastically. "You do some math, my brother and sister are still only seventeen, they just reached a standoff with how many fighters of yours down? And they haven't got a scratch. They were making sure not to kill or there'd be bodies here, everywhere. They are *that* good. We don't get an allowance, we don't need it. Spoils of war. We are set for life. The payment you will give is for their time and expertise and you are lucky we are willing to offer this much. You will be getting the best in the country."

Silence descended as the truth of my words sank in.

'*Holy hell, did you just bluff **four** Alpha wolves on their home ground? You inherited dad's balls, sis. I'm so proud.*' I looked at Zack as his dry voice joked at me through the link. Zoë giggled. A new voice caught my attention. '*I heard them! Pay attention guys, I'm sure she can link.*'

I opened a private link between Zack, Grub and myself. Zack held me up by wrapping his arms tightly around my waist when he felt what I was doing. Because Grub was lower on the food chain, he was actually harder to single out. He wasn't used to private communication like the alpha or other top animals and his second.

'*Grub, sweetie, you really need to think before you say anything else. Think. I am human. I can't link. If I could, do you think that people would be allowed to live with that knowledge, if they didn't belong to our pack?*'

Grub paled and swayed on his feet as he heard my voice in his head.

'*You made a private link? Between us?*' He was looking sick as his eyes locked with mine. Zack spoke into our link. '*We did but you are focussing on the wrong thing. The question you should be asking is: Do I want to live?*'

Grub glanced at Zoë. Zack sounded deadly. '*You must have some sense, you just looked at the only reason we haven't killed you yet.*'

'*She likes me too?*' He grinned suddenly as he looked back at Zack and me.

'*Focus, Grub. Wrong question again!*'

The blood drained from his face. '*Sorry. I want to live.*

Please. Nobody believes me anyway.'

'Hmm, strange thing is, Grub. If someone persists with something, sooner or later people are going to take note. Unless that someone is silenced permanently.' I said softly in the link.

He looked like he was going to vomit.

'We are going to spend some more time together, Grub. My twin likes you, but she won't be able to tell for sure if you are mates, until we are eighteen. I think you might be, so we will let you live, for now. If and only IF you stop mentioning my big sister when she follows conversations in your pack link.'

Grub was putting two and two together faster now. He looked scared and shaken as he softly said. *'She's the reason you guys kill whole packs. You. You're a Westlander weapon. Shit, I'm gonne die, aren't I?'*

'Don't panic yet, Grub. All you need to do is shut up. For now. And maybe if you could see if you could kiss Zoë. You're old enough and she is probably strong enough to know if you're mates. If you kiss her.' Said Zack dryly.

I heard growls but needed to know what to do about Grub. I was getting tired, my head dropped back against Zack and he was holding up most my weight. Zoë was keeping track of the conversations around us so that we would know what we missed. We felt a link nudge from Zoë.

'Fine, yes please, I mean sure, I'll happily kiss her, she's always on my mind since we first met you guys in the park, I mean I'll keep my mind shut too, my link, my opinions. I'll keep my opinions to myself. I don't want die, I wanne kiss her forever and if you won't kill me for that, that would be great.'

'Just don't hurt her, Grubby. Either of them.' Zack said, sounding once again deadly and dangerous.

'I won't sir, I promise!' I smiled in the direction of my pack, at Grub, and dropped the link with him.

'Zoë, what'd we miss?'

'They're divided, other than your teacher he's not saying much just staring at us. At you and Zack. He looks like he wants to hurt Zack actually. D and R get that look. Right now, they are figuring out who is fighting with which of us.' She meant Donnie and Ronnie and I finally knew what look she was talking about, jealousy, I'd just had my head in the sand for a long time. Hmm, interesting. Was it because of the kiss we'd shared that the teacher was jealous?

I decided I was going to take charge of the situation, I had to get home before I fell asleep, I was so tired. "Okay people let's pay attention. I'll choose the groups of fighters because you are never going to agree." I pointed at Aaron. "You are with me and so a. . ."

"No!" Dylan snapped before I could continue. "I am your Alpha, you will train our pack members."

"No. But if you have issues with Aaron I will take you, Pet's second, . .

I was interrupted again, this time by Patrick. "Nope. I will train with you as well!"

'Don't argue, sis.' Zack said in my head. *'Just get it over with already, leave them their pride.'*

"Fine!" I snapped. "Anything else?"

Dylan looked thoughtful, Patrick ginned outright and everyone else shook their heads no.

"Good. Alpha, Pet, Aaron your second and Sky your third are with me. Sky and her second with Aaron's third because they are all female will go with Zoë, there are things she can teach you that men don't use. Grub, you lucky bastard, you get to go with the girls and Zoë... and I can assure you that you will be able to disable, maim or kill anything and anyone by the time they are done with you." He grinned brightly.

"Oh man, little human, you are missing out. I can smell the jealousy already. It's lovely! I get to get up close with three of the hottest women in our school and a Westlander enforcer. I'm gonne be a legend if I survive this!"

Everyone laughed. But I knew he was only half joking.

"Great, Aaron, Brains, Sky's third and Kayden with Zack. There! Done. Not working Friday after school, Saturdays or Sunday before lunch. Training is one and a half hours, make sure you bring water and it will be inside with closed doors, you find a place."

Patrick started to talk but I held up my hand. "Later people." Zack and Zoë supported my weight disguised as a comfortable half hug each and led me home. Zoë was at my other side. "What about payment and times?" Patrick said loudly behind us. "Don't you think we need to talk about that?"

I looked over my shoulder. "I'm sure you do. You know where I am at lunch time tomorrow. Bring your proposal then and we'll amend it if necessary."

Chapter 23

Before we made it back to the apartment, I passed out, I woke late that night in the arms of my siblings. Zack was awake and linked to make sure we wouldn't wake Zoë up. *'I really think he's her mate you know.'* He said. *'I'm glad he's not too weak and he is obviously smart. I think we can trust him.'*

'I do too, Zacky. Let's hope your mate isn't too far away either.'

'I'm good but thanks.' He replied dryly. *'So, what about that wolf of yours?'*

'Euh, he's not my wolf, bro. He's my teacher and because of that he's alpha of my new pack.'

'News flash, sweetie. Your teacher has the hots for you. You challenged him and by saying you could help teach their dumb asses, you implied you are better than the best Weres at Spec Med.'

'The best Weres my boot, bro. I could take most of them blindfolded.'

'Or not. Look Juuls. I did a bit of asking around today. This town runs on Spec Med, so everyone knows everyone. Those four own most of the warehouses in that neighbourhood, four restaurants next to the park including where we had lunch the other day, one very select club that I can't get info on aaaaand...they own The Pitt.'

"HOLY_" I exclaimed out loud.

"Shhhh"

'Sorry! But that's insane!'

'Oh, it gets better, you remember that vampire you told us

160

about?'

'Hmmm?'

'He's head of the city council and member of the school board. He's old and dangerous Pumpkin.' Zack said, using dad's nickname for me. *'You have made some very interesting and powerful friends.'*

'They are not my friends.'

'In that case we are now officially in deep shit. You just made yourself a fixture with the most influential people and you don't wanna be friends with them. It's never easy with you around.'

'Zack, I, I'm _'

He gave me a squeeze and grinned wickedly. *'I love it! It's never boring with you, pumpkin. You made sure we can train with the best of Spec Med and there are sure to be fights in the future with your attitude. What more can a little brother wish for?!'*

I mock thumped him and he smiled broadly. *'Go back to sleep, Juuls.'*

The next time I woke it was time to get up. Zack started on breakfast happily humming about the overabundance of food due to the abrupt departure of our family. He loaded three plates with bacon, grinning while he put mine before me. Before I had a chance to get upset he said. "Sadness over bacon isn't allowed. Breakfast is the most important meal of the day. Maddie is a bitch and not a very good one at that! Get it? She's a bitch, not a good dog, bad dog. And if she wants to be just pack, let her. We will certainly be treating her as such from now on."

By the end of his rant, I was grinning too. "Can't let the

bad dog ruin the bacon. I get it." We laughed and ate an insanely large and unusually quiet breakfast. I dawdled and stalled until Zack offered to walk me to school. Zoë jumped for joy and begged me to come straight back after school to show her when she was training with Grub.

They walked me to the front gates, Zoë was nervous and fidgety until Zack growled at her. She flicked her hair like a pro and arrogantly looked down her nose at us while we laughed at her unusual behaviour. Poor girl looked fit to bust when Grub wasn't near the entrance of the school. Much to my displeasure however there were four wolves waiting for us. For me. Zack and I had been walking arm in arm, enjoying making fun of our sister, his twin. He pulled me a bit closer as we neared the wolves and Zoë joined our conversation in the link as Zack said. *'Wow. The welcome committee is out in force today.'*

'Great, just what I was waiting for, so much for a quiet education.'

'Things are never quiet with you, that's why you are my role model.' Zoë laughed in the link as she moved to my other side making me the middle instead of having Zack in the middle of us.

"It's very quiet for a big school like this. Surely you aren't that early." Zoë said out loud, sounding innocent as a little girl.

"Maybe the big bad wolves scared them off?" Zack replied with a straight face. I couldn't contain a giggle as the four wolves frowned at the twins. They'd heard, as expected. And Zack was most likely right too because with the twins in my grasp, my eyesight was good enough to see the faces of a lot of people behind the big, still open, entrance.

"Good morning, Alpha. Hi Sky. Morning Aaron. Hello Pet." It was barely polite but it wasn't disrespectful and that was all I was trying for. Zack wasn't in the mood for polite as he nodded his head at them. "Wolves."

Zoë immediately smiled and added. "Hello Sky. I look forward to working with you."

Sky sounded pleased as she answered. "Well hello Zoë, it looks like I got the only nice one from the family. I look forward to learning some of your moves."

Zoë wasn't human enough and it was clear as she answered. "Oh, I'm not the nice one. Until recently I would have said Donnie was but he's not really family so I guess that would explain why he's soft. I'm just as, if not more, lethal as the rest of them and I'm actually better than most of my brothers during a fight. Not Zack, we're both as good as the other."

Zack snapped. "Shut up, Zo!"

While I put my hand on her arm and said. "Honey, she means what you said is nice."

Zoë clearly thought about that for a minute as we all looked at her. Her face changed and turned feral then she ground out. "NICE!? We'll see how nice you think I am after we train. And. Do. Not. Say. Bad. Things. About. My. Family. EVER!" She barely finished the last word before she changed and parked herself in front of Zack and me snarling at the wolves. Sky in particular. Dylan laughed softly and nodded to Zack. "You must have your hands full with those two, mate."

Zack burst out laughing as he put his arm around me

and a hand on Zoë's head. "Wouldn't trade them for anything. My life will never be boring with them in it." Zoë nipped his hand and I punched his arm, he just laughed harder. "See wolves, this is why all the men in our family are Top dogs, or Alpha in your words. . . We wouldn't survive with these women any other way."

Patrick didn't laugh, he looked thoughtful as he replied. "The one that marks your sister isn't Alpha material. How does that work?"

Dylan growled at the words of his brother. I frowned but kept quiet as Zack replied. "He has potential, but you understand there is a reason why the mark isn't permanent yet."

We all turned to Dylan in surprise as he growled. "Mine is!"

Zack laughed heartily and explained in the link why he laughed before he baited Dylan's wolf and the claim he thought he had. "Careful wolf, your mark is only valid if she is in school. My advice would be, don't challenge her because she is likely to leave this school just to break your claim if you say stuff like that."

Dylan snarled, his eyes going wolf. "Contain your beast! Now!" Snapped Patrick as they all put a hand on Dylan. I heard their link and grabbed Zack tighter in despair. '*She is mine! I will have her and she will beg for more!*'

'*Calm down man, you are frightening her, she's only human.*' I heard Aaron.

'*You just need a willing little Were tonight, get it outta your system.*' Patrick, naturally.

'*D. Dylan! Think, your wolf is just wanting her because she fights back but she's human, dog raised too. She isn't challenging your status in your pack. Just back off.'*

I stiffened as he replied to his sister in the link. *'Sky, I don't give a damned about my position as Alpha to her. I want her as a man. My wolf would let her do anything she wants if we can just have her. I want to see her wake up in my bed.'* Aaron interrupted. *'Settle down bro!'*

But Dylan just kept going. *'I want to make her scream out my name. I want to wear her out, explore every part of her and then do it all again until all she wants to say is my name. My wolf likes her. I like her! She is mine, she just needs to figure it out.'*

I'd let Zack hear them in our link as the blood drained from my face so before D was finished, Zack turned me around, Zoë at our back and started marching me back home. The rancid smell of fear was pouring off me in waves I knew that the wolves could smell it too.

"Where are you going?" Dylan growled.

"I'm taking my sister home. And if you can't contain your beast better, I can't leave her here. Send one of the other human students with the work she'll miss for the rest of the week. Sky can come with your training schedule tonight, alone."

Dylan took a step towards us and this time it was Zoë that growled, baring her teeth and raising her hackles while Zack continued. "You will train with me and your second can train with Juuls. It is not negotiable, wolf. It's that or nothing. We were not in the wrong so we can walk away from this training arrangement Scot free."

Zack was using the power that could give him his own

pack. He didn't show this dominant side often and I was feeling calmer as I felt the power roll off him in waves. He was family and right now he was safety. I could feel the wolves respond but I could also hear the three trying to talk Dylan down.

'*If they walk away from the deal, they'll take her from school too, D. Think! At least she's still in your pack this way. Let them go, brother.*' Much to my surprise it was Patrick that was calming him down now. Zack started us walking again. We didn't look back.

Chapter 24

Home, the apartment that was so empty without the rest of the guys here. I was restless and the twins were quiet as I paced around the room.

"Let's swim!" Zoë suddenly yelled.

"What?" I asked stopping my pacing.

"Swim, dummy, let's go swim at Southbank. Get your mind of the mad wolf and his packs. You are further than most the people in your class, so you won't miss anything. You keep complaining that all the interesting stuff is kept for next year. Let's swim."

Dogs, unlike a lot of other animals can and actually like to swim. Zack stayed with his twin when we went swimming. She'd made him go swimming until they reached a compromise of sorts and he managed to handle his fear of water alone. I'd helped but Zoë had done most of the work. She's mangled some old quote and kept telling him that the only thing he had to fear was her and me, that fear itself feared us. Dad had laughed his butt off when he heard that and told mum we took after her side of the family. She was after all my mother in every way that counted.

I grabbed the towels and we changed into shorts and singlets. I purposely covered the mark Dylan had given me with antiseptic and water proof tape. Stuff him and the horse he rode in on. I wasn't his and he had another thing coming if he thought he could change that. Bastard mutt and his stupid packs. Lovely body and amazing kisses. Possessive over something he didn't even have. His hands had felt so good on my bare skin. What was I supposed to do now? Damned wolves. Yeah! Swimming sounded good right now.

The water was beautiful, so different than the stuff we had at home. The Channel Country has beautiful rivers, creeks and water holes but none of the waters, including the rivers are permanently full like the river in Brisbane. The water was beautiful, clear and warm enough to be comfortable. Through the water it was clear that there were more than just fish below us but we weren't bothered and we remained reasonably close to the shore because Zack freaked out if we went too deep and too far from him.

By the time we got back to the apartment Molly was leaning against the wall with her bag at her feet. I nodded at her but none of us spoke. Through the link Zoë asked a bit about her, they knew she was in my class because her smell carried home with me on a daily basis from sitting beside her in class. Zack had previously commented that the smell was amazing. She followed us up to our place and sat in the kitchen with us as Zack started the coffee machine for me. Opening her backpack, she pulled out five sheets of paper, I could see printing on both side. "Mister Hunter said that this was all you needed for the week. There is a test on Monday, the details are in this. He told me to tell you that you can come to class tomorrow if you wish, without any repercussions but you have to be back for the test at the latest. There will be no retakes allowed. Not for anyone."

"Yeah well, she's sick of that class so she can't come this week."

"Look, Zack is it? I'm just a human in a class full of sups but even I realize that there is more to your sister than what she lets on. Everyone was inside this morning but plenty of people saw and at least partly heard the argument between you lot and the Hunters. Big rumour has it that our esteemed teacher wants to mate your sister. Other rumours say that she took the vamp up on his offer and teach is pissed and my personal favourite is that you started an affair with K, the obnoxious but cute second of our mismatched pack, thereby pissing off Dylan because he doesn't want his second distracted."

Zack growled and Zoë laughed but Molly wasn't finished. "There is another rumour that is softly drifting in the Hunter Packs only. It said that you are not human and that you and those two here beat shit out of all four pack's top fighters. That rumour states that you are some sort of ninja Weres and that you will be teaching the best fighters of the packs to become better."

We shared a look and Molly didn't miss it. "Oh my lord! Are you? Did you? What for?"

We laughed and Zack answered her. "She did shit all, gorgeous, Zoë and I beat their fighters up. All true. They are cocky and only have one style of fighting each and because of that they are all predictable. Predictable will get you killed. They are lucky we didn't feel like killing anyone but they suck. Juuls beat Patrick up a while ago and she did that the same way we did, by being able to predict his moves. We were negotiating a deal with them that will have us teaching their top three but the details caused some strife this morning. No big deal really but Juuls is only human and can't handle the wolfy territorial crap."

"I thought dogs were territorial as well?"

"We are. But we are more flexible and way more fun too."

Zack had actually winked at her when he said that. Zack was flirting with Molly and it was weird to see my usually reserved little brother like that. Zoë thought so too, because she started teasing him in the link but he ignored every word not taking his eyes off the blushing Molly.

"Well, euh, I'd love to hear more about that sometime. I mean, never mind."

Zack smiled broadly as Molly hid her face behind a curtain of hair, blushing like she was on fire. "I could teach you things that they don't have in those books and I think that you should join Zoë when she is teaching the girls and Grub to fight properly. It's dangerous for a woman alone."

"Who said I'm alone." She snapped as she looked at me accusingly.

"No one. But a man can hope, can't he?" Zack asked innocently.

"Yes, I'm sorry. And you are right. I am alone here. The school protects me and the building we are in is protected by the wolves as well. Can't you teach me?"

"I would love too but I wouldn't be able to concentrate." Zack was pulling out all the stops and Zoë burst out laughing saying out loud what we both thought. "Looks like Zacky has the hots for a human from your class, Juuls. Not saying any names."

Molly choked and looked at us wide-eyed. Zack however looked thoughtful as he mumbled. "I didn't think it was that obvious."

"Zacky, Bro. You never talk outside pack if you don't have to and even then you don't say that much. Just hope that Molly here likes puppies."

"Puppies?" Molly asked softly.

"She means that Zack is younger than you and hasn't got his own pack. By choice that is, because he is strong enough to have his own pack, they both are. Zoë beat him last match, so she claims the right to call him a puppy every chance she gets."

Molly turned to Zoë. "Firstly, he isn't that much younger than I am and he certainly looks every inch a man. Secondly, I would think that he'd let you win and lastly, you might be his twin but maybe he doesn't talk much because most people aren't worth talking to." She'd sounded quite fierce as she'd stuck up for Zack and when she finished, he looked rather stunned by her outburst.

"Did you just snap at my sister? For me?"

Again, the blush spread to her cheeks as she nodded shyly. Zack didn't waste any time he stalked over to her and grabbed the back of her head as he used the link to state. *'Let's find out if she's my mate, shall we? I like her already!'*

He kissed her passionately and she got over her shock very fast to stand up and mould herself to him as she replied to his kiss in kind. I don't think they noticed that we left the kitchen with my jug of coffee, a cup for me and a bottle of water for Zoë. We retreated to my bedroom because Zoë giggled every time sounds reached our sensitive ears in the living room. We turned on the television rather loudly and opened all the windows so that we could paint our nails without the scent killing us. Then we gossiped and hung out until Zack yelled at us. He could have used the link but he must have done it for Molly's sake. Zoë tried to keep a straight face as we walked out but the fresh scent of sex and their state of appearance had her bursting out in laughter.

"Zacky has found his Matey, Zacky's found his Matey. Welcome to the family Molly as long as you don't do anything to separate us, we'll get along fine. And try not to make so much noise next time!"

Molly looked horrified with the situation but Zack kissed her gently and said. "Molly you are my mate, the other half of my soul and the Love I've been waiting for. I have a lot of flaws that I'm not proud of but you'll find that most of those are wrapped up in the shape of my twin. Get used to it. And as for you Zo, you and I will always be together because we are twins but she does come first now unless. . . well I can't think of any reason for her not too. So be nice!"

Zoë pulled Molly up from where she was sitting and hugged her. "Take care of him. If you hurt him, I will hurt you because he never would with you being his mate. Got that!"

If she had meant to intimidate Molly, she had another thing coming and the steel core I had always suspected Molly to have showed itself. She looked Zoë right in the eyes and replied. "Ditto bitch, you might be his twin but he is mine now." As soon as the words left her mouth she looked scared but Zoë laughed and looked at Zack. "I think I love her already, Zacky." We all laughed and they talked as I started making a feed while reading the stuff Dylan had sent over. Zack rang dad to tell him the good news.

Chapter 25

As the sun set the atmosphere was comfortable, the food was good and Molly worked on an assignment beside me while Zack and her kept sharing gentle touches and loving looks. The footsteps came closer and the smell of wolf reached us through the door just before the knock came. Sky was at the door and I felt like not answering at all. Zack got up after giving Molly a thorough kiss and took his time walking to the door. He purposely made his steps be heard so that Sky knew he was taking his time. When he opened the door, she was obviously fuming at the time it had taken to do so. My apartment was nothing like the big warehouse where the wolves lived.

"Close the door behind you." Zack snapped as he turned on his heel and stalked quietly and a lot faster back to where we were in the kitchen.

"Asshole." Sky muttered under her breath.

"Or you could just leave again, if you'd rather." Zack said without turning back to her.

As he'd known she would, she followed, slowly enough to take in the details of my place. We saw her take a deep breath and recognised the knowing look she gave Molly. Molly blushed realizing that the wolf knew about her and Zack. Sky looked innocent but linked as she spoke to Molly. "You stayed to help her with the assignments?"

In the link she said. '*D, the human you send here is with the boy. They just had sex too, so she might be closer than you thought.*'

'*No, Molly never went there before. I would have known, Sky. She's the most harmless and innocent creature in my pack.*'

'*Well, she just had sex and so did the boy twin and it's all over the house. Guess they hit it off.*'

'*Even better, she might be his mate. He looks too serious for random sex while his sisters are there, that would mean that the girl's mate is around somewhere too. Twins always find their mates around the same time. Julia will need me to protect her if they are busy feeling the love.*'

Zack had heard every word with me while Zoë had played hostess to Sky asking her if she wanted a drink. Zack was fuming but he showed true leadership and wisdom I never knew he'd be capable of as he said out loud to me. "By the way Juuls... Did you get a chance to check the paper for a bigger house away from this dump?"

Molly gave Zack a look and like true mates played right along with him. "I'm afraid I did, my love. I heard you two talking and looked while she was doing her school catch up. The place I found was going to be a surprise for you but I can tell you that I'm sure we can all move into something bigger by the end of the week. We will be able to shop for extra stuff over the holidays."

Zoë linked with us. '*No doubt she's his mate and she lied like a pro too, can't even smell she's lying.*' I was pretty sure that she wasn't lying from the serious look and flushed cheeks. Zack got up and pulled her into his arms for a deep kiss and then pulled her out of the room. We heard the bedroom door close behind them and the stereo turned on loudly. Zoë giggled and thumped me. "Did you see her face?!" I laughed loudly at the memory, Molly had looked embarrassed at his open, almost rude display of affection and pleased as the cat that got the canary at the same time when he dragged her away.

I turned to Sky. "Show me the roster and your proposal."

"Well there are a few changes. ."

We didn't let her finish. "No." We said in sync!

"Will you at least listen?"

"No." Zoë snapped.

"But?"

"You either state your proposal or leave. I've had enough or your wolfy shit. Her Alpha scared shit out of his student. My sister. Your brother is an overbearing, irrational idiot. She grew up with Weres but not your barbaric kind of Weres. He had no right to treat her like that. You bastards are lucky we are still willing to even consider this."

"Look Zoë, I know this, we know this. And we do appreciate your willingness to continue with our agreement."

"Euh, no. I didn't say we were. Your offer had better be damned good for us to continue. Oh, and the new stipulation is that your brother, her teacher, stay away from Juuls. He doesn't touch her or even talk to her if it isn't for school."

"I can't promise he won't talk to her but we already had a long talk with him and he won't touch her again. He even agrees that he will be training with Zack and. . . "

"And nothing! He agrees to that, or we walk away completely."

The moment Zoë said that Sky linked with her brothers, they had to be downstairs. '*You touch her they walk, D.*'

'*Skylar Ann Lee Hunter, you are supposedly the most*

persuasive of our litter. Change. Her. Mind!' Dylan snapped at his sister in their link. Patrick snapped right back on her behalf. *'You dumbshit, what the hell did you think would happen if you went wolf in front of a human? She was raised with dogs, they are practically domestic compared to us. She leaves and we'll lose her. That little human is the first woman that ever bested me in anything, hell I don't even mind that she calls me Pet. You freaking pull your head in and step back for a while. Give her a chance to get used to wolves. We have a good deal for them. They take it and they'll be bound to the city, then they'll be less likely to leave.'*

Skylar stuffed up as she engaged with her brothers and it was painfully obvious that she was used to being with them during negotiations of any kind. Zoë cut her down for it.

"I'm sorry are we interrupting something, dear?" She asked sarcastically. "If you'd rather go back to your pack and converse with them? Do so! We made it clear you were to come with an offer and that it had to be good. If it isn't, the deal is off."

Sky looked like a kangaroo in the headlights. "Okay, sorry, no!"

"What have you got to offer, Sky? I am getting sick of this beating around the bush."

"Look the offer we decided on is as follows. . .The fighting teams will be as Zack and you decided. We train with you on Monday from five thirty to seven. We'll supply dinner after."

Zoë immediately interrupted. "Fine but it had better be take-away because we won't eat with you lot."

"That can be arranged. We will also train on Wednesday

at the same time and Thursday we were hoping we could train before school because we have obligations. Unless you could split the groups so that one group. . ."

"No. We all train you guys or we don't."

"In that case we would like it to be between five thirty and seven in the morning. We run after school with our packs and have other obligations after that."

"Fine, Monday, Wednesday after school and Thursday before school. That's the time done. Move along Sky."

"We would like it to continue during the holidays, for extra payment!"

"Not happening."

"But we'd. . . "

"Not listening very well, Sky. Stop arguing, you might be convincing in some situations but after this morning your charms are useless. Only honour on our part and the recognition that the twins might have humiliated a few people keeps us to this."

"It wasn't just the twins. You might not have fought but to assume that you could teach the best Weres to fight better is, quite frankly, rather rude. *Human*."

"That's where you are all wrong. In our pack humans fight with the Weres on equal footing. As a human we get beat up more and harder and we learn better as we grow up knowing what weaknesses there are. Dad trains all of the pack. Human, female and children we can all protect ourselves and those that need protecting."

"We aren't domesticated. You caught Patrick by surprise last time to fight with him, even in training you could get hurt and Dylan won't be close enough to save you."

"Piss off, Sky, he's the one I would need saving from."

"Yeah? Is that so? That's not what he said. He told our brothers he has rights because you have already been intimate."

'Holy Chickens, sis! Did you forget to tell us something?'

'Don't say it, Zoë! Just listen when I explain to her!'

"Sky. I was taken to your brother's apartment, as you know, to have a place to get some peace. There had been some issues and I couldn't stay here."

"I did notice a lack of siblings here. What happened?"

"Just shut up and listen Sky! I showered and went to sleep on the couch. He came home and carried me to his bed because, he said, I looked uncomfortable. He woke me doing that and when I tried to move away his wolf showed up and he asked me to stay where I was. Then he kissed me while I was still half asleep. Your brother is a good-looking guy, so I didn't fight him but I came to my senses fast and got away from him faster. He is my teacher and I will not be the teacher's hussy. If I stay in this school my marks will reflect my capability in the classroom not the bedroom. As consenting adults, I agree that he wasn't a hardship to kiss but it was a mistake. A mistake that will not happen again. If he doesn't accept that and treats me like his new toy or his next prey, I will have the bond removed and leave the school completely. I am willing to give up Spec Med. I have enough knowledge for our pack and dad is only letting me do this because I wanted it. There are several trained doctors in our pack that can teach me what I need."

That wasn't all true but she didn't need to know that

and I would hate to give up my chance to study at the best Medical Institution in Australia.

"Well, just so you know, I appreciate that you didn't act like he tried to rape you. My brothers are good men. Each one of them and. . ."

"Subject closed Sky, no need for a sales pitch. Get to the business at hand."

"Okay for payment we are willing to offer you part ownership in The Pitt."

Chapter 26

The female wolf was very sure of her offer and she smiled when Zoë lost her cool. "HOLY HELL!! ZACK! GET YOUR BUTT OUT HERE!" She didn't even use the link!

Sky was smiling but her smile slipped a bit when she realized that I wasn't impressed at all. Little did she know I'd heard her in her private link. Zack rushed in. "What happened!?" He had his pants on and was still pulling a shirt over his head as he skidded to a stop in the kitchen to see us all sitting there quietly.

"They are offering part ownership in The Pitt as payment." I said in a bored tone.

"Nice and who's to say that it's running a profit? How much part are they even offering? What's the running expense of a club like that? You really got me away from Molly for that?" He replied calmly to his excited twin. In the link he replied. '*That's freaking huge Juuls. What game are they playing?*'

Sky looked at my face and then at the unimpressed Zack, it wasn't what she'd expected, what they'd expected. "We are offering fifty percent ownership to the hottest club in town. Zoë had an appropriate reaction and you two are pissing me off. We didn't make this decision lightly."

We shared a look, linked without Zoë and quickly made a decision. "No." We said together. Zoë didn't look different, she knew we'd linked without her and understood that there were hooks to this deal that she couldn't understand. She knew we'd make the best decision for us.

"Don't you get a say Zoë?" Sky asked sweetly.

"Don't need it. If they don't want it, they have a reason and Zacky is right it's probably too expensive to run and I'd get bored with business stuff. I always do."

"This is an amazing offer, what is wrong with you Westlanders?" She asked as her link went mad. It didn't take long for footsteps to close in on our door. Zack cocked his head and looked at Sky. '*There's only one of them.*' He linked me, even though I already knew.

He gave Sky a condescending look and soundlessly sprinted to the door and opened it before the person that had stopped in front of it could knock. Sky was clearly irritated with us by now. Patrick stood in the doorway. "Interesting." Said Zack in a speculative tone as he looked Patrick up and down. "Come in, Pet. Your sister is not dealing with reason."

Sky snapped at his tone and yelled "Reason? You two just. . ."

Patrick shut her down in the link and out loud. "Sky! Enough!"

She went quiet and the three of us grinned at her obedience. '*Good wolf! Now Roll over and play dead!*' Zoë quipped at us in the link. It was hard not to laugh out loud. Zack slid into a chair beside me and draped an arm around me and the other around Zoë. He gave us a squeeze and nodded at the new wolf. Patrick took his cue, sat down in the chair looking relaxed and at ease, while Sky looked tense. "So? You don't want the deal as it is? Is that because of what happened or because you don't like the Pitt?"

"Don't like part ownership." Zack said calmly. He shot

Sky a look and added. "Can cause personality clashes."

Sky's eyes went wolf and I tensed. It wasn't put on, it scared me because if we had a real fight they'd have to die. They probably thought she scared me. There was no way they wouldn't find out what I could do. We had a human in the house, one who was family now and I would do whatever I needed to do. Patrick turned to his sister at my fear and snarled at her to get out. She left without a word and Zack rubbed my back whispering softly that all was alright. He didn't use the link because we weren't alone and my fear might not have been of the wolf but it was alright for Patrick to think so. My fear was real and the smell was heavy in the room.

"I hate that smell on you. I want to kill anything that causes that." Zoë growled as she got up and slammed the windows open. Then she walked out of the room only to stalk back in and start making me a fresh coffee. When she finished, she added whisked milk and sugar making it a cappuccino. The moment it was placed before me she growled again and turned to the wolf who still hadn't said anything. "Make it good, wolf, we are still trying to be fair but that was the second one of your kin that scared her. You are out of chances here." Then she changed to her other form and laid herself at my feet.

"I appreciate that you are still open to train some of our fighters. And I apologize for Sky, she didn't think there was any way that you wouldn't want to be part owner of the hottest club in town. It is a very profitable business. Honestly though, our offer was a good one. What will work for you?"

"One hundred per person per lesson, paid prior to

commencement."

"That's reasonable but we don't have that much liquid cash lying around."

"You just clearly stated that the club was a profitable business?"

"Yes, a business. And the profits are also wages, maintenance, taxes, liquor and other beverages."

"Thought so, running expenses. That just proves our point that it isn't the best deal for us because we don't want the status that comes from the club. Fifty each per lesson, cash, prior to commencement paid by you to me. Nobody else, ever. Or training is off, don't test us on that. And a building of our choice that goes in our name completely. No sharing the building. Have you found a place to train yet?"

"We have a warehouse that can be used."

"Windows?"

"What?"

"Does it have windows?"

"Heaps."

"No good. Find something else without windows or just a few that can be covered. We will need to see the building before commencement."

"That's fine we have a large storage building that has just been cleaned out. It's on the river and we will be able to use it."

"When can we see it?"

"Now?"

"Zoë, stay here with Molly. Juuls, are you up for it?"

I finally joined the conversation. "Tell your brothers and sister to go away, you were too fast getting here so they would have to be close. Don't want to see any of them where we are going either. We tell you what needs to be done with the building and you get it done before school starts after the holidays so that training can start then."

"No, we will make all the changes before next week and we start as soon as it is finished. The rest of school without holidays leaves us one term only."

It annoyed me that the wolf was trying to get this off the ground as fast as possible, I didn't really want to do it at all. We had been taught to negotiate by dad and he was very good at it. If they didn't a few wins for what they wanted, we might end up with more trouble than we could deal with. Only good politics and the knowledge that I would be stuck with the Hunter pack for another few years had me agreeing to anything. We had to acknowledge that we had insulted them. Zack and I shared a look and got up simultaneously. We might as well get it over with as soon as possible.

Zoë trotted out of the room and we heard the bedroom door slam shut behind her. I went to pick up my coffee cup but Patrick moved faster. "Allow me." He said as he moved to the sink and washed it up for me. Charming bastards. Zack grinned at me behind his back and linked. *'He liiikes you.'*

'Shame he's the wrong species.'

'Hey sis, technically he is isn't, 'cause you, pumpkin, are human remember?!'

'Yeah and he's a wolf, dumb nut, still the wrong species!'

'From what I hear you didn't mind the taste of wolf. Not like there's anyone here that would stop you. Not like the others have for the last few years... You might have a chance to have a fling.'

I gave Zack a pointed look. *'A fling, Zack? Really?! With a wolf?'*

Zack winked over his shoulder as he walked out of the kitchen in front of me. *'They don't seem to mind, sis. Just like all the other Weres you put in dad's pack that aren't Dogs. Nobody cares what you are, they just want to be close to you.'*

I shoved him aside roughly as he pointed out the scary truth of my life. Thanks to dad's experimentations we had quickly found out that I could cast my 'sort of' magic over any Were I've met, not just the dogs. Link with them, make them change by my will and make them submit to me! It was unnatural and it was dangerous. Dangerous for all the Weres if I decided to play with it and dangerous for me if they found out I could do it.

The top dog, our father, had a dangerous weapon in me and the other Australian packs or whatever they called themselves were lucky dad didn't want more country. With my help he would be able to make any Were submit, unconditionally.

Chapter 27

Patrick didn't know what caused me to shove Zack and he raised an eyebrow in question, which I ignored completely, just I went to get my stuff to go out of the house. Zack went to the bedroom too and he shut the door, leaving me and Patrick alone. Waiting. I didn't have to wait long for him to break the silence.

"You are right, we all came to be there for Sky."

"I guessed as much, Pet."

"I'm sorry D and now Sky scared you. They would never hurt you. And you are pack, you must understand what that means."

"Yeah, dog pack and with a reasonable leader, my dad. I've never seen him go madly possessive over other women in our pack like your brother did to me."

"He likes you, as a woman. His wolf is just a bit more possessive because you are part of his pack."

"He's my teacher, Patrick. I'm his student and part of his pack for that reason only. I'm not even a Were for freaks sake."

"You aren't, true, but you are a beautiful woman and we are still men. There is something about you, something different. My wolf keeps telling me but we can't understand it. Neither wolf nor man can understand. It's nothing tangible. I think that might be why my little brother gets so worked up about you. I can't blame him."

And there it was. They could feel something. It had to be because I was part of Dylan's pack and thereby indirectly

186

part of the Hunter Pack that they all belonged to. Their old pack, one that they by rights should have been released from, when they became strong enough to challenge their Alpha. I realised the irony as my dad hadn't been challenged by anyone, like my brothers, they were all strong enough. They were old enough, strong enough and smart enough, they should be kicked out before they went for the Top Dog spot. But in dad's pack they stayed and ran smaller packs inside it. Dad had the biggest territory in Australia. There were different sorts of Weres in our pack, thanks to me. Longreach was part of our territory, it was also the base to the Guarders institution. Witches and Weres. Magic and muscle. Protection and safety. Money, papers, antiques, jewellery, even full home content if you had to go away. It would all be safe at the Guarders Buildings that were everywhere in Australia. Our family had been part of the founders of the Guarders and Longreach was far enough inland, close enough to the forests and deep enough in Were territory that everyone was well protected. The Witches lived in the actual town with some humans and some of the less territorial Were species, like the crows.

Good lord, dad would pull me out if he even got the slightest whiff of this, the first hint of them suspecting anything would see me locked up in our territory for life. Grub was right, I was a weapon, but I was the daughter of Cameron Westlander first and foremost. Without apology, dad would protect me as he saw fit. The worry must have shown to some extent, again Patrick immediately assumed that he knew the reason for my worry. I didn't need to risk lying as long as I kept my mouth shut, he would make assumptions. Most people did when it came to strong emotions like fear. In this case it worked in my favour.

"Look, I know that I didn't make a very good impression when we met, and I am more sorry than you could ever imagine, but I am a strong wolf. I am as strong as D, faster and more in touch with my wolf. I am only a year older, so I'm not that old compared to you either. I chose not to fight because for some reason my wolf didn't feel the need to argue when you pinned me. That has never happened before, I am Alpha, I don't let a challenge pass. Everyone thinks I didn't take it serious but I know that when you call me Pet, it is because you think you could have taken me. It intrigues me because my wolf still agrees though you are not my mate, so that isn't the reason you got away with it."

He looked at me for an answer while I contemplated how bad this situation was.

"What do you want me to say?" I finally asked.

"Ah." He sighed. And it took all I had not to speak as he looked at me thoughtfully.

"It intrigues me, but my wolf tells me to just let you be and we are one. My wolf is clear in our direction. I will protect you, be your friend and make sure that nobody else gets into the position I was in, so you don't have to deal with more like me."

"And what are you, exactly?" Asked Zack from the doorway, he stalked into the room silently.

"I am the brother of her Alpha, a pack leader and teacher at her school and I am a son of the strongest wolf in Australia. My blood is pure and as a wolf I do not submit to anyone beside my father. Yet what I want her to know is that

I am hers to do with as she pleases... and I do believe that it would be regardless of what I want or am ordered by my father. My wolf crawls in her presence like a pup wanting her touch, just a scratch behind the ear, anything. And before you get upset, it isn't because she is my mate, it isn't sexual though, as a man, wouldn't mind... "

Zack growled.

"Down doggie, just letting her know the lay of the land and if she would like to take me up on it, I'll be happy to please. She's a grown woman. They have needs too, just like men do."

I blushed at his implication; he continued like he didn't notice. "I haven't told my siblings of how you make me, and my wolf, feel. I've let everyone think I was playing with you when I submitted so easily. I won't dig but if you ever want to explain, I will be ready to listen. I managed to reign in Dylan for the time being but I can only do so much for you so don't lead him on."

"My sister didn't lead him on!"

"No but he showed us the memory and she didn't resist him outright when he kissed her."

"JULIA! WHAT THE HELL?"

"Dude!" I blushed madly as Zoë stormed into the room laughing. "He woke me up, kissed before I had a chance to understand what was happening and I might have kissed him back a little before my sense kicked in. He does look very good!"

Zack and Zoë followed my memory of the event as it rose while I told them. Patrick didn't know but I feared my sister's big mouth as she said. "Might have? Just a little?"

Zack used the link and growled. '*Where the hell were your clothes?*'

Thankfully Zoë wrapped me in her arms as the blood rushed to my face with more vigour than previously and I hid my face in her neck with my hair hiding me further. Patrick laughed and Zack growled dangerously. "If he does that again I'll. ."

"You'll what, dog boy? You don't think she could control him? If there was a way that I could show you the memory my brother showed us you'd know the temptation your sister presented and that she didn't get forced into anything."

"She was hurting, he abused his position and her vulnerability."

"He kissed a beautiful woman dressed in . ."

"SHUT UP!" I yelled. "It's happened and it won't happen again! Ask him how it ended!"

Zack was smart enough to remain quiet but Patrick grinned and mumbled. "Uhuh, sure."

"Take care of Molly, Zo. Stay in contact and we'll be back soon."

Zoë didn't reply but released me fully and stalked back to the bedroom without another word. Zack ran after her, probably to kiss Molly judging by his swollen lips when he returned, and then we left.

There was a hummer on the curb, shiny black with tinted windows. He had informed his siblings of our terms and we couldn't smell them. We didn't talk as he grabbed the keys out of the hand of the dark broody looking Were beside the car and we didn't talk as he drove us up to the industrial district on the river. I sat in the back like a good little girl and linked with Zack. I asked. *'Do we need to kill him?'*

'Do you want to?'

'No!'

'Good because I didn't smell a lie, his wolf submitting to such an obvious human must annoy the hell out of him but he made the right choice. The only problem is that we can't put him in dad's pack, so we'll have to be very careful. If anything looks like it could cause trouble, you'll need to kill him. He might be too strong for me, sis.' It had to hurt Zack to admit that but he was always brutally honest and as a predator he knew what was needed to survive, including when to back down.

'You'll need to promise me this, sis. We are taking a risk here.'

'Okay.'

'No, I mean, a stray thought on telling the others. A careless word about his submission to you. A mere hint in his behaviour that you are higher on the chain and he knows it. Anything to jeopardise you. You kill him!'

Zacks power was leaking into the air as he sat there looking at me with his head turned to look me in the eyes. I was sure that the wolf could feel it. I bowed down to my little brother and made the vow he needed to hear. *'If at any time this wolf so much as hints that there is anything more than human about me, I will use my power to kill him.'*

'Good girl.' He sounded like Dad and Richard with an edge. He would always be more dangerous, more feral, more animal.

"Is there anything I need to know about?" Interrupted the wolf that had just been put on notice without knowing I now held his life in my hands.

"No." Snapped Zack without breaking eye contact with me. Daring me to get smart.

"Why are you letting your power out? Are you trying to prove something to me, pup?"

"No."

Patrick bristled and his power now started to fill the cramped space of the car as he slowed it down. "Are you using it to threaten your sister?"

"No."

"Listen, you damned Dog, I don't know what you are playing at but reign yourself in before I make you do it!"

Zack turned to look at Patrick as the car came to a full stop and I could smell the anger and testosterone filling the car. I had to make sure that this wouldn't go any further. If Patrick said anything wrong now Zack would kill him himself and if he looked like losing, I was bound by my word to finish it. This was sooo bad. Thinking about it, Zack would probably expect me to kill Patrick if he did anything so I did the best I could to defuse the situation.

"Zack, honey, are you missing Molly? You know that Zoë is with her."

The wolf pulled back instantly, there was the excuse that he needed to explain what was happening to Zack. The new mate bond. Patrick started the car and took off grinning as Zack quietly fumed at me in the link. *'Low sis, very low.'* I grinned at him and winked at Patrick who was glancing at me in the rear-view mirror. Patrick burst out laughing and the power that was coming from Zack didn't challenge him anymore.

Chapter 28

We didn't go much further before he pulled up in front of a large warehouse. There were four big burly men waiting for us and they bowed in respect for Patrick. They were lower on the food chain that much was obvious, it was also obvious that they didn't belong to the pack that he'd made for his students. But the wolf was definitely connected with a pack of his.

They politely said hello to us and bowed to Zack to indicate they knew he was a strong Were. Three of them were dogs too and one was a wolf Patrick was linked with via a pack. It was strange to see these big men bow to my little brother. In our pack at home there were so many dominant males, and females too, that dad didn't ask for shows of respect unless there were outsiders around. Without outsiders everyone was the same, even dad. He was approachable and kind, respected and well loved by everyone.

The dogs looked at me and Zack and rather unexpectedly one asked. "How are you human and related to him?"

"He is my brother."

"Not twin?"

"Hey Zacky, they know you!" I laughed.

"Oh yes, I was in clean-up when you Westlanders came to our territory for a visit. He's the only one I saw with Mr Westlander and I'll always remember that day. He was barely a teenager then."

"Pack?" Zack asked shortly.

"MacKellar, Southwest near the border of NSW."

"I remember. Some of your pack wanted to use my sisters for sports. You are a good man if we let you live. I'll be in town as long as my sister lives here. I see you are with the wolf but if you ever need me, let me know."

"Thank you, Sir, it means a lot. And just to clear it up, we aren't with the wolves, we are security."

Zack laughed but Patrick frowned. "Why are you laughing at that?"

"You need security. And if we wanted you dead, they wouldn't be the first to die. Then you'd all be gone. Security is useless."

"Zack, could you, like, not provoke him every chance you get just because you'd rather be with your mate. They might be here as security for the building or even to help protect us. Pull your head in."

I had grabbed my little brother by the collar and yelled up in his face, stunning the other men with my audacity. I was after all, to them anyway, a mere human.

"You are right, I am sorry, Juuls. I'll be good, not that we'd ever need security. Let's just get this over with."

He bowed down to me and I patted his head grinning. "Good doggie."

He laughed and turned back to the five stunned looking men. "Lead the way." He told them, like I didn't just pet him on the head like a domesticated, trained animal.

The warehouse had some high windows that we told them needed to be blacked out. As it was night the lights were on and the place was lit up like a summer's day. Nothing needed to be fixed with that. The floor space had to be divided into four areas, one with a boxing ring and three with mats. We needed four ropes in the middle that went to the ceiling and twenty boxing bags of leather filled with sand and rocks would need to be spread out near the side with the ring, hanging on chains, not rope. They asked why twenty and we replied that it was in case any broke because training would continue regardless. We asked for a fridge near every mat and that there would have to be change rooms with showers for those of us that didn't want to start school smelling like we'd been sweaty with a heap of people. We also added the need for five patrol people to surround the building. Our training style would remain ours because we would be sealing the premises in magic. Each and every one of them would be making a vow not to talk about it.

Nobody even blinked as we relayed our wishes and I could faintly hear Pet use his link to pass the information on to others. One of the men took notes as we detailed our instructions. Really, it wasn't much, the only time they blinked and asked questions was when we told them there would need to be a Were cage in the furthest corner of the room. "Why?" Patrick voiced their doubt at the instruction.

"Julia is human."

"That doesn't explain anything, Zack." He replied patiently.

"What he's trying to say is that I am human, yet I will be kicking your asses regularly while I am teaching you. In our pack we humans fight and train with the Weres our whole lives. We learn to make up for the fact that we are not as strong or just as fast. No matter what you think now if it isn't you Alphas that snap at me it will be a second or third that breaks when I hurt the Alpha or when I humiliate them. It could be that one of the men snaps at being beaten by my little sister in the ring. It could be that they are closer to their animal because something happened at home or stress at school could have them on edge. One way or the other, sooner or later someone will snap. To prevent someone needing to be killed, we will need a cage. Or two. Yes, make it two cages, Pet."

"One more thing." said Zack. "On Mondays I want these dogs to train with us and on the other days I want these guys to be part of the patrols for the building. They will be under the vow regarding training as well."

"What about the wolf?"

"Is he your pack?"

"My original pack, yes."

"Then no. I want the dogs."

"Are you planning on taking them as your own pack?"

"No, not at the moment but I remember them too and if they are here, they didn't leave their original pack because they wanted. Therefore, I would like to offer my help to them. For if their past ever comes knocking. Because I know one thing and that is that the past is never far away."

"Pet, the incident they referred to was one of the gentler ones that we've been in. Their Top Dog allowed us to hunt the culprits. One of them was related, a nephew, I think. There are bad feelings because some of the men from his pack agreed with ours hunting their own as we demanded the blood to be settled."

"It wasn't his nephew, it was his youngest, bastard child.

The situation was bad enough to see us released from the pack the moment your lot was over the borders. Us was four of the council and our families were kept." The men were hurting that much was clear. I asked the next logical question. "Where is the fourth?"

"He went feral without his mate. We haven't got mates, our families were blood only."

Zack growled as the wolves looked sad and angry at their story. "Westlanders didn't cause this!"

"We know that, Sir." The dogs bowed down to the angry Zack, his power caused them to cower down. The power of a half feral Top Dog was an intimidating, unpredictable thing and with them not being bonded to pack they had no protection from him. I put my arm around my baby brother as he ranted in the link at the injustice of the situation they were in and the fact that Westlanders would be bearing the blame, if not theirs then others for sure.

"We did not cause this. But we shall talk to dad and our council and then we shall fix this!"

"Sir, we appreciate it but our families are well, so it isn't needed. We have contact regularly."

"It should be settled."

"Choices were made, consequences were accepted, this matter was settled." The man replied quietly, being careful to keep his demeanour submissive.

Zack growled again, longer and louder, his frustration clear. Patrick and the other wolf were looking at me in question. Could I settle my brother?

I moved in front of him and wrapped my arms around him whispering in the link and out loud. "Baby, we talked about this, sometimes the human way is the humane way and it needs to have its place. They don't need us to save them, baby. Calm down. We will make them stronger and better fighters. We will give them the company of our kind without strings while we are here in town and we will let dad know that they might need a pack so that, if they find a mate, they can get the safety of a pack, of a family, once again. Leave them their choices baby, they are older than us, respect their knowledge."

Again, Zack bowed his head to me and again I rubbed his head like I used to do when he was a little boy, mostly dog. "Good boy, calm down, baby, I'm here."

The man that had told us they knew Zack nodded his thanks to me when I let Zack go. "I am Ned, this here is Dirty Harry and the short guy is Weasel."

"Guess you know us. It's nice to meet you and I do believe that it will be a pleasure to work with you guys. Zack means well, I hope no offence was taken by his behaviour."

"None at all Miss, it's good to see that the younger Westlanders are taking after their daddy. Cameron is a good man. And you, my feral little friend, have developed great control."

Much to my surprise Zack laughed and replied. "It's a work in progress Ned, every damned day. But at least I'm getting better, my sister is letting the side down."

"Hey, don't look at me, he's talking about his twin. You'll meet her soon enough, they are never far apart."

Zack looked proud as punch as he said. "She's with my mate!"

The men looked happy for him and congratulated him

with manly thumps on his shoulder.

"See you when we start or if you wanna meet up sometime, we are normally at the park during school hours. When Juuls is busy. Now wolf. You may take us home."

Patrick grinned at his command and replied playfully. "Yes, your highness."

Chapter 29

The moment the car stopped at our building Zack shot out and left me with the wolf. "Next week is the last week. It's testing and tournament week next week, Julia. If you miss it without being on the brink of death you will be expelled. He will control himself."

"You can't promise me that, Patrick." I said, feeling my fear of my teacher resurface, I looked at the ground.

"Your fear of my brother saddens me. He showed me the memory and I do not understand the fear you have. It seemed pretty mutual to me, for a little while anyway."

"He is my teacher!"

"He is a man."

"He is a wolf!"

"He is still also just a man."

"He is being crazy possessive!"

"Well, you said it yourself, that's his wolf."

"You don't have that problem!"

"You aren't marked by me."

"Bull! Freaking Bull! I'm not his mate. It's a school pack, it's not real."

"Yes, it is real, but you are right it isn't standard pack structure. Maybe it's because I haven't kissed you like he has. That might have something to do with it."

"Don't you dare!"

"I don't know... you are competition in the tournament next week, it might leave you off your game if I do."

"Might leave you castrated too!"

He burst out laughing. "You can take a girl out of the Bush but you can't take the Bush out of the girl. Raising girls on a cattle station is dangerous for men."

I grinned back. "And don't you forget it, wolfy."

"Should be illegal to raise girls in the Outback."

I laughed with him and relaxed in his presence. "Thanks, Pet."

"My pleasure, Julia. Enjoy time with the twins for the week. He could use the lesson but make sure you are back and ready for the exams and the tournament next week."

"Yes sir." I replied with a smile.

He winked and got back in his car. Looking at him drive away, he left me wondering when I'd gotten comfortable with him. His life now depended on him being able to keep his mind and mouth shut to his pack mates, all freaking pack mates and there seemed to be quite a few of them because the moment he'd driven off I'd heard him open to the conversations in his links. Siblings, students and his father's pack. There were people other than his siblings from his father's pack in this town. His life and whoever he could tell were on the line. Worst of all, he didn't even know it.

I took a deep breath and shook off my doom and gloom thoughts as I felt a presence heading my way from the left. I turned to look as he rounded the corner with a huge grin. I blocked his link to the school pack and opened one to him with Zack and Zoë in it. *'Put some clothes on Zack, we have a visitor.'*

He growled before he felt Grub and he noticed at the same time as Zoë, if her happiness that flooded the link was anything to go by. *'Hey'* she whispered in the link. *'Open the door for me?'* Grub asked her in reply. We got to the top of the stairs and my floor at Were speed, Grub didn't seem surprised I could keep up. But more to the point he picked up that it made me tired to link him into our link.

"Thank you for not killing me and giving me a chance with your sister. Julia, I, well I, euh"

"It's cool, Zack just found his mate and I think that you'll like the irony of it. Destiny has a funny way of working things out." I said grinning when I saw Zoë standing at the doorway to my apartment. She was dressed up nicely and even had shoes on, she was really trying to look like a grown woman. Grub had a crappy name but he looked anything but grubby. He was actually quite good looking and I was happy for my little sister to have found him. She didn't move aside much as we neared the doorway to go in and I squeezed past. Grub hesitated. "Zack found his mate." Zoë said proudly.

"So I heard."

"We are twins, Grub."

"I know that too."

"Twins usually find their mate around the same time. Did you know that?"

"Yes, Zoë, I actually did." He smiled at her and then he showed another side of himself as he said. "I hope you haven't found yours yet, Zoë."

"W What?" She asked. It was clearly an unpredicted turn of the conversation.

Grub stepped closer to Zoë and said. "I want that title, Zoë Westlander. The reason I came here is because you've haunted my dreams since the first time I saw you. You've been on my mind every waking moment and on the days I didn't see you, I felt like part of me was missing."

Zoë tried to interrupt and finally managed to say. "Zacky and I are not as human as most Weres, Grub."

He replied with. "Every time I look at you, I know that there is a Goddess out there somewhere because you are perfect just the way you are."

"I. . "

"Shut up, Zoë, and don't fight me because I'm going to kiss you."

He took the last small step to close the distance between them and kissed my little sister as her twin and I watched with bated breath.

She kissed him back, thoroughly, she wrapped her arms around him and when he tried to move away a bit, she growled. He laughed loudly, happily at the growl and said. "You, my love, may call me anything you wish but I would like you to know that I am Benjamin Isaac Hollows."

"Mate! Benjamin Isaac Hollows. My mate! Mine. I will call you mine." Zoë was grinning from ear to ear. "You taste great and feel great and look great and I love how you have no fear of me and I didn't think I'd like to be bossed around by anyone but these two but it sounds great when you are bossy."

He laughed even louder. "I have a woman that speak her mind, and so far, I like the way she thinks. Now comes the problem. Will you move in with me at the pack house?"

"No, you will move in with us. Zacks mate is looking for a house we can share. We will need a room without him in it." She sounded so matter of fact that we all burst out laughing. That was when Grub finally spotted Molly, she was wrapped in the arms of Zack.

"You?"

"Yeah, problem?" She snapped at him.

"Yeah." Zack growled but Grub continued. "What are you?"

"Human." She replied, but it didn't have the same fire. Still, I know the others couldn't smell a lie. Grub nodded at me and said. "That's what she calls herself too. Neither of you are human to the full extent. I can feel her and I've always felt you as well. Difference is she feels more animal. You feel like shadows."

Molly looked pale now. She wormed out of Zacks embrace but he caught her quickly and sat down with her in his lap. Zoë pulled Grub inside and closed the door. They all looked at me, all with different questions in their faces.

"Molly, I can link with the pack. Any pack. And I can, to some extent control any sort of Were creature. Grub felt me in the school pack link. Zack and Zoë almost went feral when they were little and I pulled them back. They are always on the edge of animal. They don't think like a human does, they can't. Grub is mate to Zoë, he bonds with her or he gets killed, those are his only options. You are mate with Zack. Thankfully both of you are accepting of the mate bonds but if you are not human, we need to know. It's probably better for you if you aren't fully human with Zacky, he gets a bit out of control sometimes."

The silence that settled in the room when I finished speaking was a heavy one as we waited for Molly to answer. A howl split the air outside and it was picked up around the streets, coming closer.

"Shit! They are looking for me. You killed the link and they couldn't reach me. Kayden probably followed my scent here. Shit! What do we do?"

"Well, I could help you guys kill everyone or we could knock him out before they get to the door." Molly said calmly. "I have a dark fey father but my mum knew how to hide my scent as one, so I have always lived as a human. Mum was born from a witch and a human. I do have some extra abilities but if I use my magic, I will draw the dark fey to me because it isn't diluted at all. I'm one of the crossbreed freaks you hear about. I just wasn't killed because my mum loves me and my dad doesn't know I'm not only human. That sums it up, now, what do you want to do?"

"Knock him out. Zoë, quick move aside. Zack needs to be the one to do it. Let me talk when they get here." Zack got up and approached Grub.

"Just don't break anything Bro." Grub grinned just before Zack knocked him out cold.

Chapter 30

Zoe was clearly conflicted as her brother had hit the love of her life. She was angry and her dog was close to the surface as the door burst of its hinges. In the opening stood a half-naked Kayden and at least four other guys from our class including the one that was called Jordan. All the blokes looked fit to kill us as we were seated calmly in my little living room and Zoe was still flickering between dog and human. She settled in her dog shape as Kayden stepped aside for Dylan.

"What is my third doing here, knocked out, in your apartment, Miss Westlander?"

"I'm sorry, Mr. Hunter, it's all just a big misunderstanding." I couldn't keep the grin from my face as the boys looked at Zack as if he was the only threat in the room. I made sure to stay out of their link because I could guess well enough what was being said. Kayden meanwhile tried to get closer to Grub but Zoe nearly bit his arm off.

"Zack saw Grub kissing Zoe and knocked him out. They are mates so please stay away from him, Kayden, she'll kill you or die trying. Either way you'll lose."

I'd left out a few details but I hadn't lied so when they took a deep breath to see if it was the truth there was no lie there to catch. Molly grinned at Dylan. "Thank you for sending me with the work, Sir. I found out humans can have mates too and Zack is mine."

She never said she was completely human, she never said that she only just found out, she never lied. Instead, she

206

snuggled closer to Zack and cooed at Zoe. "Darling, I am sure that he'll come around soon. Why don't you let his friends see that he is fine for the rest."

Zoe shifted to human and snapped. "He's mine, don't touch him."

Dylan laughed suddenly, breaking the awkward silence that followed her words. "Grub with a Westlander, who would have guessed. And dear sweet Molly. Good luck with them, I think you'll find that you'll get the lot, not just the mate."

Molly smiled back sweetly. "Isn't that the loveliest thing, Sir, an amazing mate and such a strong pack to protect me. Julia and I are already friends and now we will be family. We'll both finally have family in class. Someone not of the Were variety."

"He's practically feral! I can smell it from here!" One of the boys growled behind Dylan.

I stood up and snarled in a close impression of a Were Dingo. "Talk about my baby brother again, you freaking lap dog." A warm hand landed softly on my shoulder. Pancakes and maple syrup, help me, Zack! Zack pulled me firmly into my own pack link with the twins.

"He didn't mean it like that, Julie." I shook the hand off and turned to Dylan. He was too close. "There aren't many ways to take that."

"And he's sorry. Will Grub be alright?" As he asked, I heard Grub in my head telling me. '*Let me in their link or I can't wake up for them.*'

I complied and followed him into the pack link. Out loud he groaned. "Baby, every second was worth it. Kiss me again, I need you."

Zoë happily complied as the guys from our class laughed and cheered him on in the link. *'Nailed a Westlander and the enforcer too. You movin' up my man.'* Kayden quipped.

'What happened?' Dylan asked finally in their link while Grub was still kissing my little sister.

'Kissed my mate, got knocked out by her twin.' He laughed at Dylan. *'She's worth anything they can throw at me!'*

Dylan chuckled. Out loud he said. "You have four days as a school rule for the new mate bond, that gives you the rest of the week. I will expect you back in class by Monday, Mr. Hollows, and ready to take the term exams."

"Yes, Sir." Grub replied, coming up for air. Kayden took a step in his direction and my little sister suddenly growled with her canines extended, going for Grubs throat. He grabbed her just in time, by the hair. Then he roughly pulled her hair and got his face close to hers. He also had his teeth out. "We will mate properly. You are mine! But we do it when I say and not with all these people here. Is. That. Clear?"

My sister submitted as we all watched in awe at the feral girl, suddenly tamed by the normally so quiet Grub. There was a reason he was third in the pack hierarchy but this was the first time I saw it. He was pleased as she dipped her head at his command and he repeated the question. "Is that clear?"

"Yes Benji. I'm sorry."

"Good girl, we'll go now." He pulled her up and she followed obediently. Zack was smiling but even in the link it was quiet. He obviously approved of the situation. As her big sister I wanted to kick his ass but having grown up with a pack of dogs I understood that she needed his dominance and strength and he needed to show it. He would now be the one to keep her from going feral. He respected Zack, out loud. "I will be keeping her safe, we'll keep in touch so don't worry."

Much to everyone's surprise Molly answered "That's alright, Grubby. He'll be busy. You just take care of his twin and I'll keep him happy for her." Zack laughed and kissed her but she pulled away to say something else as Grub led Zoe past the guys from school, the pack that had busted down my door to find him.

"Looks like I have the rest of the week off too, Mr. Hunter. I've found my mate. You boys make sure this door gets fixed for Julia and keep her safe. I am taking my mate home." She started pulling Zack to the door but he stopped next to me looking in my eyes like that was how we were communicating but we linked.

'Will you be alright? I can stay, I'll explain it to her later and she knows that we are here to protect you, she doesn't really know what you can do. I. . '

'It's alright Zacky, go with your mate, just tell them that Kayden, not Dylan stays please.'

'That's fine. Done. Thanks, Sis.'

'Have fun, baby brother.'

'Oh, I will and so will she!'

Then he spoke out loud turning to the other men. "You!" He snapped at Kayden. "Will protect my sister. You should be capable enough to do this without the wolf or any others. And You." He said turning to look at Dylan. "Will make sure someone fixes this door. Tonight. And stay away from my sister while she isn't in school."

Dylan bristled and I felt the fear of him finding out rise again while I thought of his possessive behaviour. They didn't know it was because I was afraid of my own carefully guarded abilities being found out, they assumed that it was the fear of my Alpha that caused my reaction.

Zack growled and my classmates looked offended at the sour smell of my fear. Kayden was talking to Dylan in the link and whatever he said worked as Dylan nodded to Zack, taking a step back. "Two of mine live in the building, I'll make sure they keep an ear out too. The door will be done within the next hour at the most."

"Aaand?" Said Molly sarcastically.

"And you need to be careful how you speak to me. You are pack!" He snapped at her.

Much to everybody's surprise she laughed. "I suppose you are right but really. . It's crazy isn't it? I go to school, become part of a pack and then meet my mate. Damned, who would have thought my life could get so interesting?"

Zack relaxed and looked at Dylan pointedly while my fear left a sour acidic smell around me. Having the senses of a Were now and with so many around made me very aware of what they would think of it.

"I will see you ladies in class next week." He turned on his heel and stalked off, other than Kayden who walked in further and sat on the couch like he owned the place. Zack didn't respond to his audacity and gave me a quick hug. Molly did the same and then they were gone. Stepping over the broken door and going to Molly's house. I stood for another second, wishing I was home before I went and opened the rest of the windows to let the smell of fear out. Kayden raised an eyebrow in question, I replied. "I know that being scared smells and I know it puts you guys on edge. I was scared, Kayden, I am sure you can still smell it on me so I thought I'd air the place out. At least I don't have to open the door."

He laughed and nodded at my bad attempt for humour but stayed where he was, letting me do my thing. I got some drinks from the fridge and some Anzac biscuits and placed them between us then I sat as far away from him as possible without leaving the room.

He had a sad smile on his beautiful face as he looked at me, but I remained quiet, he wasn't wanted here even if I understood it was sort of needed. It was the first time I was in my apartment without any of my siblings and for a quick second I felt afraid again.

"I'd never hurt you, Julia Westlander. Your last name is enough to make sure of that. You might not be a Dingo, but you are in every way that counts, a Westlander. Why are you afraid of me now? We've fought and you had not an ounce of fear in you then. Was it because it was at school?"

"I'm not afraid of you, Kayden. I haven't been here without my siblings since I came to this town. It was just an irrational fear of them being gone, that's all."

"And why are you suddenly so afraid of D?"

"He behaves like he owns me, Kay. I'm in his stupid pack because I want to train at Spec Med where I was hoping to just fly under the radar and do my time, now look where I'm at."

"Yeah, you do seem to have a knack for getting attention. But look, I knew D before he became teacher. They were at the school as students and all four of them excelled despite being so young. That they were offered a position when they finished came as no surprise. I am here because he asked me to come in as a student so that he would have a second in his pack that he could trust. I was working at the Pitt and was interested in the school so it wasn't a hardship. Only Patrick didn't ask a friend. He found Brains and connected with him instantly when he met his batch of students. It's funny that Brains took an instant liking to you as well. You seem to be interesting to a lot of people Julie."

"Aaah yes, the transfer student that refused to be in the Black Hunter pack. . ." A new voice interrupted from the doorway.

"What the . .?" Kayden exploded off the couch.

"I remember you. I didn't realize it was because you knew Dylan prior to starting school. We all thought it was your competitive nature and Patrick that just didn't match. Interesting. Your stunt caused a major shakeup in the classes and ended up creating the most diverse classes we've ever had."

"You bloo. ."

"Careful, Kayden Blair Johnston, I am not one to forget. Anything. Think before you speak."

Chapter 31

I appeared neither of the men would shy away from a confrontation so I tried to defuse the situation before it came to a head.

"Julien, what are you doing here?" I asked in my most bored tone. Hoping to prevent them starting a fight.

"Why?! Miss Westlander! How rude. I had assumed you were raised better."

"Oh, you know what we're like, kids raised after Anarchy just don't understand how lucky we are. So ungrateful and rude. All those wonderful manners and respect were buried under a tide of bloodshed and change." I replied in a sweet voice and a sad look.

"Sarcasm is the lowest form of wit, Miss Westlander."

"Well, I am only human."

"See, I actually agree with young mister Johnston here, you seem to have an inhuman ability to draw super naturals to you, however we will speak in private. It would be nice if you'd invite me in and Mr Johnston... leave."

"He needs to stay until I have a door."

"From the smells here, he is one of the reasons your door is broken in the first place."

Much to both their surprise, I stuck up for Kayden saying. "To make a long story short, the third of our pack came here and kissed my sister. My baby brother, her twin, knocked him out and because of that Grub had fallen from the link and then couldn't be reached due to being knocked out. He's her mate by the way. Kayden came looking, worried about our reputation as Westlanders. He broke the door in his worry for a pack member."

It was a thin line between truth and lie and I walked it like a pro. Kayden looked smug but I could see a new respect in his eyes as he looked at me. Julian looked speculative. "How noble that sounds. It smells of truth. Yet somehow, it feels false. A matter for another time perhaps. Do be a good girl. Invite me in."

There wasn't really much I could do. This was a teacher at our school and a very influential member of the community, according to Zack. I had to be polite. "Julian, just for tonight, would you like to come into my living room?"

He laughed. Quite rudely I thought. The invitation was a proper one and even if I added the part about the living room, it didn't mean he had to laugh at me. An open invitation was like giving them the right to enter at will. Kayden looked fit to burst as he watched the vampire enter and sit on the couch beside me like he owned the place. It took me a lot of will power not to get up and show my unwillingness to be that near the man. The vampire. Another teacher too. But I didn't get much time to think as he said my name softly putting a hand on my arm. The moment I turned to him he was in my head.

'I suspect you can hear me, Julia. We need to talk, without the dog.'

I was shocked, tried to hide the emotions and without a word, out loud or in this strange link, I turned my head to Kayden. He still looked angry. It wasn't his facial expression, it was the tense way he was sitting up straight, the way his hands were clenching and unclenching and the smell.

Unknown to them I could smell his emotions like they smelled mine. The open windows helped but the situation was tense. I had no intention of breaking the silence either. They had practically invited themselves into my apartment and that thought was my anchor to sit there in silence. Kayden broke first, he got up and started pacing. Julien looked amused as he listened to Kay mutter under his breath. I had a hard time keeping a straight face because I heard every word clear as day. He was complaining about vampires, doors, school and me being an idiot as well as a trouble magnet. I was human to them so I shouldn't hear him. After seven minutes, I timed it, he rounded on me.

"How can you just sit there? You're like the damned vamp. Say something!"

"Fine!" I snapped. "Thanks for taking care of pack and breaking down my damned door in the process. You could have knocked, we would have opened the door. Thanks for wearing a track in my carpet. I know for a fact my furniture isn't that bad to sit on. But thanks for at least being quiet while doing it. If they keep the bond when I move out, I'll send you the bill. Thanks for insulting my other guest. I let him in and that should be enough for some decency."

"You defend him?"

"That's all you got from everything I said?"

"He's a vampire!"

"He's a teacher at our school. He's a member of the council and he asked nicely."

"Then why isn't he speaking now."

"Maybe Kay, just maybe, he is waiting for you to leave."

"I'm not leaving you alone with that! I promised your

brother I'd_"

I stood up fast and stalked closer to Kayden until I was in his face. The only drawback was that he was much taller than my human self, so I had to look up into his face to yell at him. "That! The term is HE! He is a person and_"

"A vampire!" Kayden yelled back interrupting me.

"Zack asked you to take care of me so that my house wasn't filled with a pack of strangers and only until my door is fixed. Just ring someone for crying out loud! Then piss off! Better yet..."

I turned to the vampire we were so rudely yelling about. "Julien, you want to talk to me? Swear that you will protect me and see that no harm comes to me from you or any other for the duration of this night! Then Kayden can go and do his thing somewhere else." I opened my phone about the same time and rang Zack. He answered third ring and I put him on speaker.

"What's wrong?"

"Tell Kayden that he can go if I agree to be protected by someone else."

"Who?"

"Julien, he's_"

"I know who he is, Juuls. Why?"

"He wants to talk?"

"What did he say?"

Julien shot Kayden a glare as they both started to talk as one.

"Shut up Kayden!" I snapped. Kayden shut his mouth with a glare and Julien replied to Zack.

"I hereby swear an oath to protect Julia Westlander and

keep her from any intended physical harm for the duration of this week as she does not return to the safety of her school pack until Monday and her closest family is newly mated. If any try to harm her, or do so, I will defend her to the best of my abilities and they will give their life."

He looked at me with challenge in his eyes and it was quiet for a while. I knew that he had added the word intended so that he wouldn't be punished by the vow if I stubbed my toe. Then Zack broke the silence. "Mental harm, manipulation or spells?"

Nodding Julien asked. "Anything else?"

"Any harm that befalls my sister will find you in twice the amount by the end of the next day. That should give you the time to find a safe place for her, if anything happens to her in your care."

Julien didn't hesitate, he repeated the oath and made the adjustments Zack had given. Kayden's anger rolled off him in waves as Zack agreed with the simple words 'do it' and I replied to Julien.

"I accept your oath and safety offered to me for the duration of this week with the terms you stated."

Magic wind whirled around us as the universe accepted our words. Zack said a gruff goodbye and hung up on me. Kayden gave me one last glare and stormed out of the apartment. Julien smiled. A real smile and suddenly he looked younger and more at ease. He had dark blond hair swept back from his gorgeous face and I relaxed at the warmth of the smile but immediately tensed as his voice entered my head.

'Do you know what you are?'

I tried to relax again but his eyes told me that he had been looking for a response and had seen me tense up.

"I need to change."

"That would be nice. You reek." He replied bluntly to my retreating back. I knew he was right but it still annoyed me so when I went to look for a new shirt, I purposely grabbed black one with fangs in the front. Nathan had a crazy sense of humour and always bought the coolest shirts. He'd bought this one as a going away present for school. It had the words 'Bite me...' written in the mouth and the fangs had a drop of blood on them. On the back of the shirt it said. 'And die painfully!'. I chuckled at my own childish wit and finished putting on different blue jeans, clean undies and socks and some makeup to finish my look. Julien raised an eyebrow at my choice of shirt but didn't reply.

"So, do we talk now?"

"Come with me."

It wasn't a question and I had no reason to fear his company, the oath he made had ensured my safety as long as he was near, through the pits of hell if needed. So, I turned to get my phone and wallet and walked to the still broken doorway. I heard his soft laugher as he saw the back of my shirt. There was nothing in the apartment that had sentimental value, so I didn't really care about getting robbed. Anyone dumb enough to rob me would just be hunted down by Zack and Zoe anyway, so I glanced at the vampire behind me and walked out.

We didn't talk as he walked down the steps, he let me set the pace as we left my building behind and the people we passed all stepped well away from us. This vampire was well known. I had the senses of a vampire with his close proximity and could tell there were people following us. Other vamps. He let me lead and I walked with a purpose. He let me think in quiet and I appreciated it. When we reached the 24/7 shop, he stuck to my side as I grabbed a sandwich, some chocolate and a drink. At the counter he paid while I was grabbing my wallet. The look on his face was enough to ensure that I didn't argue, at least not while we were in public. If he thought, for even a second, I'd let this slide he had another thing coming.

Chapter 32

The moment we stepped outside a car pulled up in front of us. The guy that had driven it stepped out of the car, leaving it running, and simply walked away. Julien opened the passenger side door and closed it for me before getting in behind the wheel.

"What do you know?" I asked. I'd taken the time to think of questions and dismissed most of them because it would tell him things I didn't know if he knew. He obviously knew something and much to my surprise he laughed. Loudly.

"Okay, I could feel you in the hallway that day. I could feel your fear and anger and I could also feel the extreme need to release you. That's what gave you away."

"Gave me away?"

"Oh, that's a classic. That explains why your daddy let you go to Med school here. You have no idea, do you?"

He let it hang and I didn't say a word as I waited for him to enlighten me.

"Would you like to hear a story about my race?"

He glanced at me waiting for a reply.

"Sure, I love stories."

"As you would be aware, most of my kind are made. We are made by others and we are picked. Not everyone survives the transition either. The people capable of changing a human to a vampire are old. Young vampires do try on occasion but they aren't strong enough mentally and usually die with their chosen one. To make a vampire you have to be able to deal with another person's emotions, so we tend to be very careful in choosing. A long time ago there was another race of super naturals. They didn't really fit in. But they were treasured and taken care of by most races. They had no real power, most of them were weak and scared of life. They had only one gift that made them supernatural. They could feel the emotions of others. Empaths. If the race was prone to using mind magic, they could hear them if the thoughts were directed at them, in rarer cases even if it wasn't. Those stronger ones could block out the emotions of others and could live like normal humans. Are you seeing any resemblance?"

"Maybe."

"Hmmm, anyway. The stronger ones could act human, ignore those around them and work with the information they felt. They were the ones that wouldn't go insane and they bred a stronger race in their survival. Every upside has a downside. It made them more treasured because during negotiations for territory it was handy to have someone that could tell if the other party lied in any way. They could also influence the emotions of any race. They became much sought after advisors and the whole race became hunted because of that."

He looked at me again and I shrugged, making sure to sound casual as I summed up. "Empaths, mostly human, inbred, advisors, hunted, got it."

He scoffed at my summary but continued without counter comment.

"Some of these stronger empaths were very tempting. They made others feel calm and happy around them. They managed emotions without thought, to make their own life easier. But as advisors they were hunted by all races and that led to new information. If a vampire attacked an empath the empath would defend themselves. They would fight like wet cats in corner and if they were bit the vampire would actually feel bad. The vampire would end up on the ground with the pain of the empath. I didn't feel your pain. I did, however, feel your anger, your disgust for yourself because you ran and your fear that I'd bite regardless of everyone there. I didn't let go because Dylan Hunter told me to, I let go because you made me feel bad. You replaced my anger with your feelings."

"Well, huh!" I puffed. "Sorry to have made you feel bad." He took no note of my sarcasm as he replied with a straight face.

"Apology accepted. It took me a while to get the information I needed but I went back into your family line and I must say. . . .it is remarkable that you can't turn into a dingo because your father comes from the oldest and strongest line of Dingos in our country. Cameron Westlander is pure bred. Not a drop of dilution in his Dingo genes. But then on the other hand your mother isn't a strong witch. Her line is unimpressive and they are more intermixed with humans than most. It took weeks of digging to find where the empaths came into your heritage. I'm not even sure yet but I'll let you know when it gets confirmed."

"Gee. Thanks!" Again, my sarcasm was ignored but this time I noticed a twitch of his lips before he continued.

"Where was I?"

"Empaths should not be attacked."

"Ah yes. But as you might be aware some people like

pain. Draining an empath is like suicide without death for a vampire but then, just before they die, there is remorse and I understand it is so incredibly strong that they ended up turning the empaths. It was like an open season for old vampires. You see, feelings dull over the ages. To feel becomes a luxury. Even if it's pain. But it had a downside that reduced the number of vampires dramatically. More than the human hunters ever had. Empaths were terrible vampires. They were full of rage and absolutely ruthless when they got turned. Also, they were strong enough to survive killing their masters. Even the weak empaths were stronger vampires. They were so much stronger than the normal fledglings. There were suddenly a lot of young vampires without masters and they were set on drinking from other vampires while they were still learning to control their bloodlust. Some drank only from other vampires and that is unsustainable because we need the life force of other creatures despite the incredible high of drinking from another vampire. With no one to guide them not many made it through the first year. Then the other old ones started hunting them, simply to kill the race, so not many lasted past their first century. Not when the councils got involved and the hunts were in packs. It was brutal and it happened twice in history."

He paused clearly remembering something, possibly from that time. I had no idea how old this guy was and the hint of blackness that I had felt in his head was enough for me to thank my lucky stars that, for now at least, I was under his protection. The pause continued so I used it to ask. "Did you ever meet one?"

"A turned empath? Yes. I know more than one. It was a while ago but I was also around when they were the main topic of our society. . . They come in groups now. Dangerous groups." He smiled to himself as he said the last bit. I didn't ask anything else so he continued. The car had left Brisbane inner city but he didn't speed up like I expected. He resumed his story. "The empaths that remained alive as humans disappeared from the radar and most races lost their advisors because of it. Now all that remains is the myths. They were forgotten by the world. The vampires that were alive during the second hunting don't speak of it and the young ones are only told that if a human makes them feel different than normal when they feed, they are to report it immediately. With the easy access to fresh blood from willing donors no empath has been reported for a very long time. They tend to steer clear of our kind because they feel our needs, even the ones that don't know what they are."

I mulled over his words, he remained silent. Waiting. Knowing what my next question had to be I finally asked.

"What is supposed to be done if an empath is found?"

"The council declared they should be killed without prejudice. No feeding allowed."

"Then why am I alive? Why tell me this and swear to protect me? It can't be due to the school. Surely the vampire council would be able to kill me without a trace."

"Surely? The council is made of vampires and they have only one flaw that follows them from their human time. Pride. And with pride, most of the time, comes arrogance. You asked the wrong question."

I thought and he slowed the car right down. Turning

into what must have been an old neighbourhood mall once upon a better time. Now there weren't enough human and there was no attraction for most of the other races. I looked out the window but stopped seeing as I thought again about what he'd told me. Then it dawned on me and I asked.

"What exactly happened to the empaths that survived the hunts by their fellow vampires?"

"Good. But too late. We're almost there."

"And where is there exactly?"

"My home away from home. Do you want to keep your secret?"

"Yes."

"What do you offer in return?"

"What do you need?"

"Need? I don't need anything."

"Yes, you do. You came to me. You chose not to tell anyone and you are asking me for an agreement of some sort. You need me for something. Now you tell me. What?"

"Smart girl. I like it. Okay. Here is the deal. I teach you about your kind of people. I keep you safe outside school and eliminate any threat to your secret, by any means necessary."

"In return for?"

"You pledge yourself to me."

"No."

"Hmmm, it was worth a try." He smiled.

"Not funny. What do you want in return for your silence?"

"Not just silence, assistance as well. Knowledge is power, little pup." I refused to reply and raised my eyebrows in an attempt to show him that he should get to the point. "One night a week you will come with me as my escort. I will attend meetings and you will use your gift to advise me."

"Not possible. I have other commitments and I think every week is too much. Every month maybe and with plenty of notice too."

"There are less than six months left for this year. I will need you at, at least, eight meetings. I will give you twenty-four hours of notice where possible and make sure that you have appropriate clothes at all times. In return for your acceptance, I will introduce you to the turned empaths I know and teach you most of what I know of your race."

Chapter 33

With everything he told me I realized I wasn't exactly an empath. I was an evolved version of what he described. I also realized that I had to let him think that we didn't know anything before he told me. I'd need to meet with Richard ASAP. I couldn't let Dad find out, he'd would go insane and bring me home under lock and key. The rest of my life would be spent imprisoned on our lands. No way dad would let me go anywhere if he knew. And no way that Julien would let me live if he found out what I was capable of with my evolved empath gift. I was much more dangerous than he realised.. And I thought it funny too. He would never know that I was an E.E., an empath evolution, instead of an E.T, an empath terrified. I didn't mean to but I laughed softly at my own joke. It was his turn to raise an eyebrow. I blamed his ancientness on the fact that he did it so well with only one. My eyebrows always go everywhere together. Nice, stuck between a rock and a hard place. I thought fast and replied to his unspoken question.

"You still won't tell me everything. I noticed the 'most' in your sentence. And introducing me? Doesn't say they'll talk to me. They might hate me for being what they once were."

"All true. But I know they won't hate you. They'll adore you. Most of them anyway."

It was my turn to hum.

"So? What do we do, Julia?"

"I can't. What about the holidays when I go home? And

what if I don't like the clothes, I've got enough of my own and_"

"We'll make a contract like normal people, the only oath involved will be for your safety and mine."

"Yours?"

"You will need to have my back too during these events."

"Events? First they were just meetings, now they are events? Make up your mind." I smiled at him.

"I am a vampire and we are old and stuffy. Because of this, most meetings are events just because we make the effort to get together." I laughed at that and he grinned. He didn't look old or stuffy and he knew this very well.

"How about we worry about that after you meet my crew."

"Crew, really? That's what you call them, that's so BA!" I grinned at him. He grinned back and I looked at him. For the first time I really looked at the vampire that was now sitting, ever so relaxed, at the wheel beside me. He had dirty blond hair that curled at the collar of his white dress shirt. He had rather high cheekbones but not in a way that made me think Asian. His skin was pale but that was understandable, it wasn't like he could work on his tan. His eyes were very dark brown and I could see his amusement, he knew I was checking him out. I made sure not to let my eyes drift down his body. I couldn't help ask. "How old were you?"

He didn't ask what I meant, just replied. "Twenty six." He hadn't been much older than I was now.

"Willingly turned?"

Before he could answer I quickly said. "Sorry. Don't

answer that. That was rude." I wasn't even sure why I asked. The whole time we'd been in the car together I'd had the great smell and better eyesight of vampires but I'd heard nothing else from his thoughts. I'd actually felt mellow and safe.

"It was a long time ago. I made peace with what I am. But to answer you, I was turned kicking and screaming the whole way. Most of my crew were." He looked sad but snapped out of it and started the car forward again, into a covered parking garage. He opened his window, yelled something in a strange language and proceeded upwards. I saw them and he noticed regardless of the fact that he was driving. "We park at the top covered level. The other stuff is here to give us an advantage if we have an infestation problem. Guards are on every level, the number varies. A few of the old ones take dayshifts with the humans we have."

"Do you have your own humans?"

Again, my question was out before I thought about it. My father would be so disappointed, I'd been taught better.

"Would you be jealous if I did?"

"No."

"Hmmm, that's fine. I don't. I don't need or want them. The connection with those I teach is very limited because they are all immortals. Having humans would require a connection that works mostly in favour of the vampire but there are drawback to it as well. They can make you weak. Oh look! We have a welcome committee."

The welcome committee wasn't what I expected. There were about ten vampires standing at a parking spot closest to a door. Julien drove in and they moved just in time not to be hit. Julien smiled touched me and thought at me. '*Stay close, puppy*.' It was strange to hear him in my head and he smirked knowingly as he turned to open the door. I didn't open mine, in a flash he gracefully held out a hand as he opened the door for me. I smiled shyly at the old-fashioned gesture. He put his arm around me and with the vampires that surrounded us I didn't put up an argument. Somebody opened the door and Julien took the lead. None of the vamps at our back spoke and one moved to my side. Closer and closer. I moved closer to Julien and he finally noticed the man at my other side. We stopped.

"Axel. Is there a reason why you are getting so inappropriately close to my guest?"

The guy grinned, if he hadn't had his fangs on display, I would have said he was gorgeous. "Just trying to get to know what we'll be eating?"

"Oh, you misunderstand, Axel. She is my guest." The guy responded by running a finger down the side of my arm before looking back at Julien. I shivered under his touch.

"Can I have her when you're done?"

"No one can have her. At all. Ever. She is here and will return here, at all times, as my guest. She is not here for refreshments. Is. That. Clear?" His voice had dropped to a menacing growl by the end and I heard a few soft replies. It didn't make sense, because the responses weren't about what was said; instead, they all centred around my responses.

"Ahhh. . .Come on Juuls. I like new toys." I thought he was talking to me and my eyes widened. The guy grinned misunderstanding my surprise. "Yeah, I get to call him a nickname. I bet he makes you call him sir. We've been friends longer than you could possibly begin to imagine, little girl."

I had to stand up for myself, that was the same with all supernaturals, even with humans, show no weakness. So I quickly replied before Julien could. On a hunch I said. "You would know better than anyone then... that you wouldn't be the first friend he's had to kill. But I'd be happy to do the honours myself if you touch me again. Now..., is that clear?" Instead of menacing, something I would never be able to do as well as I just heard Julien do it. I'd spoken softly in a sickly-sweet voice. There were a few chuckles and Julien laughed softly. "That's my girl." Then he started walking again, pulling me deeper into the vampire nest.

Axel stayed beside me looking at me the whole time instead of where he was going. I, on the other hand, was doing my best to ignore him while hoping he'd trip. He didn't touch me but he was perfectly in step with Julien and myself. He said a few words in a strange language and Julien replied before looking at me and switching to Australian English. "Miss Westlander comes from the school and has a remarkably good sense for business my friend. We have made an agreement to help each other for a while. We're still working out the details. If she is as good as I think she is, business will improve for us. We spoke of this." He switched back to his other language and said something else.

We stopped moving and the others spread out in a circle. I kept my eyes on the floor and stayed tucked up under the arm of Julien. Axel replied.

"Nice. Just a heads up. Dev is causing trouble. Again. I am getting sick of him, Juuls. Pick another one to take the seat. We've already agreed."

"If he doesn't back down. Who did you guys decide on?"

"Misty?"

"Seriously?"

"Oh, come on, Julien. She'd be good. Think about it. . .She's manageable. She liiiiikes you!"

"Grow up, Ax. Was it unanimous?"

"Not really."

"Thought so. Who else was put forth?"

A voice beside us quietly said. "I prefer Evelyn. Outspoken but manageable. Pretty and politically savvy. A decent name too."

"Did we approach her?"

"No, just vetted her. It'll have to do. Dev will most likely try to take you now that you are home."

"Let's do this."

I still hadn't looked up when the same person spoke again.

"What about the girl. You know he won't let go easily. They never do."

"What better way to introduce her? She holds up here in this situation, she holds up in other territories. But just so you all know, I swore an oath to protect this one. Isn't that right, Miss Westlander?"

He forced me to look up and I decided to go for attitude again. "Yes, you did." I looked around briefly before looking back at him. "And if any of your 'friends' draw blood you'll need to deal with them on my behalf. So, I can just sit back and do nothing if I don't feel like it. Come to think of it that probably means anyone here is, like, I dunno, my servant." I grinned broadly up at him. "Sweet!"

Julien's voice entered my head as he looked at me. '*Please behave yourself, Julia.*' He sounded exasperated. I'd never expected that tone from him so I laughed softly as I boldly put my hand on his cheek. "Don't worry Julien, I'll be a good little human."

He chuckled. '*You are a pain in the ass, miss Westlander.*' Out loud he just sighed. "Okay then. Let's go get this over with."

Chapter 34

Someone shot ahead while we walked in quiet contemplation. Then they opened a roller door to what turned out to be a big area with a load of vampires. The moment we entered silence fell. The door was lowered shut behind us, most of the vampires around us dispersed. There was an honest to goodness throne at the far end of the room with dais and all. On it slouched a blond-haired guy that looked like he could have been a part giant. The man was built like a brick shithouse. Huge muscles bulged as he moved to sit up straight. "Julien, what a pleasure to see you home. We don't see enough of you. And you brought a snack. She does smell lovely, thank you for the present."

"Devon, you are not making a good impression on my guest. Everybody knows that if I bring donors, I bring enough for everyone and the survival of said refreshments. Nor do I ever escort them, Miss Westlander is my guest."

"Fuckbuddy?"

"I can remove you from your position even easier than putting you in it. Do not push your luck."

"You haven't been home much lately and I do run the place now. What makes you think they'll even listen to you?"

To my surprise it was Axel that spoke, still on my other side. "Newbie. There is a good reason why none of us argued with his choice to put you in charge, regardless of how much older we are. If Juuls says she is our guest, then that is what she is. Doesn't do to push your luck."

In a flash the big guy was before us. I had their senses

with so many around and because of this I didn't jump as he appeared before me. He pushed me to the side, away from Julien and turned to the man that had brought me here. There was no emotion on his face at all as Julien looked at me, ignoring the big man. "Who would you like to talk to as I settle a little domestic matter?" He was asking me who made me feel safe. He was asking me to use my gift. I could feel a lot of them wanting my blood. Some smiled invitingly and if I hadn't been able to read them with my gift I would have been tempted. I didn't look behind me at the ones that were there when we arrived but looked at the vampires that had been lounging around. Then my gaze fell on a guy with silver eyes, he shook his head 'no' just a tiny bit when I wanted to point to him, so I kept looking. The next person I saw that didn't seem to want my blood was a beautiful woman, tall and angry looking wearing tight jeans and a black shirt with writing on the front finishing it off were black biker boots. Even her pose, leaning against the wall, was screaming Bad Attitude! I caught her eye and saw surprise flash through them as I pointed at her. "Julien, I would love to introduce myself to that lady over there, if that is alright with you?"

He followed my finger and nodded. I'd made sure to look at him as I pointed and caught a flash of surprise in his eyes as well. But he seemed to agree without question. "Axel be a good man and introduce Miss Westlander to Poppy please."

"Sure. Interesting choice, Miss. If I may?" He held out an arm to escort me.

"What? Do I look that unstable?" I asked with a frown

on my face. He just laughed and grabbed my hand. I felt him immediately but even knowing I had no reason to be scared I still felt it. Julien wrapped his arms around me from behind pulling my hand from Axel's. His calm infused me right away. "She's had bad experiences with dominant males, Ax. Don't touch her, she doesn't know you."

Axel let go right away but there was a look that passed between the men that let me know that this would be taken up at a later date. I didn't stop to think that I was very comfortable with Julien now and felt the loss as he released me to give me a gentle shove to Poppy. Axel stayed beside me but didn't touch. Poppy nodded and Axel left without a word. There was a low rumbling growl behind me and as I started to turn Poppy decided to speak to me forcing me to look back at her. "What are you doing with Julien if you don't like dominant males?"

"Therapy." I replied with a grin. She laughed. "I like it. But I would like to know why you picked me."

"I wanted to know what was on your shirt."

She uncrossed her arms. And I read. 'Sunshine makes me happy.' Then she turned and on the back it said. 'When I think of you in it.'

"Harsh!" I smiled at her as I said it.

"I like yours too." She smiled back. "Now let's get you to the bathroom. Humans always need to pee when they meet too many vampires at once."

I'd heard the fight continue behind me and I didn't let her distract me as I looked this time. There were now several fights going on. Julien wasn't actually doing much fighting; he looked like he was having fun, so did Axel and some of the others I recognised from the welcome committee. There were some people that were fighting for life and death it seemed. Devon was serious in his attempts to get Julien. It was almost sad to watch. The outcome was clear. Poppy stepped closer and whispered in my ear. "It's hot, isn't it? The way they move? The way they just dance around their victims. I've been with them for centuries, they saved me from a bad master. It amazed me then and it still amazes me now. I am just happy I'm accepted by them, I'd never turn on them. Some forget what they are capable of." She smiled dreamily and continued softly.

"Devon got arrogant. Bossy too. It's only been forty something years and he's forgotten that he's only a figure head." Suddenly there was a blur to the side of us and when I looked that way the silver eyed guy I'd noticed before had another vampire on his knees, by the hair. He looked at me calmly, said 'sorry' and sunk his teeth into the man that was on his knees. I stepped back in shock and into Poppy. Her fangs were down when she grabbed my hand and I felt a sliver of fear. But then I realized that I felt her fear. They were too old and too strong. Her mind was flashing with similar events where the same group was wearing different clothes telling me that they were in different times. They killed ruthlessly when they got carried away. Then she settled on a nicer memory. It was brutal for me but she liked it. It calmed her down. This had never happened to me before. I'd never felt or seen memories without trying. And it seemed like she didn't even know I was in her head. I saw everything from her point of view. And despite the disgust I felt, I made myself pay attention. They had slaughtered her master after he tried to kill one of the women in their crew because she'd refused to join him. They had given the ones that survived, and those that had tried to help them, a place in their crew. The rules were different and they didn't have a master. But they had a figure head, never one of the fierce ones, and they all knew that if they disobeyed, they'd die. Painfully. But it seemed that none that chose to join minded the threat because they got to live. They got to be their own person again like it had been when they were human. Nobody else controlled what they did or thought. The figure head was for political reasons and as long as the council didn't have proof that there was no master, they were fine.

I pulled my hand from Poppy. There was something in what her thoughts displayed as she remembered her introduction into this nest. Something that was important but just out of my grasp, the memories too overwhelmingly real. As I'd pulled away Poppy came to herself. "Let's get you to the bathroom, darling, too much blood here for a sweet little thing like you. Wouldn't want you caught up in the argument as it's going now."

We left quickly and behind me there was a loud crack followed closely by an ungodly scream. "Just in time!" Poppy said, relieved, as she shut the door quickly behind us. She proceeded to march me down a corridor and actually dragged me into a bathroom. "I'll turn around if you need to use the facilities. We don't really use them much so when there was a fight and the door was broken to the stall we sorta didn't bother fixing it. We just took it out. I can't believe Devon would be so stupid. I wonder who's to replace him. Do you think they already picked someone? Never mind you wouldn't know. Oh, I just hate this. What I don't understand is why. . " Suddenly she stopped, I guessed that she realized that she was babbling. She looked flustered.

"What's the problem, Poppy?"

"I'm worried, what if you get hurt? Not everyone was in the meeting and we have guards up here too and you smell very nice. And there are traders here too. I mean you smell very, very nice but if Julien has you here as a guest. Well, it doesn't make sense. He never had guests before that weren't vampires. Never. And you see, that means if I stuff up. ."

"It's alright, Poppy. Everyone was pretty busy back there." I smiled kindly and changed the subject to her life.

We talked for a fair while sitting on the counter next to the sink and I found out that she was originally from Europe. She left there with most of the ones she was with now. The fierce ones had no trouble traveling over water regardless of age. She'd not long been turned in her opinion. Something that amazed her but still there was something that I was missing. It was just out of reach. Like a word at the tip of your tongue. This thought kept eluding me, teasing my brain just at the edge of being clear.

Poppy had some funny stories about her time in the settlements when she first came to Australia. A knock on the door startled us, like the footsteps before, we'd thought that whomever it was would pass. Poppy unlocked the door in a heartbeat. Then she got upset. "Go away!"

A beautiful woman pushed her way into the bathroom not taking any notice of Poppy as she pushed her out of the way. I heard the crack as Poppy hit the wall. The woman had straight, blond hair down to her waist and spoke with a posh English accent. "Let's get right down to business, shall we?" She never gave me a chance to reply as she continued. "I don't know if you are aware but when we bite, we can heal the marks so that nobody'll ever know it happened. It aids in our survival. It also means that I can't know for sure if you've been bitten before. I can smell Julien all over you and frankly. . .I am disgusted."

Without another word she attacked. It was so unexpected that Poppy didn't have time to react either when the blond sank her fangs into my shoulder without further ado. Pain exploded and I screamed with Poppy. Mine was of pain, hers was of anger. I felt the blond, got into her head without thought and transferred my pain. It was instinctual, it was habit and it was hell. Her mind was dark and empty. But unlike Julien who had such a calm mind, her mind was scary dark, angry. I flooded her darkness with pain and she released me clutching her neck like she'd been bit instead of me. A split second later I was engulfed in the arms of Julien. "Drain her, SLOWLY!"

Chapter 35

He turned me to watch as Axel and three others descended on the blond woman. She didn't stand a chance against the four men. She couldn't make a sound because one of the men had clamped a big hand over her mouth but nevertheless her agony was clear. I tried to look away so Julien clamped a hand on my chin and forced me to watch. Right up until three men pulled away while Axel stayed in place. Axel looked up at me. She'd hollowed out like a terminally ill human. She was at the verge of death. Julien asked me if I wanted to have the kill and I shook my head while whispering 'no'. Axel pulled his bloody mouth further away from the victim to say. "For you, Miss Westlander." And then took the last of the blonde's life force.

She turned to dust and even the dust all but disappeared. She'd been old to turn to dust, very old. On death a vampire body went to the state its human body should have been. The older the dustier and the fresher the bloodier. We'd learned that in school already. To my surprise Axel spat out a heap of blood in front of me. The last of her blood. the most potent part of a kill for vampires.

I'd been in some gruesome battles, I'd been in life or death fights, and I had killed plenty of people. It was the way of the world. Kill or be killed. But my traumatised brain was stunned by the pain, the fear and the unreal events of a vampire telling me he killed for me and spitting out the life force in the last blood. Their greatest high. So, my mouth moved before my brain came online. "Well, that's a waste of a perfectly good vampire high, isn't it?!"

There was a moment of absolute silence before the men started to chuckle. Axel replied with a bright smile. "Just for you, Miss Westlander."

There was a soft whimper but I heard with the vampires enhancing my senses. They all looked at Poppy, curled into a ball in a corner, her face in her hands. The tough woman reduced to a whimpering mess. I pulled myself away from Julien and he let me go easily. I rushed to Poppy and threw my arms around her, asking. "Are you alright, Pop? Did she hurt you badly? Talk to me Poppy... You're scaring me here. It's all good now. We're safe."

She looked up with bloody tears running down her face. Her voice void of emotion. "I'm dead."

"Euh? No? You are a vampire, Poppy, technically you aren't dead. Did she hurt you? Did you hit your head too hard?" I turned to Julien. "What's wrong with her and why aren't you guys helping?"

"They'll kill me. Please just go. Let them get it over with." Poppy still sounded emotionless.

"Don't be stupid. They killed the blond bitch that hurt us."

"You still bleed, Miss Westlander." She said timidly.

"You know what, Poppy. I trust you. I want you to fix the wounds, please."

There were a few gasps behind me and Poppy looked like I'd just hit her over the head with fairy wings on a turtle shaped bat.

"Look, there are five other people in here. I heard about vampire men, they use sex as a feeling when they feed. Four just fed already. I don't want them near my neck in that mood. And Julien is scary on the best of days so honestly, sweetie, I don't want him to get a taste of my blood. Ever! That leaves you. Please?"

She looked at the men behind me with fear in her eyes. I turned and snapped. "Julien! She told me you lot saved her. She's always been loyal and she respects your rules. She thought Devon was stupid and she tried to protect me from the blond bitch. Tell her she won't be punished."

"You got hurt in her care."

"Took four men to kill the bitch. Look at poor, innocent, sweet Poppy, she wouldn't be able to hurt a fly. It all happened so fast and goldilocks hit Poppy really hard. Look at the dent in the wall for crying out loud!"

He raised an eyebrow at my choice of words, she looked anything but sweet and innocent. "You got hurt in her care." He repeated coldly. I frowned at him.

"No, I got hurt in *your* care! You made me her problem by letting me pick a babysitter while you settled your domestic. You took me here while you knew there would be problems. You caused this while she never had a choice. If you hurt her, any chance of a deal is off!"

He shared a look with Axel. Then looked at the other men, each of them nodded yes.

"Well, it looks like you have a champion, Poppy. Clean her up and we'll consider it past."

In reply Poppy mumbled.

"And the past should always be remembered because that way mistakes shall never be repeated."

Then, without warning, she pulled me closer in our

embrace and licked my neck. I shivered. She licked again and mumbled softly. "So sweet." As she started flicking her tongue all over my collar bone and neck to clean it up. I couldn't help moving my head to the side to give her better access, it felt good. Finally, she closed her mouth over my wounds and sucked. I moaned, I couldn't keep it from happening, it felt so incredibly good. A light, pleasant tingling sensation was shooting through the wounds and I heard some chuckles behind me. My hands found their way into her hair, pulling her closer. I didn't care. I heard footsteps. But I really didn't care anymore. I felt Poppy, her pleasure at my blood, her worry for my safety, her worry about her own safety was second to mine and I felt lust. I wasn't into girls but my hands were caressing her, pulling her closer. I felt like we should be. . .

Hands grabbed my shoulders. Calm intruded on my mind as they did, then I realized I was in the black, bleak, empty place that was Julien's feelings. There were never thoughts or memories in his mind, he simply supplied me calm. I completely came down from my sexual high when Poppy let go. She was smiling shyly. "Sorry you had to find out this way."

I stupidly shook my head at her. "Huh."

"It's not just the men. We can only use pain or pleasure. Those are the only two ways we can use our venom to feed and heal. Pleasure or pain."

"What? . . . Oh... Oh! Right, euh. Well. You learn something new every day. I hope I didn't make you uncomfortable."

She laughed and replied like the girl I first met. "Not at

all. Any time baby, any time."

I laughed with her while I felt Julien growl lowly against me. "I don't know, Pop. I might never go back if I take you up on that. You were great."

"It would be like that with any vampire. More with the ones I promised you, so you won't need Poppy." Julien growled. "Go away, Poppy. Evelyn is in court. Pay your respect."

She dashed off and I was left with the men. Julien turned me under his arm and led me in a different direction than where we'd come from. Axel was again on the other side. We went down several sets of stairs in quiet. Then they led me into a big room that managed to be cosy despite its size. About fifteen people were spread out around the room. I could only feel Julien and then I freaked out as he spoke. "She's an empath."

I turned on him with speed I shouldn't have and slammed him into the wall behind him with a strength a human couldn't possess. I was in his face. "We had a deal. You just broke it in front of a whole bunch of freaking immortals! You know how hard it will be to kill all of them!"

He was still so calm and my hands against his chest made me calm regardless of my fear and anger. A hand touched my arm and suddenly I thought it was the funniest thing in the world that I had attacked such an old vampire. I started laughing but Julien said. "Stop it, Axel." The hand, and the joy that had come with it, disappeared.

"We are all empaths here, Miss Westlander."

And it clicked. The memory I had found in Poppy, the stuff he'd told me too. How he'd said he'd protect me, introduce me, how he'd been turned kicking and screaming. Julien was an empath. He'd been turned against his will, he had no master. This nest didn't have a master. The way they fought, graceful, deadly, and like they were playing. Ruthless. He'd told me. I'd had all the pieces the moment they had spoken of a chosen leader but I hadn't put it together.

I felt the blood drain from my face as I looked up at him. "You can control what I feel."

"Only extremes and you'd learn fast enough which feeling is your own. You are very new at controlling this." He sounded so kind. He made me feel safe and calm. I let go like I burned myself.

"You've been making me feel things!" I accused.

"Why, Miss Westlander. How very forward of you." He smirked.

"You! I. . . You. . I am not! You did, didn't you?"

"Shut up, Juuls. Calm down, Miss Westlander. And let us explain.." Axel shoved Julien aside.

"Would you like a drink, dear?" Asked a burly, black-haired bloke that had helped kill the blond. He looked imposing but sounded like a teddy bear.

"Yes, please. A water if I may?" I smiled politely.

"I'm Dermot by the way, have a seat." He said as he turned.

"Yes, have a seat." said a woman from somewhere. I carefully chose a chair that faced everyone in the room. Too late I realised that they had left that one open for me. I'd been herded like a sheep and I'd fallen for it. Dermot returned with my water and went to lean against the wall near Axel and Julien.

Chapter 36

"Hello. I'm Sarah. And I'm a vampire." She giggled. "Sorry, joke. I was turned fighting every step of the way because I was an empath. I was afraid to touch people, I couldn't shut them out. As you may be aware there is always more pain than happiness. Unlike the stronger empaths, I couldn't shut out the others, or influence them. So, when I became what I am now, I made use of the turnaround. When we are turned our skills turn too. Instead of feeling what others feel we make them feel what we want them to feel. The thing is that vampires do that naturally, so we are enhanced. We are also faster, stronger and because each and every one of us was turned against our will, we are all more ruthless. We can survive without a master from the moment we are turned and all of us chose to do so."

She suddenly looked lost in thought and Julien took over.

"It's like I told you".

"No actually, you might have missed a few vital pieces of information there."

"I promised you answers and a way to learn to deal with what you have. We are it. You are strong enough to make it away from your family and their protection."

Axel happily interjected. "Actually, your control is impressive, making it with a school full of sups. The only ones of us that ever managed anything like that were advisors before they were turned. But we are a rare breed."

"And who were the ever so special advisors?"

"Dermot here, Charley, Nicoletta, Freja, Beth, Gordon, Christina - Chris for short, Sid, Henley, West, Julien and me."

"Let me see. There are about a dozen that were advisors. So that makes you, if I understand correctly, some sort of super vamps? Even the empaths that weren't advisors are better vamps than the vamps in general. None of you have a master and there is some sort of truce because you go about business in the open, or at least that is what I assume from knowing about Julien. So then why are you all together like this, wouldn't that be like an invitation to get slaughtered? I take it that they would still want you all dead, age would make you more dangerous not less."

"Oh! I can see why you are interested, Juuls. She is fast. Fascinating, little human, aren't you?"

"Axel, was it? Put yourself in my shoes for a second. I had a shitty afternoon and it didn't improve in the evening, being dragged here wasn't in the plans. I had to make a deal with Julien to protect something that is apparently enough to put a target on my back with vamps and then he proceeds to introduce my extremely well-kept secret to a room full of people. People that happen to be super vamps with a target on their own freaking backs due to what they are. If you aren't answering my questions, don't say anything."

There was a scattering of chuckles around the room and the woman that had told me to sit started talking in a soft melodious voice. "I'm Chris and I'll start with the most important part. Yes, there is a truce and yes, if they knew we came together like this they would perhaps try to eradicate us. But of the super vamps that were advisors, the ones that

Ax just told you about, only half are here. We hardly ever meet in person and we are fairly spread out. We started looking for others like us during the hunts. And when the opportunity came, we moved to Australia. All of us had fought together. Of all the vampires in the Asian Pacific more than a quarter started as empaths. The chance that the council comes after the empaths is small, we would eradicate them. Julien told us about you several weeks ago. Last week he called the meet for tonight and Devon thought we came as guests to trade here. Eva, the blond they killed for you, was the only other 'super charged', as you call it, that lives with Dermot, Axel and Julien in this territory."

"Oh, euh, well that sucks, pardon the pun! Didn't mean to break up a happy home by getting attacked while Julien was under oath."

Another woman grinned wickedly and replied.

"No great loss dear, most of us didn't like her. That is why Dermi, Ax and Juuls got stuck her. She never got past the fact that she was a princess in her day. I mean that was obviously centuries ago and on the other side of the world. We all know she was royal alright, a royal pain in th_ "

"Enough Nicoletta, she's here for a reason. Do we agree?"

There was a mumble around as they spoke super softly, unaware that I could hear them clear as day. It took all my training to keep a straight face as they spoke of whether I could be useful as their advisor. Someone they had searched for, for a long time after losing the last one they had. Someone stated that me being a woman would cause problems while the women and a few men stated that it would be an advantage. Julien and Dermot wanted to present me to the community as a partner so that none would guess that I was an advisor. The women agreed but to my surprise it was Axel that brought up the fact that I would have to agree with that idea. Julien said I had no choice. They mumbled under their breath and glanced my way occasionally. They were doing this on purpose too, I realized. I was being tested. So, I let my gift roam a bit. It had been a long time since I could use it and not be judged if found out.

I got up and walked to Axel, I didn't stop but continued while running my hand over his softly as I went to lean against the wall next to Dermot, shoulder to shoulder. They fell silent to see what I was up to but Julien walked to someone else, away from me and mumbled to the others. "She is curious, this is what we wanted, an empath that can block and use at will. Let's see what she comes up with, she is obviously comfortable with Dermot. I don't want her unhappy. Let us see what she can do."

The arguments continued about how to introduce me and when. Even my clothes were up for discussion and they wanted to know if I would be able to remain quiet if needed. What to do with me during feedings and where I would be staying.

I listened for a bit before walking past the couch running my hand along the edge behind the people sitting there. I got another glass of water and bumped into someone, it seemed accidental. I made my rounds and whenever I came close enough to officially hear them, they fell silent. I didn't take long before I sat back on my chair, my head leaning back against the seat and my eyes closed. I relaxed and let them at it. I didn't agree with everything they decided on but overall, I could see they were right with their final decisions. They had my best interests at heart, that much was abundantly clear to me.

Silence fell.

"Julia?"

Laughter erupted as Julien said my name.

I opened one eye and glared at the biggest culprit, Axel. "Yes! And people call me Juuls too. I wasn't impressed with you nicknaming him when we met. I thought you were talking to me, idiot!"

He smiled sheepishly as laughter flowed around the room at his expense now. "Well, Miss Westlander, it seems that I will need to find you a different nickname."

"That's fine. And when you do find one, make sure you remember where you last used it because that will be where I'll leave you balls!"

"Feisty!"

"And serious."

"Definitely hot!"

"But not amused."

"Aroused then?"

"By you?" I took my time checking him out as he was still leaning against the wall. He was built like a runner. Long legs wrapped in a nice pair of proper pants, white dress shirt with a few blood spatters and a tear near the shoulder. A shirt that was incapable of hiding a well-built chest, broad shoulders and brown hair down to the collar of his shirt. He had bright emerald eyes and a few cute freckles on his nose. It went well with the pale skin. Yep, he was gorgeous. Thankfully I was used to gorgeous men, so I didn't lie when I replied calmly. "Nope, not doing it for me."

He laughed softly along with the others. "What do you know?"

"About what?"

"Us, wanting your help."

"You actually care that I might have a different opinion, whereas Julien, Dermot and most of the others don't care what I think. Julien wants me happy because you guys need me and there is a very big meeting coming up soon that requires all of you in the same building. You fear it. Despite the fact that it is a centennial ball, mostly because there have been whispers about you guys still refusing to be masters to your individual nests. Meaning the people that are in your care can not be used as a bargaining chip. This isn't confirmed but it is rightly suspected. The council worries as your strengths grow. You worry that they will figure out who is *actually* one of you because other than Axel, Eva, Dermot and Julien, they haven't got confirmation on anyone. You are alive because they want to find out who is like you and because they fear Julien. Which I find pretty bloody amazing if I may say so myself. You guys killed almost a whole generation of vampires to ensure your secrets were safe. But it seems the council has a list of suspects and you need to know who is on it, because they have a way of testing for super vamps." I looked around the room and continued looking at Julien this time.

"I am not the first empath you've found and now that I told you why you need me, you tell me what happened to the last one you had at your service." I glanced around and found them all suitably impressed. I grinned back at Axel. "Well?"

"Well, I must say, and I do believe I speak for everyone here and those not present, you are incredible. Better than we could have imagined and that means a lot. We were all capable of the same things as you, so to impress us is very impressive."

"Whoop de doo, now answer my question."

"He isn't here but he was turned and is part of our inner circle. His name is Cyril. He was good but arrogant, spoke out of anger and gave away what he was. The one he was with got killed and he was turned. They forgot, in their intense remorse for almost killing him, what would happen if he lived. He murdered two nests and burned the bodies, leaving enough of everyone to make them think he died as well, at the hands of hunters. Then he came here. He grew out his hair, shaved his beard and became Sid. Don't worry he's keen to meet you too."

"Too? Julien how long exactly have you been talking about me?"

"I told you, since the incident in the hallway."

"Shit. I don't suppose I can get out of having to deal with you guys?"

"Not really, but you do have enough to think about and we should finish this off for tonight. There is still much to be done before bedtime."

"Your bedtime maybe, mine came and went hours ago."

"Well, we'll arrange accommodation for you here. We don't know if the door is fixed yet."

"It should be, Dylan promised."

"Dylan Hunter's pack is the reason the door broke in the first place. There is something off about his pack and those of his siblings. But that is a matter for some other time perhaps. Right now they are not a threat to us."

"I want to go home."

"I want a lot of things, Miss Westlander. One of those things is to be sure you are safe. I happen to know you will not be attending school for the rest of the week and your siblings are gone. You shall stay here as our guest."

"Someone who is held against their will is not a guest, that is the definition for prisoner."

"No, Miss Westlander, they go in the cells, they don't get a room or any luxuries. We feed on prisoners, we don't feed on guests unless invited to do so. I assure you, our definition of prisoner is somewhat more.... Arcane."

Then I heard the mumbles of someone. Directed at Julien. "Don't upset her, but please get her out of here. I am starving and I need to feed. We're all hungry and it's been a long night. We can't let her find out what else changes when we get turned. Just move the girl, Juuls."

Dermot spoke to me directly after the mumble stopped. "Miss Westlander. If I may? I would like to have the time to discuss a few things with you. There is however the matter of our dinner that needs to be seen to and I can only assume that you may be a bit peckish by now. Perhaps we could see to the basic needs of both parties and then we can perhaps persuade you with our logic?"

"Dermot, your manners are impeccable, your logic sensible and your tone reasonable. If you would do me the honour of escorting me to a room where I can rest, I would be most obliged."

"It would be my pleasure, Miss Westlander."

"Lovely. Goodnight all. And Dermot? Can we perhaps see if Poppy is alright on the way?"

He replied that it wouldn't be a problem and led me from the room. They were blissfully unaware that I could hear them behind me as they started talking before the door closed.

It was a nice feeling, that they were all worried about my wellbeing. None of them wanted a repeat of what had happened to Sid. It seemed that these vampires valued my humanity more than they wanted my blood.

Chapter 37

Dermot led me in the direction of the meeting hall and left me behind the door as he put his head in to call for Poppy. She was there in a flash, he left me with her, closed the door behind him for a minute where Poppy and I just smiled at each other and then Dermot pulled me into the room. The meeting hall was now filled with way more vampires which surprised me because there were a heap in the room I'd just left. This was larger than any nest I'd ever heard of.

"As was stated before. This woman is here as our guest. Poppy is her companion and any that bleed or harm her, or Poppy, will be punished by Evelyn, Julien, Axel and myself."

I could feel the fear skyrocket in the room and the looks in my direction ranged from awe to hatred. Just what I needed! In a room covered in blood stains, surrounded by vampires. Only the woman on the throne smiled at me kindly, her voice floated to me. "I'm sure you're tired, please enjoy your stay. We'll catch up at some later time, in a more private setting. We're just about to do some housekeeping, no need to stay here and be bored."

Dermot nodded to her with a kind smile and led me out with his other hand on Poppy's arm, practically dragging her along. She was on the other side of Dermot and I couldn't feel her, so I moved to her other side. Dermot let go of her arm and I threaded mine through hers. The skin contact opened her mind to me. She still felt threatened by the fierce ones. Strangely enough she was more worried about what I had to do with them and the feelings she had for me were like we'd known each other for life not for a few hours. I was curious and I fell into a memory. This time it was a memory from her human life. It was a different time.

There were men and women all around us and they were dressed rather strangely. There was a young girl clinging to my hand as we manoeuvred ourselves across a marketplace. She had big doe eyes and curly long brown hair, her face was very pale with a light sprinkle of freckles and I was looking down at her with a smile. It wasn't my memory but I could feel it like my own and this girl's innocence reminded me of, strangely enough, me. I was getting Poppy's emotions with her memories. The girl spoke in a strange version of English yet somehow I understood it clearly. "Are you sure about this?"

"He'll be able to fix you, people say he works miracles."

"Oh aye, but what'll 'e want in its stead."

"Do nea you worry about that wee one. I need to see you well."

The memory skipped to a dark room, the sun had set for the night and the little girl was clutching to my hand, Poppy's hand. The man in front of us was clearly a vampire and I felt fear at the look in his eyes "That's the deal!" he said calmly.

The little girl looked so scared as I replied, Poppy's voice was strong. "I'll do it. But I want your word she will be protected from all your kind and I want the money up front."

"Done and to show you what a nice person I am, you will get to see each other one day, every month for as long as she lives. I promise it will be a long, long time." The evil glint in the man's eyes didn't escape me, but the little girl was dying.

The memory zapped again. The little girl was older now, healthy, but she looked so sad as she broke away from my hug. "I didnea want this for ya."

"It's alright, get married to him. He's a good man, be happy and donea ever forget I love you more than life."

"Do you have to leave?"

"They killed Master Robertson. I'm free, but with them I'll be safe."

"Will you stay for the wedding?"

"Oh aye, I wouldnea miss it for all the tea in England!"

The memory zapped again. This time it was an old woman, she was at her deathbed.

"You've nea changed a bit."

"I know."

"I've had a good life. Donnea be upset."

"I know."

"Are they still taking care of ya?"

"Oh aye!"

"Good because that man that changed you was evil."

"It was worth it, every second of pain. He saved your life."

"Aye, but he took yours."

"Your children are coming back."

"Oh well. You are my sister's daughter and you look so much like her too." The old woman chuckled softly as more people entered the room.

The memory faded when the old woman died and I saw Poppy, beside me now, look at me with a wishful smile. "You remind me of my sister. She was so sweet, yet so strong. Life takes funny turns sometimes. Thank you for saving me by the way. If you are alright with Dermot, I would like to just go and feed before the night leaves. I just. ."

"It's alright Poppy. I'll see you again. They are keeping me here for the rest of the week it seems."

Her face turned fierce. "If it's against your will. . " She turned on Dermot.

"NO! POPPY, STOP! They protect me too!"

Dermot hissed at her while I yelled over them both and it took a moment for her to look at me. Whatever she saw on my face was enough. She turned and left in the blink of an eye.

"Interesting effect you have on people, Miss Westlander. She's normally so docile around us. Come, I'll show you to your rooms."

We strolled in silence until I realised that I hadn't felt anything from Dermot. At all.

"Dermot?"

"Hmmm?"

"Are you upset with me for having to kill Eva?"

"Nope."

"Why can't I feel anything from you?"

"Because I don't let you."

"Oh."

"Hmmm. Does it bother you, little one?"

"Nope. Just not something I am used to. I guess I've gotten used to feeling other people around me, it's strange that there aren't any feelings from you."

"Here we are." We stopped in front of another roller door. This one had a smaller door to the side. He opened it with flourish and waved me through. There was a huge space with three doors spread across the back wall. It seemed Weres weren't the only species that liked their open spaces. Everyone was able to live in buildings like my smaller apartment, but with choice and money they all picked big. My choice had been to be close to the school. I smiled. This was clearly a bachelor pad. Leather furniture, several big televisions spread around because some had different gaming consoles attached. A huge table with a big paperwork mess scattered across the surface. There was nothing homely about it but it was very nice. There were mismatched pieces of art and knickknacks spread about the room and I laughed at some of them. Dermot looked at me in question and I pointed to a Greek looking statue of a naked woman, she was dressed with a polka dot bikini with a big straw hat. "Axel?" I asked.

"The statue is mine actually, but yes, Ax decided it was inappropriate to have my naked woman in the main room for all of us to see, so he dressed her. I removed the first few sets he put on her but he just dresses her more scantily and outrageous every time, so I decided to leave the bikini." He looked at me seriously and asked. "She pulls off the look, wouldn't you say?"

"It looks great, Dermot." I giggled. He just nodded, a smile tugging at the corner of his lips. I looked the big man over again. He was solidly built, his skin was dark for a vampire, his face was solid too, strong square jaw with a dimple in his chin, he looked dangerous and had pitch black hair to complete the look. His eyes, the only thing that didn't match. He let me check him out. His eyes were soft and gentle, worry about me clear, as he looked down at me. I couldn't feel a single emotion from him though. The moment was rudely interrupted when my stomach growled loudly. I looked away, feeling my face flush and Dermot chuckled.

He disappeared for a few minutes and I got comfortable on a big chair that let me see the door. When he came back with a tray piled with food, I slowly set about devouring it as he watched quietly. When I finished the meal, I couldn't control myself and yawned.

"How about I show you the rooms?"

He helped me up and led me to the door at the right of the far wall. I could smell Axel all over the moment Dermot opened the door. The room was dark with a huge bed at the centre, it was sort of scary all on its own in the dark room. The frame that held the bed in place was made of thick sticks at the top third of the bed. The headboard was solid at the bottom and had the same thick sticks pointed down from the top. The covers on the bed were deep shiny red and I flinched when I noticed the things that covered the wall. There were chains and all sorts of other scary things there. I didn't linger but pushed back out and slammed the door shut. "Axel has serious issues." I mumbled. Dermot let out a surprised laugh. "You called it." He didn't know I'd smelled the man that occupied the room. Dermot then led me to the middle room. It was totally different. The walls were light and the furniture was different shades of blue. It was quite beautiful. The light had been on when we entered and there was a book open beside the bed. I breathed out a soft 'wow'. The room was so airy. There was one door at the other side but nothing on the walls, no shelves or other furniture. Just the bed.

"You like?"

"It's gorgeous." It really was despite the emptiness. I could smell Dermot in the room, it was his. These supernatural senses were a big benefit in knowing things that a normal human nose would never pick up.

"I leave the light on for a reason. Do you trust me?"

"Euh, sure?"

"Go lie down on the middle of the bed."

I looked at the bed and only now saw that it was the same as the one in Axel's room. Yet it didn't look scary in this room, it looked stylish. I walked over to bed and crawled to the middle.

"Lie down on your back." Dermot said from the doorway and I did. He turned off the light and the room lit up like a night sky. Whole star systems that I actually recognised immediately. A breath escaped me. I was in awe of the details. It was almost like the real thing and at one side of the room there was a light peeking over the skirting boards. A sunrise. It looked so real. I sat up and walked to a wall. Someone, most likely Dermot, had painted the whole night sky at the point of daybreak. It was amazing. I could almost imagine that it was a real sunrise. I hadn't noticed the colours on the wall but there were colours in the sunrise. "Incredible,. . . This is amazing!. . . Wow, I mean WOW. Dermot this is. . . wow! This must have taken forever to make."

He opened the door and turned the lights back on. "I have forever, why not use it to make something beautiful.

Just don't tell anyone, I don't wanna ruin my reputation."

"Your secret is safe with me." I replied seriously.

Chapter 38

Dermot had shown me two of the room and now he led me to the last room. This would be Julien or Eva's room I presumed. The moment he opened the door I carefully took a deep breath but it didn't tell me much. The room did have a trace of Julien but I could also clearly smell Axel in here and it was more recent, stronger. There wasn't even a trace of anyone else. I realised that the whole space had only carried the scent of the three men. Looking around this room I immediately noticed that the bed was the same again. I asked without thinking first. "So? Why the matching beds?"

"Glad you noticed."

"Dermot. That doesn't tell me anything."

"Do you like them?"

"In your room and here, yes. In the first room, not at all."

"Well, to answer your question I would again ask you to lie down on the bed, not the middle, closer to the headboard or the side this time."

I did as he asked and kept an eye on him as he grinned broadly, fangs peeking out.

"Hit the side or the headboard."

I did as he told me, hitting it softly.

"Do it like you mean it, little girl." He goaded me so I rammed my fist against the side of the bed.

I jumped back away from the side as Dermot burst out laughing. Two of the spikes had burst out on either side of where I'd hit the bed. I rolled back and softly grabbed one only to see they were stakes. Very sharp, wooden stakes. "OH

264

Goddess, Lord almighty and Christ in a basket! You have a bed made of stakes? What the hell?"

I punched the headboard and the same thing happened, two stakes either side of my hand. I touched the tip of one this time and my finger started bleeding right away, I hadn't even put pressure on it. Sleep forgotten, I looked at Dermot as he was still looking very pleased with my shocked face. "We are known by our people as the fierce ones. We take no partners to our beds as a rule but have learned that even if we trust someone enough to bring them to where we sleep, sometimes we are wrong. We designed these ourselves, there are only three and they have been useful over the ages."

"Useful?"

"We have been attacked where we sleep, there is no master to our clans. They can make their own decisions and Devon was not the first to think he could throw out the way we do things. He was just more direct in his approach. We clean house regularly."

"Why not make them yours, like normal vampires?"

"Because we are not normal vampires and there are,. . . side effects. . to us having mark someone. Also, none of us were changed because we wanted to be, so we do not take slaves. That is basically what you are to a master, no free will. Not all masters treat their people badly but there are those that do horrible things and they can. Poppy had a master like that, it's disgusting."

I yawned again and he looked worried. "I'm sorry, I forget this isn't day for you. Go, sleep."

"Here?"

"Yes." He put three of the stakes back where they came

from and handed one to me. "Sleep well, little one. You won't need this but I know it will make you feel better."

I smiled at him and put it back where it came from. "I trust you. I trust Julien, I mean he made an oath and I trust he'll keep it. You have all worked to keep me safe. If I need that I might as well use it on myself because you would all be dead."

"Thank you for your trust. Sleep well." He softly closed the door behind himself and I took off my shoes as I prepared for bed. Absentmindedly noting the muted colours of the wood floors that matched the dark wood furniture and the earth tones to compliment the room. It was peaceful and beautiful I thought with a yawn as I put my jeans down beside the bed with my shoes and settled into the heavenly fresh bed.

Something was interrupting my slumber, it was a lovely feeling. The arm that was lying down on the bed was tingling with it. I moaned softly as the blissful feeling extended from my wrist to the crook of my elbow. Such a gentle touch. "Julia?"

"Hmmm." I replied as my other arm followed the hand that caused these feelings and pulled someone closer. There was a shift and suddenly there was a body against mine. I was pleased with how nice it felt and started to doze off when nothing else happened.

'*Julia*' it was a soft voice, almost a feeling instead of a voice.

'*Wake up, you lovely, little pup.*' I decided it was a feeling and I could ignore it for the comfort of sleep.

Something brushed my neck and I wrapped my arms

around the body beside me. "I don't wanne get up yet." I mumbled as I snuggled into the arms of. . .The fog of sleep started to descend again despite the hot breath on my neck. I still refused to open my eyes but then there was another hand and when it touched me the most erotic feelings flooded my body. Arousal went from one to a hundred and I was instantly wide awake as my body instinctively moved on the body in my arms. I turned, rolled on top and ground against it with my hips as I opened my eyes to kiss. . . I closed my eyes, pulled back, slammed my hand against the sideboard then grabbed a stake without thinking, only opening my eyes as I moved with the stake in hand. Then I was pinned to the bed, hands in an iron grip and the stake loosely plucked from between my fingers by the second man. My body was pinned under one much bigger than mine and my eyes were wide open now. Adrenaline pumping through me as my heart worked over drive. From asleep to awake. From full arousal to intense fear.

Loud laughter, from Axel right beside me, as he returned the stake to the headboard. I glared at him but it only made him laugh louder. Then I focused on the body that had me pinned down. A hint of fang in the smirk, beautiful dark eyes, pale face with dark-blond hair swept back and a playful voice. "Miss Westlander. You sleep like the dead."

"Let. Me. Go!"

"Now, now. Manners. I let you sleep in my room. Let you get all indecent with me and then you use my own bed to try and stake me."

"Get. Off!"

Axel laughed louder and I heard the soft chuckle that

indicated that Dermot was most likely here for my humiliation. I was so embarrassed I turned my head to the side and closed my eyes tightly. He shifted and grabbed both my wrists in one of his hands then used the other hand to turn my face back. "Open your eyes, please."

I didn't. He kissed my lips and my eyes shot open.

"Always be alert to your surroundings." He grinned, still rather close.

I frowned at him and turned my head to the side again, this time with my eyes wide open.

"I'm sorry. We shouldn't have woken you like this. If I remove myself from this lovely position, will you leave me alive?" He asked with a smile in his voice.

"I have to leave you alive to get out of here." I growled.

Laughter erupted around me from all three of them. I glared at Axel. "I don't have to leave him alive to be protected."

Axel slowly brought a hand in my direction and I flinched.

"Baby, if I let you get close enough, you'd fuck me before you kill me. You have no defences against my strong emotions and I am horny as hell!" He grinned before moving off the bed.

Julien slowly released pressure on my wrists but instead of getting right of me he ground his hips against me sensually, much like I had when I'd straddled him. I felt my face catch fire from embarrassment. He gently caressed my cheek before languidly rolling to the side with an arm around me keeping us together. "So innocent." He murmured.

"A good reason to release her my friend." Dermot, my current saviour, said blandly.

Julien let me pull away and I got up from the bed to lean against the wall to my right. Slowly I pulled the sheets to my waist. They had already seen my knickers but I could pretend they hadn't. I kept breathing deeply to calm down and the men quietly let me.

"Euh, so what time is it?"

"It's morning. You slept for about three hours but we need to rest soon so it's better to talk now."

"Oooh-kay?"

"There are a fair few of us that can stay awake during the day. It would not be safe for you to wander around without one of us with you. Even Poppy won't be enough. The others have gone and that means there are a lot less vamps here but everyone is restless after a changeover and Evelyn needs to establish her dominance without our interference."

"So? I need to stay in the room?" An involuntary yawn escaped me. That didn't sound so bad. I was still pretty tired. The adrenaline was already wearing off.

"One of us will keep you company at all times, while you are here. Does that sound alright?"

"Well yes, but, euh. . . well, whatabout when I, you know?"

"Oh, well, yes. There is that." Dermot looked embarrassed for me as he replied looking at the other two.

"I've heard about this. The joys of having humans." Axel grinned broadly.

"Excuse me but you don't HAVE a human!"

"Human. Empath. Same difference."

"I meant_ " I started to get pissed with him but Julien interrupted me.

"Ignore him, he just wants to rile you up. You are your own person, but you are under our protection. If it makes you feel better.... that means you *have* three vampires."

"Oh. . " The thought of having these three, so different but each so good looking, men had me blushing again. Several inappropriate thoughts danced into my head. Something that didn't go unnoticed if their chuckles was anything to go by.

"To answer your 'not really question' . . ." Axel said with laughter in his voice. ". .we have a beautiful shower here and there is a fully equipped working bathroom a few doors from our quarters. We don't need those facilities, so we didn't see the need to have it installed. We have made sure there is fresh food in the living room, fridge and all, and we have clean clothes for you too."

"Thank you?"

"No problem. Who would you like to have first?" Axel grinned.

"What?!"

"Naughty girl! I like it! I actually meant, just to keep you company but I'm happy to comply if you have other... endeavours... in mind." Axel purred, then he outright laughed at my horrified face.

"NOT you! That's for sure! And I don't really need company, I think I'll just go back to sleep." I squirmed a bit, thinking I might need the bathroom first. Dermot took pity as he ordered the other men out and told me he'd show me the facilities before I went back to sleep. When he closed the door behind him I quickly got my jeans and socks back on and went out of the bedroom. Julien and Axel were playing a video game, rather intensely and Dermot was waiting by the door for me. He quietly led me down the hall, a few doors was a fair distance, he leant against the wall as he pointed to the toilets on the other side, giving me the pretence of privacy against the enhanced senses of the vampire.

I washed my face and my reflection looked just like it always did. But so much had changed in the last few months. The last few hours even. I ran my hands through my hair trying to tidy it up and rinsed my mouth, all the while staring at my face. I had a strange sense of excitement knowing that I would be spending a lot more time with these vampires from now on. It didn't scare me and a tiny part of me was telling me it should. The girl looking back at me smiled brightly. I was with people that knew what I was and didn't mind. I had always made sure that I didn't pry into the minds of my pack but this place, these people, they had been like me. Sorta. They could *actually* affect me, instead of me changing their feelings or thoughts. Maybe they would let me try to do it to them.

The bright smile turned into a wicked grin. I should see if I could instil the fear of God into Axel, he had it coming. I straightened up and gave a saucy wink to the girl in the mirror with the 'Bite me' shirt before going back to Dermot.

He smiled at me. "Feeling better?"

"Much, thank you."

A vampire strolled our way, keeping his eyes on me the whole time. He was dressed in black and had a dangerous air about him. He nodded to me and he stopped in front of us then turned to Dermot. "Last of the guests have left. Perimeter is secure, watch has been rolled over without incident, second watch is in hands of Drip."

"Good, thank you, Jeff."

Even though Dermot sounded like he dismissed the man he didn't move to let us pass. Instead, he held out a big hand to me. "Jeffrey Addison Francis Sebastian Middleton the third. At your service, Milady." He suddenly spoke in a posh English accent and I was amazed with the change.

"Oh wow. That's quite a mouth full. Euh, hi. I'm Julia Westlander..., the first."

The man grinned wickedly, showing his fangs and told me he wouldn't mind being called Jeff by a beautiful lady such as myself. I smiled, not because I was flattered but because when he held my hand, I could feel his intense curiosity. His mind flashed with the moment he first saw me surrounded by the fierce ones and some of the group that came to trade as I got helped out of the car by Julien. He suspected that they were fierce ones as well but he would never mention that. The look of Axel, me and Julien together, Dermot bringing me in to see Evelyn and now, my smile at Dermot just before I'd noticed him coming our way. The last time they had introduced a woman it was Eva. She'd been a pain but they had protected her as well. I was human though and Jeff was intrigued.

"I heard you were there for the management changeover. Are you alright?"

"I am, thank you for asking."

"And will you be staying long?"

"Just the week. You are security?"

"Second in command to Dermot. I was not trying to pry, Milady." He actually looked, and felt, worried that I'd get upset.

"I know, its fine." I smiled. He'd let go of my hand before, so I touched his arm as I said it and suddenly I was in a memory of him being severely beaten by the woman. The same woman who had attacked me. I didn't wait to see the whole memory as I quickly pulled away and put a steading hand on Dermot. Dermot was clear, calm and empty. A bit like Julien.

"Thank you Mil_"

"It's Julia. Please, I must insist, Sir. For you to be second only to Dermot for the security of the whole property you must be an important figure. I am merely a guest and, as I will be staying here, you will also ensure my safety. Back home, in our pack, the security is run by our enforcers. They are faster, more cunning and much more dangerous than the general pack and that's saying something as our pack prides itself on the sheer number of lethal fighters we have. I don't know much about vampires, but I can only assume only the best and brightest have a chance at being security as the welfare of all depends on them."

"Thank you, Julia. You will be safe with us, I vow on my honour and life." He bowed and walked away not waiting for a reply from me. I looked at Dermot.

"Well, that was something else." Dermot smiled. "Jeffrey is normally quite reserved." He didn't say anything else as we walked back to their living area. Axel and Julien were still on their game and they were swearing in a strange language and laughing at each other. Julien looked so different to what

I'd ever seen him or ever expected. Carefree, happy. I softly said goodnight to Dermot and walked to the room I'd slept in before, leaving the door open just a tiny bit. Again, I left my shirt on but removed my jeans and socks. Again, the wonderful bed welcomed me in. I drifted into sleep with the sounds of laughter from the other room.

Chapter 39

After a deep sleep I slowly drifted back to a semi wakeful state. I was in a tangle of limbs, much like the puppy pile I'd slept in most my life. My head was on a somewhat cool chest and my leg was over another leg, there were two arms over my waist that weren't mine and somebody was spooning me from behind. It was peaceful. I'd draped my arm over the other two and made a soft sound of pleasure. There wasn't anything sexual about this this was comfort, companionship, this was how I liked to wake up. It was a dog thing. I snuggled and heard a chuckle from one of the bodies. This wasn't family but they smelled so alive, musky and masculine. My mind slowly put the pieces together as I heard footsteps come in from the other room. "Guys? She up yet?" Dermot asked.

"Hmmm, I'm awake." I replied softly. I was a second too late to realize that I shouldn't have heard him being human. The door opened. "Who's awake." I mumbled again. I rubbed my hand down the chest and heard a groan. Ha. "Who's doing breakfast? I don't wanne cook today." I happily kept my hand tracing the body I was draped over and slowly started on the arms around me. I knew they were vampires but the feelings I got from touching them were minimal. I was pretty sure I was laying on Julien, that body was calm and there were barely any emotions. A hint of arousal came through but that was manageable. That meant the other body was Axel. Time for some fun. "Nate, be a good boy and make me pancakes." I mumbled as I patted the body behind me awkwardly.

"I'm not Nate!"

"Well then go find him and tell him I want pancakes. I'm comfy here." I replied in a mumble.

I was ready for what he did the last time he woke me up. I focused my mind, years of practise. The moment I felt a flicker of his mind touching mine, I responded. I grabbed his arm as it tightened around my waist and then I thought of pancakes on the veranda, in summer, while the sun was already hot in the sky. His body flew away from mine in a flurry of curses. I rapidly sat up and looked as innocent as possible when I asked. "Axel?"

Both the others were stunned into silence as Axel stood there looking like he'd seen a ghost. "You!.. You just... I... What did you do, woman?" I slowly sat up and stretched as I answered.

"Wake up?"

"No!"

"Ask for pancakes?"

"Pancakes. I saw them!"

"I want them."

"It was mid-morning!"

"It should still be." I smiled innocently.

"You were there!"

"I am still here."

"She put me in the sun. Not shady, barely there. Full, summer sun, breakfast! With pancakes! I felt it!"

Julien rolled into me and put his head on his arms, on my bare legs. He was looking at Axel with a gentle smile. "You're not making much sense."

He calmed down and a wicked grin made its way onto his face. "She's so much more like us than we could have ever guessed. She's not just a strong empath. I do believe we've got ourselves an honest to Goddess, old school, real advisor."

Axel and Dermot jumped on the bed and crawled closer, smirking. I stiffened as Julien pushed himself up with one arm on each side of my legs. His face close enough to kiss. "Miss Westlander? Have you been holding out on me?"

My heart sped up, I shuffled backward and asked innocently. "Whatever do you mean Julien?"

"Did you understand the difference between the empaths that were advisors and the ones that were not?"

"They were better in crowds?"

Dermot put a hand on my foot as I pushed my back against the headboard. "Oh, there is so much more to advisors. Julia. So much more."

I felt a rush of happiness and pride. "I would like to know what you are feeling, Miss Westlander."

"Euh, whatever you are doing is making me happy and strangely enough, I feel a bit proud too."

"Good. I was just thinking that it would be fun to work with you." The sentence hadn't finished when I felt terrified. The feeling washed away in a blissful wave of happiness.

"Now I was thinking that you might not be part of your father's pack. But looking at your expression that was a nasty feeling. So, I thought you look like your father. Do you understand what I do?"

"Not really?"

"I cause other people's emotions to rise in response to thoughts I have, to what I need or what I want from them."

Axel put his hand out to touch me and I kicked at him sideways. "I know what you do! Don't touch me!"

"Oh, but it's different, I give my own emotions to others. Times a hundred!"

I suddenly realised that I was leaning into Julien to get away from Axel. I was too late trying to pull away. *'Shhh, little pup. I won't hurt you. I used to hear the thoughts of others. I used to feel their emotions and take their pain. Now I project my thoughts and create emotions, like Ax does.... And I can give them pain, emotional and physical pain.'*

I looked up at his face, focused and thought. *'Can you hear me too?'*

'Amazing, you are very capable. That's good. I can now but until this moment I have heard nothing from you. It's been a very long time since I've heard thoughts. It changes when you become a child of the darkness.'

I used my voice next. "Then how can you hear my thoughts?"

"Jesus! You can hear her? She projects? What else?" Axel sounded like a kid in a candy store, completely excited and extremely hyper.

"Axel, calm down!" Dermot snapped.

"Mate, she only just found out she can project thought. Remember she didn't know what she was until yesterday. I'd say she only ever calmed the animals, for her own peace. Remember she grew up with link-thinkers, they are the loudest and most irrational."

"Link-thinkers?"

"As Empaths we found link-thinkers the most emotionally interruptive of species. They are a collective.

Because you grew up with them you must have developed a natural resistance at an early age. That explains your ability to calm them down so effectively. You wouldn't have even noticed because you never met another empath or vampire for that matter. It's really rather incredible. We will have to find out what sort of empath you are but I would guess you are like Dermot. You affect them by what you expect around you and your thoughts about a person. They respond to your needs. You want quiet, they settle down, you want to play they get energetic. You fear something, they get protective."

I looked at Dermot then back at the other two. They had settled around me, pleased as punch. They had no idea how wrong they were. I was in deep, I would have to talk to Richard soon. It was an opportunity to learn about others like me. An opportunity to find out what else I might be capable of. I would be protected by the vamps and it would actually be safer for me than the pack from school. It would be possible for the twins to be with their mates more. I had to think about their lives as well. These guys couldn't read my mind, so my secret was safe. I realized the risks of making a deal but. . . if I was an empath, and I was evolved, the basics of what I was, was here with these people. Choices. Answers!

"Well boys. You make interesting points. I must admit that I think I'm probably a tiny bit like what you were..." I couldn't give in too easy. "The thing is, if you are right, I should have gone mad ages ago. So instead of a strong empath I think that maybe I might just be a tiny bit like that."

They all started to protest as one but Axel was the one to make his point when the others went silent. "Nope. Insanity is level three. The lowest form of empathy is a masochist, they get happy by making others happy, at any cost to themselves. Then there are the ones that go for suicide due to depression because they can't make everyone happy and there is so much misery. They can't deal with the input of emotions and opt out. Level three is too aware of themselves to let them want others happy at any cost and too strong to kill themselves, but they can't deal and go mad. The fourth level is self-aware and strong enough not to go mad. They are usually depressed hermits that live in fear of others. Level five is capable of dealing with the emotions from others by blocking them most of the time. Level six blocks when needed and uses information to make themselves happy instead of others, they do this without thought. Level seven does those things on purpose and the next levels are capable of doing these things to sups too. Nine can easily communicate with anyone telepathically. Ten is the highest level, the advisors of old, capable of manipulation and alteration with humans and sups regardless of the surroundings and amounts of people there. There were obviously different thing that different advisors excelled in but that's it in broad lines."

"Wow, levels? Okay, well, that euh, that's cool?"

"Cool? Seriously. That's all you've got?"

I flipped myself forward, pushing Julien away and sat up on my knees, the move was faster than human but not too much. I got into Axel's face. "You just drop this shit on me and expect me to have something better than cool? Whatdayawantmetosay huh? I haven't got a clue about this, levels, I mean levels had to be determined, who did that?

How long ago did you guys find Sid? Are you always looking for empaths? How can I be one, if dad is a dingo? Why doesn't anyone know about them, I've never heard of sup like an empath? How am I supposed to tell dad? Does my teacher know about my species? Should I tell them at school, where I'm registered as human? Just how dangerous is it for me to be one? What a__"

Axel grabbed my arms just as Julien put a hand on my shoulder and Dermot did too. "You're probably a six right now or seven, but we can teach you. Train your abilities to become a nine, you already affect the sups, all you need to do is learn to do so on purpose."

I felt comfortable, calm, happy and realized that they all tried to calm me with a different emotion, each in their own way. And then I focused and felt them, all three, they were worried about me. Simply worried about me, about how I felt. No ulterior motives drove their worry, they simply wanted to protect me because they had lived in my shoes. That moment I realized I finally found a safe place. I wouldn't have to fight my nature. My family pack would be safer without me. I wouldn't have to hide myself as much. I decided....

This would be the first step to an independent and stronger me. I smiled wickedly at the though and met the eyes of each of them.

"How about we talk about a mutually agreeable arrangement?"

Chapter 40

A mutually agreeable arrangement. These vampires were stronger, faster and more ruthless than regular vamps. They were hunted and these three were already on a watchlist from their council. They made it clear that they wanted me to help them in situations where they had to negotiate with other vamps or species. I would be at risk in those situations, because I had to be human to everyone else. They promised to protect me but at the same time the deal put me at risk. They didn't hide what happened to Sid. They didn't try to sweettalk me, instead they outlined the risks in excruciating detail. Just the risk of a human in a vampire meeting. The risk of an empath in a vampire meeting. The risk of being with them and their kind while their council wanted to exterminate their kind. Taking everything into account, the risks were huge. Not to mention my school pack and the possessive Dylan Hunter. He would not be pleased if I spend too much time with Julien. Dermot had an easy solution to my teacher, one that actually made sense. There had to be a reason for me to hang out with the vampires.

Dermot grinned when he told us. "I think, we should pretend that I am a love interest. Your teacher won't like that you are choosing to hang with our kind but he won't mind me nearly as much as Julien. I'm not well known here and the council only suspect me being an ex advisor because I am close to these two. Julien is the only one they know about for sure. He's the only one they've tried to have killed.. a lot of times."

I looked at Julien and he replied to my unspoken question. "They send a few assassins after me every few centuries. They haven't tried to outright kill me since the last hunt. I was quite well known before I was turned, there was no way for me to hide my past. They never confirmed Axel but he was already in my entourage before I was changed so they can't know for sure. He was my backup for the meetings where I worked as an advisor. They suspect everyone in our nest of being empaths changed, it is why they don't attack here, we would slaughter them."

"Whatabout people like Poppy, the ones you liberated? She calls you the fierce ones."

"Most of them are incredibly loyal to us, we have killed quite a few bad masters over the centuries without blood-binding them to us. They don't want to go back to being bound but they wouldn't make it alone. The ones that aren't loyal generally don't last long. They know we are incredibly strong but they don't know what we were before we were turned. They all think we are just *that* old."

I giggled. "Aren't you?"

Julien shoved me. "Twenty-six, I told you. Barely older that you are now."

"Yeah, but you never told me *how long* you've been twenty-six."

He shoved me off the couch we had moved to, to talk, and laughed at my shocked face. "I'd tell you but then I'd have to kill you."

Then we had to discuss what they needed from me. I would be getting protection when I wasn't with my school pack and I would get training about the race they thought I was. By the time they had finished explained what an empath was I was convinced that they would be able to help me. I was an evolved version but that didn't matter to me. Our pack had done all it could to train me with Weres of all varieties. Now I could safely train on other species.

They needed me to come with them on trade meetings. To find out what the other party was asking for and whether they had what they offered. Julien's nest, Evelyn's as it was now known, offered training in surveillance and computers to vampires and other races. They were hackers with experience dating back to the invention of computers and the internet. Axel hinted that it was very different from BA.

Then he fell into stories about how they had become hackers, it was in a time working nights needed an excuse. They had been part of the developments made in the computer industry, so they knew everything about them. At the time there had been something called emo and humans had idolised vampires. In those times they didn't stand out in everyday society. Vampires moved faster so typing at speed was easy for them and they earned good money. It helped that they had nothing to fear from working as hackers for questionable individuals because in the end, they were more dangerous than any human.

After anarchy they had kept the internet running and adjusted to the needs of the new world. Made websites for species that had always hidden themselves. Housecleaning services for brownies. Masonry and smithing work for dwarves. Heavy lifting and building for giants. There were all sorts of jobs that specific sups excelled in, some went into business with surviving human businesses and they all thrived.

Now the nest dealt with all other species as well as other vampire nests and the trouble was that there were demons. Most of the time the demons used marked ones to do their wheeling and dealing for them. Marked ones weren't possessed but the demons could access them as a vessel or use their magic. The vampires didn't matter doing shady things but they didn't want to work for demons. Nor did they want to deal with the vampire council. It would be needing my magic to ascertain if their business partners were who they said they were. And to find out if the council was onto them.

They still hadn't wanted to discuss how the council could figure out if they were turned empaths. For some reason that was a touchy subject.

Poppy got to spend time with me and Jeff also made the time to talk to me after he briefed Dermot. I had an audience with Evelyn. She was pleasant to me but she made it clear that it was only because I was with Julien and the other two. She was honest about being a figure head for the outside world and explained what that entailed for me during meetings. I would be brought as a human. In no uncertain terms it meant that I was for sex or food. I was a tiny bit offended but because I was raised with Weres I was fully aware that humans were of limited use as far as sups were concerned.

Dermot chuckled when they had me back in their area. "I told you. You need a love interest. I mean... if you'd rather be Axel's companion..."

Axel grinned at me wickedly. "I'd love to have you as my human. You'd have to be completely submissive... I like the idea of that."

I shuddered at the thought and they all saw it clearly. "You don't come near me, pervert."

"Hey, Hey, I am happy to *be* submissive for you too... if that's what you're into."

"No. Just... No!"

"Your loss, puppy."

"I told you that I would be the best option. Juuls can't do it, from what I heard, your teacher will blow a fuse if he pretends to be your interest. I generally run security here or travel to trade with our figure heads. Juuls has to be careful where he goes outside the city. Your teacher won't know how close we are so I can pick you up from school."

I spoke to Zack and managed to get a hold of Richard too. We had a conference call while I was in a soundproof room. The vamps understood that I needed privacy but didn't want me to leave their compound. Richard talked me through a procedure to check everything before we spoke, to make sure that they weren't recording us in any way. Even so we spoke in our own code by using references that nobody would be able to understand.

Richard was more worried but also understood that I needed as much information as possible about empaths. Zack and I would be seeing each other while we trained the in the mornings. He gave me a few reminders and a few tips and then we hung up. It was good to know that my brothers supported this course of action. Now, if dad ever found out, at least I had backup. Anyone facing off with Cameron Westlander needed backup, even his kids.

After the call, Axel tried to find out exactly what we

had spoken about and because of that I had my first lesson about what I could do. When he tried a light compulsion on me, I found out I could feel his intentions. As a vampire their magic was compulsion, to make it easier to subdue prey. As an empath they had felt everything from others. As an advisor they had been able to manipulate the feelings from others. On turning to a vampire their magic turned that they could affect others with their own feelings instead. Combined with the vampire compulsion they got on turning they affected supernaturals as easily as humans. They turned empaths could also enter the minds that used to enter theirs, with emotions and pain. The turned empaths got the vampire hunting instincts, sharper. Their aggression, stronger. They speed, faster. Their compulsion, more intense. And their empath gifts turned outward.

Trying it on an unturned empath though, Axel was hit with his emotions twisted. The compulsion he tried on me didn't only fizz out. The vampire compulsion seemed to backfire, it was almost as if I had used compulsion on him. He was open to any suggestion I made. He became softer and attentive to my needs. Dermot was the first one that figured out what had happened, it took us a while to catch up to him because he was laughing too hard to tell us.

The moment Axel dropped his compulsion he slowly became aware of what had happened. Again, only due to Dermot. Julien kindly offered Poppy as a test subject to try compulsion on me. When I refused due to our budding friendship he found another subject for me to practice on. It was interesting, when the woman left, she had no idea that she had been completely submissive to all my needs, as if I had her under compulsion.

By the time it was Sunday, the day before I had to start school again, they had helped me study for the tests as well as taught me more things about being an empath. The tests wouldn't be too hard anyway, I had already learned most of the subject matter for this year. Julien kept teasing me in between all the learning, telling me I would be better in his class.

The next morning Dermot drove me to school. He laughed and kissed my cheek, so close to my mouth that anyone looking would have thought that it was on my lips. It was seen. It was discussed too, when I set foot in class but Molly intercepted me loudly. Dylan gave me a hard look but nothing was said. All the teachers shut the mind links down for the testing period and at lunch I was dragged away by Molly and Amy before anyone could say anything to me about my vampire escort.

The topic of conversation during lunch, at the human table, was Molly mating with my little brother. After lunch we went back to more testings and at the day's end Dermot was waiting at the front gate to take me home.

Patrick was the Hunter Alpha that caught up to me. He introduced himself to Dermot and to my surprise Dermot acted completely different to how he normally was. He was chatty and light-hearted. If I hadn't known any better, I would have thought he was a freshly turned vamp with no power at all. He was also touchy and possessive in his behaviour, like a new boyfriend would be. Patrick obviously believed it and I felt him talk to his siblings in the link. They now all thought I was hooking up with a newly turned vamp.

School would be so much more interesting and fight training with the top three of every pack hadn't even started yet.

On the bright side, Molly had really found a house for all of us, she had also paid a deposit to secure it. After we met up at the house for a tour, Zack asked Dermot to move in as well. It was a beautiful house, more than enough rooms and a view of the river. It was also within walking distance of the school. Zack was aware of Dermot's status as an enforcer of sorts but the vampires had no idea I had told everything to my brothers. Dermot acted like a fresh vamp, a young, clueless one, because he thought my siblings had no idea what he really was.

Dermot liked the idea of moving in so he could work with me and he could escort me to the vampire meetings I had agreed to. Zack liked the idea of vampires in our house because it meant more protection. But when I agreed, I had no idea that it meant that Axel would be moving in too. Because Axle and Dermot had had different skills as an empath, before they were turned, they could teach me different things now.

The future had changed. I knew Spec Med would be a challenge and I knew that it would change me before I went there. But I knew that the moment I agreed to a deal with the vampires my life would never be the same again. Nothing could have prepared me for everything that would happen though. Nobody had told me demons were in Australia.

Don't miss out!

Visit the website below and you can sign up to receive emails whenever Gabrielle Monego publishes a new book. There's no charge and no obligation.

https://books2read.com/r/B-A-LNSY-DJUJC

BOOKS 2 READ

Connecting independent readers to independent writers.

www.ingramcontent.com/pod-product-compliance
Lightning Source LLC
Chambersburg PA
CBHW030647020726
47493CB00006B/1916